## 'TIS THE SEASON TO POISON

I pondered what Olivia could have meant as I made my way back to Thistle Park—and was greeted by the sight of Truman's police cruiser in the drive.

*Out of the frying pan into the fire.*

The chief was already sitting at the kitchen table addressing my sister. Rachel wore a worried expression atop her green-and-white striped minidress and red tights.

"I was just telling your sister about Lacey's toxicology results." Truman beckoned me to take a seat. The local radio was blasting Chipmunks Christmas music. I snapped off the dial for this macabre conversation. The cheery, ultra-falsetto voices seemed discordant with what might be depressing news.

"As I was telling your sister, it was no accident. Lacey Adams was poisoned."

My heart skipped a beat in morbid anticipation.

"How?" I asked Truman.

He shook his head, already baffled by what he was about to say. "By drinking antifreeze mixed with Hawaiian blue punch and blueberry vodka."

My heart beat in my rib cage like an agitated bird. I recalled my mother's shaking fingers unscrewing the top of a bottle of electric blue juice, Lacey glowering above her atop the bar. Luckily, Truman hadn't yet noticed my panicked expression . . .

Books by Stephanie Blackmoore

ENGAGED IN DEATH

MURDER WEARS WHITE

MURDER BORROWED, MURDER BLUE

GOWN WITH THE WIND

MARRY CHRISTMAS MURDER

Published by Kensington Publishing Corporation

# Marry Christmas Murder

## Stephanie Blackmoore

KENSINGTON BOOKS
www.kensingtonbooks.com

KENSINGTON BOOKS are published by

Kensington Publishing Corp.
119 West 40th Street
New York, NY 10018

All Kensington titles, imprints, and distributed lines are available at special quantity discounts for bulk purchases for sales promotion, premiums, fund-raising, educational, or institutional use.

Special book excerpts or customized printings can also be created to fit specific needs. For details, write or phone the office of the Kensington Sales Manager: Attn.: Sales Department. Kensington Publishing Corp., 119 West 40th Street, New York, NY 10018. Phone: 1-800-221-2647.

Kensington and the K logo Reg. U.S. Pat. & TM Off.

First Printing: October 2019
ISBN-13: 978-1-4967-1753-5
ISBN-10: 1-4967-1753-8

ISBN-13: 978-1-4967-1754-2 (ebook)
ISBN-10: 1-4967-1754-6 (ebook)

10 9 8 7 6 5 4 3 2 1

Printed in the United States of America

# CHAPTER ONE

"I'm at the airport, Mallory. Please come get me."

I felt a rueful smile on my face as I heard the trill of excitement in my mother's voice.

"Very funny, Mom. You were here just a couple of weeks ago at Thanksgiving."

I wasn't due for a visit from my sweet but meddling mother until a few days before Christmas. It was only the first week of December, and I wondered what had put her in a joking mood. I gazed at the kitchen of my B and B, tucked atop a hill in Port Quincy, Pennsylvania. I soaked up the holiday milieu. A skinny, flocked tree, one of seven in the mansion, stood attention in the corner of the room. This specimen was the most casual Christmas tree of the bunch, decorated with all the handmade ornaments my sister Rachel and I had crafted in our youth. There were misshapen snowmen and snaggletooth angels, fuzzy reindeer, and glittery pinecones, all lovingly made by our small hands a few decades ago. Hundreds of red and green twinkle lights blinked back at me in merry rounds. The sweet, piquant smell of cardamom cookies baking vied for olfactory attention with the sharp scent of evergreens from the garland hanging above the window seat. The ledge overlooking the back porch was filled with a dozen candles in silver, red, and gold. Their electric flames cast a warm glow against the frosted glass. The MP3 player on the island blasted out a stream of Motown Christmas hits. All was calm, all was bright. December was my favorite time of year, and I was making the most of it.

My mother snapped me back to reality. "I have news. We finally sold our house! Your stepfather and I are moving to Port Quincy immediately. That is, right now."

*She's one hundred percent serious.*

The neat row of cardamom cookie men and women I'd just retrieved from the oven slid to the ground, where many met a crispy death on the black-and-white checkered floor, broken into cookie smithereens. I managed to rescue a few with my oven-mitted hands, stifling my yelp. I nervously bit into one of the cardamom army's brethren that hadn't perished on the floor. The cookie was delicious, and noshing on the crispy little confection gave me a certain satisfaction. Talking to my mother Carole sometimes reduced me to stress eating.

I placed the portable phone on the island so she couldn't hear me chew. My sister, Rachel, breezed into the room and glanced at the caller ID feature. She pushed the speaker button, a smirk lighting up her pretty face.

I was distracted by my sister's getup. She wore a red velvet jumpsuit, complete with bell-shaped sleeves and a daringly cut neckline. Her feet were ensconced in gold high-heeled boots, and she completed her look with glittery red earrings nearly swishing to her shoulders. Her caramel waves were perched atop her head in a jaunty genie ponytail, and one brow was arched, a silent question begging me to fill her in on our mother's call.

I should have known when the phone rang it would be my mother. I'd recently installed a landline so my guests at the B and B would have an infallible way to contact me without dealing with the vagaries of cell phone outages. So far the only callers had been random telemarketers ignoring the line's unlisted status. The only other person who had the number was my mother, for use in case of emergency.

*And Mom moving to Port Quincy definitely classifies as an emergency.*

I loved my mother dearly. Don't get me wrong. But she was a bit of a meddler, and we'd had a fantastic relationship these past few years since she and my stepdad retired to the Emerald Coast of Florida. We'd see each other about four times a year, catch up and reminisce, and I'd be treated to a healthy dose of unsolicited advice. I thought she'd been half joking about moving to my adopted hometown of Port Quincy. Rachel and I assumed she and my stepfather would opt for their old stomping grounds in Pittsburgh, a safe and pleasant two hours away.

"Mallory, this isn't a joke. Come get us!" My

mom's voice resonated around the room via speaker, a little shrill at having been ignored. Rachel jumped back, nearly dropping her own cardamom figure, this one a squat snowman. She testily bit off his hat and sent a sigh toward the phone on the island.

The airport west of Pittsburgh was hours away. I felt myself growing a bit testy.

"I'd love to pick you up, Mom. But I have an appointment in . . ." I glanced at my watch, "fifteen minutes." I did have a business to run.

But I couldn't tamp down an undeniable thread of amusement. I giggled that of course my mother would hop on a Southwest flight from Pensacola post haste in a bid to get started on her move ASAP. She didn't do anything by half measures.

My stepfather drily explained my mother's hastiness. "I realize this is short notice, girls. But your mother believes all the good houses currently for sale in Port Quincy will be snatched up if she waits any longer."

My mother had a keen interest in real estate, having been a stager before she retired. Rachel and I exchanged a glance and shrug.

"Fine. We'll just rent a car. I thought my only daughters would be more excited." My mother delivered her speech with a healthy dose of petulance. I heard Doug soothing her in the background. I felt myself soften by degrees.

"It's not that we're not excited! We are." I glanced at my sister, who nodded vigorously, despite my parents not being able to see her gesture over the phone. Her long, sparkly red earrings clanged against her shoulders.

"It'll be so fun to see you all the time rather than just holidays," Rachel chimed in. Then my mom had to go and ruin all the warm fuzzies we'd just cultivated.

"I hear you munching on something, young lady. You need to watch your figure and keep the interest of that fellow of yours!" My mother's voice of censure rippled through the air, and I stopped mid-bite, another half-eaten cardamom figure momentarily spared. Rachel tried unsuccessfully to tamp down her giggles. I was simultaneously annoyed at my mother's antiquated views on my cookie consumption and my figure, while also being amused at her use of the word fellow to describe my boyfriend, Garrett. That's how it usually was when I interacted with Carole, a confusing mix of annoyance and appreciation. Rachel and I said our goodbyes and waited three seconds to start laughing.

"No doubt it'll be a blast to have Mom here for the holidays." I removed a second tray of crispy cookies and slid them more carefully onto a cooling rack.

Rachel nodded her agreement and plucked a jaunty soldier from the rack. She blew a stream of air onto the cookie and popped it into her mouth.

It would be a treat to spend the whole month of December together rather than the short visit she'd booked for the week of Christmas Eve through New Year's Day. It was the one time of year my sister and I had refused to book a single wedding. We had a few events to throw, but nothing major. And no one did Christmas like my mother. Not that she would have much help to lend in the decorating arena. The mansion was already decked out from top to bottom. I hadn't let Christmas influence me prior to Thanksgiving, but as soon as the sun rose on Black Friday, all bets were off. When others were rising at dawn to score deals on gifts, Rachel and I tore around Thistle Park with boxes of greenery, tinsel, and mistletoe.

The spirit of the season was woven into the very fabric of the mansion. And I owed my zest for the holiday season to my mother Carole. She had made the winter holidays extra special for my sister and me because that's when our father had left. I tamped down a wince of pain, remembering presents under the tree, but no dad. My mother had gone into typical decorator overdrive that December to stamp out the indelible mark made by my father's absence. She'd drowned us kids in ribbons, tinsel, cookies, and Christmas tunes to numb the pain and redirect our attention. It had almost worked. Little by little, year by year, the sorrow subsided. A tradition that had been born of sadness morphed into a joyful, boisterous, over-the-top celebration.

Our B and B bore that familial legacy. Green twinkle lights winked each evening from the trees and shrubs surrounding Thistle Park. Stately candles lit each window, and giant twin wreaths with cardinals nestled within the boughs greeted visitors at the double front doors. We'd woven fresh and artificial garlands through the spokes of the grand staircase. A massive tree, nearly worthy of a

White House lawn, stood sentinel in the front hall. It was decorated with glass ornaments fashioned in the factory owned by the family that had originally built the mansion. While the trees outside of the B and B and the one in the front hall were tasteful and traditional, the other six scattered about the mansion were kitschy and fun. Rachel and I had holiday music blasting in our third-floor apartment, and we reveled in the season and the tradition our mother had cultivated for us.

Still, a tiny frisson of doubt nestled between my shoulder blades at the thought of my mom and stepdad taking up permanent residence in Port Quincy. I'd gotten into some crazy situations over the past few years, and my mom was the empress of worry and catastrophizing. It was easier to allay her fears and concerns from afar.

Rachel seemed to channel my thoughts and let out a breath with an audible gust. "It will be interesting when Mom and Doug are here all the time."

I gulped.

*Make that forever.*

I glanced at my watch and confirmed we had a few minutes before our appointment. There was no time to ruminate, as we had a planning meeting to attend. My sister and I did a 180-degree turn and focused our attention on the pastel parade that would be my best friend Olivia's spring wedding. Last night Rachel and I had finished up our presentation of ideas on my tablet. I'd recently switched from using heavy, tactile idea books to share planning ideas with couples and their families. The tablet was sleek and efficient, but I still gathered a neat and tidy bundle of fabric swatches for brides and family members to examine. I didn't want them to miss out on personally examining all of the small touches. It was fun to observe their faces lighting up as they brushed their fingers over luxe fabrics with surprising textures, whether rich brocade or slippery silk. But I had to admit I didn't miss ferrying around the heavy tomes I used to use, the massive three-ring binders groaning with sketches and swatches. Couples still got to experience a glimpse of the styling of their big day with precise place settings at wedding tastings, their five senses stimulated with a representative meal.

And that was the experience I'd designed for Olivia and her family. I swelled with pride as Rachel and I ferried minute portions of a meal perfect for the springtime feast Olivia and her fiancé, Toby, had requested. We'd assembled a cucumber, citrus, and dill roulade for the salad course. Next was ginger mahi-mahi with grilled root vegetables for the main dish, followed by a citrus-and-berry angel food wedding cake. The food and theme seemed somewhat discordant, all light and effervescent springtime amidst the explosion of evergreens and cheery Christmas decorations, while outside the chilly wind whipped around the grounds. But we'd suspend disbelief and be transported to a sneak preview of Olivia and Toby's big day. We placed the dishes on the sideboard in my office and awaited our guests.

The doorbell clanged, and I ushered in Olivia's parents and grandparents. Olivia's mother, Goldie March, was as quiet and dignified as always. Her dark hair was done in a sophisticated chignon, her brown turtleneck sweater dress subdued and refined. Olivia's father, Alan, was more animated. The tall man gave me an affable hug, his wire-frame glasses slipping down his nose, his gray hair perfectly coiffed.

"Goldie? Like Goldie Hawn?" Rachel's smile faltered when Olivia's mom dropped her hand like a hot coal. Mrs. March may have shared her name with the celebrity, but her affect and style were the antithesis of Ms. Hawn's. Goldie March was buttoned up and staid.

"Yes," Goldie admitted, her face somewhat dour. "It's short for Marigold. We have a tradition of botanical names for the women in our family."

I hadn't met Olivia's grandparents and smiled at the older couple who emerged behind Goldie.

"I'm Clementine March, Olivia's grandma." The woman before me shrugged off her sporty, silver parka and hood with a flourish. She had pretty silver hair, cut in a short, spiky style. I blinked in the light of the hall's chandelier and realized the tips of each spike had been dyed a vibrant green. Somehow Clementine March avoided looking like an exotic southwest cactus and had landed in the territory of bold, grandma chic. Large diamond studs twinkled in her ears. The rest of her attire was understated, close-fitting black exercise garb.

"Clementine! I had no idea you were Olivia's grandmother!" Rachel squealed and rushed forward to exchange air kisses with the older woman, who dispensed with formalities and gave my sister a hearty hug. "Clementine is my favorite yoga instructor at Bodies in Motion."

"And Rachel is my best student!" Clementine bestowed a fond look on my sister. Both women were tall, and their styles were similarly bold. Clementine had finished her all black, beat poet yoga getup with blinking Christmas light earrings. My sister and Olivia's grandmother were two peas in a pod, style wise.

"And I'm Olivia's grandpa, Rudy March." The most arresting guest of all shrugged off a large Sherpa coat. He took in the bird chandelier, a fixture formed of concentric rings of glass birds chasing each other around and around. He next scanned the colossal Christmas tree and let out a low whistle.

I felt like doing the same. He was the spitting image of a Norman Rockwell Santa Claus, complete with a shiny bald head, thinning white hair, a voluminous snowy beard, tiny spectacles, and a jolly affect. The man looked like he'd just come to life and walked off a holiday edition Coca-Cola can.

Rachel and I hung up our guests' coats in the small vestibule to the left of the door. We ushered Olivia's family into our shared office and took seats on the poofy chintz and striped furniture arrayed around a low, walnut oval table. And we began our wait for the bride.

*She's not going to show.*

Half an hour later, we'd run out of polite chitchat to sustain our guests.

"Oh, let's just get on with it," Clementine announced. She gestured with her green-tipped manicure to the food on the sideboard. "Olivia obviously isn't coming."

"You know how hard she's working in her final push to make partner." Alan frowned at his mother-in-law as he defended his absent daughter. "I'm sure she has a good reason for not being here."

And on cue, my cell phone buzzed with a text from the bride.

"Something has come up at the firm," I murmured. Olivia and I had met at the high-powered law firm where we'd both once been starry-eyed associates. I'd lasted half a decade at Russell Carey before decamping to become a wedding planner. Olivia had stuck out the grind of corporate litigation with its long hours and pressure-cooker atmosphere. She was on the cusp of making partner this winter. I knew her excuse was one hundred percent legitimate and no fault of her own, if not ill timed.

"Sorry I'm late." The groom-to-be ducked into the room, a warm smile gracing his handsome face. Toby Frank, a tall redhead, was just as busy as his fiancée. Toby was a surgeon at the McGavitt-Pierce Memorial Hospital in town, and his work and shifts on call made his attendance at this wedding meeting just as unlikely as his busy bride's.

"I'm sorry my mom couldn't make it. She's got a trial she thought would wrap up yesterday." Toby's mother, Ursula Frank, was Port Quincy's most notorious judge, a woman who was fair and honest, but fierce in her decisiveness both on and off the court.

"Well, both women with careers in law are absent today." Clementine subtly drew censure at her granddaughter and gave a pointed gaze at the large cuckoo clock in the corner. With the groom in attendance, we began our meeting.

Olivia's family and fiancé gave appreciative murmurs as they tucked into the springtime menu.

"This will be lovely for our daughter's April nuptials." Goldie's pronouncement was tinged with as much excitement as her buttoned-up demeanor allowed. I began my presentation of ideas on the tablet, and smiled as Clementine donned a pair of sparkly green reading glasses to better see the screen.

"That's the March family dress!" The older woman beamed with delight as a photograph of herself, then one of Goldie, slid onto the screen. "Each woman in our family has worn the gown since the turn of the last century." Clementine frowned. "But Olivia is quite small boned. The dress will need to be cut down."

"And we'll have plenty of time before April to do so," I soothed. I finished the presentation, and Olivia's family chatted excitedly about the wedding.

"I'm sorry to cut and run." Toby stood and glanced at his heavy nautical watch. "I'm on call soon, and I'd like to be a bit closer to the hospital with the roads growing slick." He gestured outside, where a fine sheet of sleet slithered down from leaden clouds. "Give Olivia my love." He offered his future in-laws a winning smile, asked me for directions to the bathroom, and ducked into the hallway.

Clementine waited a moment before he was gone. "I knew Olivia would put that career of hers ahead of her wedding." She held up her hand as Alan began to protest. "I know she has no choice. And I'm as proud as anyone that she'll make partner. But this is a special time in her life, and her absence, well, it's a bit telling."

I tamped down a similar feeling and took a deep breath. I'd been so pumped when my best friend had excitedly tasked me with planning her big day. I'd introduced her to Toby and had a hunch the two would be a perfect match. They'd agreed and had gotten engaged in lightning-quick fashion. But I'd conveniently forgotten that as long as Olivia worked for Russell Carey, her allegiance was to the firm, first and foremost.

I recalled trying to plan my own defunct wedding to my ex-fiancé Keith, all while striving to be a model associate. We didn't marry, but it had been an exercise in extreme multitasking to try to pull off planning a wedding while working eighty hours a week. Olivia was on the precipice of making partner, and I had to excuse her absence today.

Goldie and Clementine must have read my mind.

"She won't be able to keep up these hours when she's wed," Clementine sniffed. "She ought to take up a second career, like my yoga. Then she could be an attentive wife and eventually a mother—all while feeling personally fulfilled."

Her daughter Goldie rolled her dark brown eyes so forcefully they nearly ricocheted out of her head. "Come on, Mother. Olivia's worked so hard for this. And Toby understands more than anyone else could, for Pete's sake. He's gone at the hospital just as much as she's at the firm."

"Which is why she needs to leave that horrid place and relocate to Port Quincy. There's no way her new marriage can withstand a long commute to Pittsburgh each day on top of working such inhospitable hours."

*She has a point.*

I'd wondered how Olivia and Toby would rearrange their lives after their wedding in the spring. As of now, the busy careerists saw each other on weekends only. Olivia had made no mention of cutting back on billable hours or moving south to Port Quincy. And Toby seemed quite committed to remaining at the hospital, unless something had recently changed.

"Will Toby be taking the March name?" Rudy stroked his white beard from his perch on a rose love seat. I did another double take, expecting to see a red hat atop his head to complete his Santa affect. "It's important for our family legacy. At least their children could carry it on."

"I don't think that's going to happen this time, Rudy." Alan drily arched a brow above his wire-framed rims and threw back the last of the scotch he'd been consuming. I realized with a start he must have taken on the March surname, as he shared it with his wife's parents.

I hadn't heard any cars advance down the drive. I hoped Toby hadn't stuck around to hear any of the current conversation.

"Well, one thing's for sure." Clementine folded her green-tipped manicured fingers together. "Mallory, since Olivia won't be an active participant planning her own wedding, I think it's time to deputize you to make all of the choices."

I gulped as the rest of the attendees swiveled their gazes in my direction. Little did they know

Olivia had made a similar request of me just a mere week ago.

"Absolutely not!" Twin spots of pink appeared on Goldie's cheekbones. "This is Olivia's big day. I'm sure she can find time to make a few key decisions." Goldie shot her mother a glare and sank into her wingback chair with arms crossed.

I felt myself grimace and quickly made my expression neutral. If this was the kind of atmosphere Olivia faced within her family, maybe it was better that she cast her lot with the hostile climes of my former law firm. It might be safer for her to reside there than bask in the cruel rays of her mother and grandmother's dueling expectations.

I swallowed and waded into the fray. "It might be necessary to make some decisions to keep the ball rolling. And if Olivia—"

"Good. And now let's turn to the auction." Clementine rolled over me like a freight train and redirected the conversation to other matters.

In addition to Olivia and Toby's wedding, I'd be hosting a holiday auction to benefit the local animal shelter. The auction was tomorrow, and all of the details were nearly wrapped up. The auction was sponsored by the company Olivia's family owned—March Homes—and would be the company's formal foray into Port Quincy society.

"We're ready to host a wonderful gala," I promised. "Paws and Poinsettias will be such a success that you'll want to make it an annual event!"

Rachel nodded beside me, her red bead earrings jingling. "You'll be the toast of the town."

Clementine beamed at my sister's declaration

and clasped her husband Rudy's hand. "This is our chance to introduce ourselves to the town of Port Quincy properly."

Olivia's family helmed one of the largest real estate development companies in Western Pennsylvania. I'd grown up in a March Homes house myself, surrounded by a maze of March Homes developments carved into the green hills and countryside of the suburbs north of Pittsburgh. The style of the company's homes had changed over the decades, from neat split-levels and colonials in the seventies and early eighties to peaked and gabled McMansions in the nineties and aughts. The homes Olivia's family built now were more customizable, but there was a serious contingent of Port Quincy citizens who were wary of their onslaught into our small town. March Homes had already broken ground on two behemoth housing tracts in Port Quincy last month. Like it or not, the March family was here to stay. And if the Paws and Poinsettias auction and gala went off as well as I was sure it would, then Olivia's family would endear themselves to the doubting denizens of our town in no time.

I distantly heard the double front doors open. A frigid gust of air slipped into my office. I excused myself and found Olivia sharing a sweet kiss with Toby under a sprig of mistletoe in the hallway. They parted, and Olivia gave me a beatific smile.

"I made it after all! I'm so happy you're still here, Toby." Olivia shrugged off her cheery red pea coat. The couple were like two ships passing in the night, or mid-afternoon, as it were. "Do you have a minute to stay?"

Toby glanced at his watch and then his fiancée's face. "How are the roads? If they're not icy yet, I'll stay and keep my pager on."

The happy couple followed me into the room, and Olivia's family exclaimed in delight at the bride's appearance. I served a remaining portion of the tasting, and Olivia dug in with gusto. My best friend was tiny and bird-like, with big brown eyes, dark near-black hair, and a pretty smattering of freckles. She could put away an impressive amount of food despite her small frame. She momentarily blanched at the fish, which I found odd. She'd been so excited about the proposed dish in her email response. She saw me take in her reaction and gamely recovered. "It's all lovely, Mallory. This is the perfect menu." She took a swig of pepper-mint tea and settled back into a chintz couch, Toby's arm wrapped protectively around her. She gave him a portentous glance, and Toby cleared his throat.

"Olivia and I have a surprise." He bestowed a warm gaze on his bride.

"Toby and I are so in love." Olivia sent a melting smile Toby's way. "We can't wait to marry. Mal-lory," her smile wavered, and her eyes turned pleading, "we'd like to marry before Christmas."

A swig of peppermint tea from my own piping hot cup went down the wrong way. Rachel patted my back as I attempted to stop sputtering.

*Christmas is in less than three weeks. No way, no how can I whip up a winter white wedding.*

"We want to take advantage of the festive season," Olivia rushed on. "And we'll downgrade the guest list from two hundred to just fifty." She dragged her eyes from her lap and seemed to peer plaintively at mine.

*I can't say no.*

Olivia and I had been through so much at the firm. She'd personally held my hand when my own engagement had imploded in my face, and along with Rachel had nursed my injured psyche back to good health. We didn't see much of each other these days, but she was a dear friend.

Rachel rubbed her hands together next to me. "What day were you thinking of?"

The bride and groom exchanged a glance. "How about December 23? That's the day before you leave for Key West, right?" Olivia directed her question to her grandparents, who slowly nodded in unison.

"We'll be able to see our dear grandbaby get married before we leave town." Rudy beamed his assent, while Clementine wore the beginnings of a smile, slowly seeming to warm to the idea. Goldie and Alan looked confused. They swiveled their attention between Olivia and me.

I counted down the days in my head and stymied another panic attack. It was December 8. That left just fifteen days to pull off a super sped-up plan for Olivia.

Toby seemed to pick up on my hesitation. He sought to reassure me. "Less guests will actually attend the wedding so close to Christmas."

"It'll be so dear and intimate," Olivia promised. "Just family."

"Of course." I felt a small smile tick up at the corners of my mouth. "It'll be a blast!"

Now that I'd officially agreed, Olivia's family was

ecstatic. Well, everyone but Goldie, who seemed flummoxed by her daughter's rush down the aisle.

"Where will you hold the wedding on the twenty-third? And what will be the theme?"

"Why, Christmas, of course." Rudy slapped a large hand on his knee and shook his head, his white beard swishing against his plaid shirt. It was as if Santa himself had decreed the wedding theme.

"And we Marches are British on one side and German on the other. We can have Christmas crackers as favors and real candles on the Christmas trees."

Alarm bells rang distantly in my head. "Um, real candles? I'm not sure how that will comply with the fire code."

"And my family is Italian on my mother's side," Toby mused. "So we'll need an elaborate cookie table."

Olivia's family and her fiancé began to chatter excitedly about the menu, a proposed glorious culinary mishmash of holiday traditions.

Olivia spoke in a small voice. "I'm not really sure what my ethnic heritage is."

I recalled for a moment that Olivia had been adopted. She rarely mentioned that fact, and I hadn't considered it when her family planned the menu based on their cultural affinities.

"Nonsense! You're one hundred percent March." Clementine left her seat beside her husband and plopped next to her granddaughter.

Goldie followed suit and crossed the room to clasp her daughter's hands. "These *are* your traditions."

Olivia sent her mother and grandmother a wavering smile.

"Where will we hold the wedding?" Goldie turned to me expectantly.

"We could have it here." It would encroach mightily on my personal plans for the holiday, and it would break my December wedding moratorium. But I'd do anything for my best friend.

"Actually, we were thinking of the cabin." Olivia turned expectantly to her grandparents. "It's two miles west of town, close to where we're breaking ground for one of the new developments."

It was the first I'd heard of the cabin, but I was game. It would be easier to set up and break down the wedding off-site from the B and B, without the worry of the event impeding on Christmas with my mom and stepdad.

"I do have an idea for the theme," Olivia quietly put in. She pulled a small glass figurine from her pretty red leather bag. "This was my first ornament. It's a tree topper, actually. I'd like to incorporate this into the wedding decorations."

She solemnly held out the piece of glass, which took up the length of her palm. It was a vibrantly colored angel, designed to perch on the highest branch of a Christmas tree. The vivid blue, gold, and white glass was heavy and unique, exactingly cut into thousands of etched lines that sparkled under the subdued office chandelier.

Goldie blanched at the appearance of the ornament and shook her head. "Oh, Olivia, that old thing? I think you could come up with a better muse for your wedding."

Olivia's face momentarily crumpled. She recov-

ered from her wounded expression and shook her
head. "No, Mom, this is what I want." A small smile
returned to her heart-shaped face. Her big brown
eyes sparkled beneath her heavy fringe of bangs.
"This is the first ornament I remember. It means
Christmas to me."

Alan retrieved the piece from me and removed
his wire frames. "This is good Czech glass. An old
world piece." He returned the angel to Olivia. "I
think you've made some fine choices today, honey."
He beamed at his daughter, who seemed to glow
with her father's approval.

But Goldie wouldn't let her irritation go. "It's
such a common piece, sweetie. Are you sure you
don't want something more sophisticated to plan
your wedding around?"

"Mallory, hello!" My mother Carole's voice
thankfully broke through the tense undercurrent
brewing between Olivia and her mother. "We made
it!" She burst into my office, my stepfather in tow,
laden with luggage and a half-empty bottle of antifreeze. Her pug, Ramona, trotted dutifully into
the room. She wore a toasty-looking snowflake doggie sweater. The little gal settled next to the gas
fireplace, no doubt exhausted from her travels.

My mom didn't seem to notice I was having a
work meeting. She plucked the large plastic bottle
of blue liquid from my stepfather's gloved hands.
"No thanks to the rental company! We nearly perished on our trip here. The car was out of antifreeze,
and we had to stop to get more." She shrugged off
her electric blue wool coat and seemed to realize
she'd crashed a planning meeting. "Oh, I beg your
pardon!"

"Hello, Mrs. Shepard." Olivia stood to give my mother a hug, blessing her appearance. The rest of Olivia's family seemed somewhat amused at my mother's shenanigans.

"Congratulations, Olivia. You are a lucky fellow, Toby." My mother beamed at all assembled. She was soon chatting amiably about Florida with Clementine, comparing the March family getaway in Key West with the home she and my stepdad had just sold on the coast of the Gulf of Mexico.

"Did you say you were a stager?" Clementine seemed to perk up at some morsel of my mother's conversation. "We could use some fresh ideas for our newest developments in Port Quincy."

Goldie shook her head at her mother. "I'm sorry, Carole, but that's not true. We have a stager, and we're quite happy with her work."

Clementine raised one artfully plucked gray brow in challenge. "Some of us are not, as it were. This is something we need to discuss, Goldie."

My mother swiveled her head from Clementine to Goldie, trying to determine which woman wore the most powerful pantsuit at March Homes.

"For instance, the decor at this B and B. It's lovely." Clementine sent me a warm smile, and I appreciated her praise. "But it's utterly predictable. This is just the kind of thing Lacey would come up with."

I shriveled at her rescinded praise and bristled on Lacey's behalf. I'd worked with the Marches' stager, Lacey, planning Paws and Poinsettias. She'd given me some ideas for the very setup I'd put in place at the mansion.

"What would you have done, Carole?" Clementine left my office, and we all followed her into the hall.

"Well, for starters, I'd place a more daring tree as a statement piece." My mother flicked her eyes over the decor and licked her lips. She was just getting started. "Perhaps a teal and fuchsia tree, to echo the rose tones in the bird chandelier. Something that would pop."

Clementine nodded, her green-tipped spiky hair more vivid under the brighter lights.

"I'd focus on a bounty theme. The mansion would be filled with sparkly fruit ornaments in a panoply of warm, tropical colors. I'm not afraid to mix more bold items against a traditional palette. Then I would—Ow!" My mother yelped and stopped her speech. My sister had thankfully pinched my mom, and she stopped her verbal deconstruction of my carefully crafted holiday decorations.

"I think it looks great," I put in with a small voice. "I wanted to honor the architecture and history of the mansion and make it festive but not overpowering."

"We didn't want it to look like Father Christmas vomited all over the mansion," Rachel spat in sisterly solidarity.

I plucked a large framed photo in mellow sepia tones from a marble table. "The decorations echo the past nicely." I thrust the picture of the original inhabitants of Thistle Park, the McGavitt family, into my mother's hands. "I even consulted with our town historian, Tabitha Battles. We checked out photos of parties here in the past and designed the holiday decorations with that in mind."

She gave it a quick glance and set it firmly back on the table. "Different strokes for different folks."

*Oh my goodness, she's auditioning for a stager position at March Homes.*

I decided to shrug off my mom's traitorous teardown of my decorations in light of my realization she was directly appealing to Clementine March for a job. I had to stifle a giggle as she continued her pitch, detailing how she'd meld her preferred Emerald Coast decor with traditional elements to create Spode on steroids with a tropical flair. And Clementine was eating it up, much to Goldie's chagrin. Olivia and Toby watched with amusement, stealing more kisses under the sprig of mistletoe.

Rachel and I soon doled out coats to Olivia and her family.

"I'll see you tomorrow at the Paws and Poinsettias auction," I promised. Rachel opened the heavy double doors, letting in a gust of damp wind. The hinges whined in the cold, and I made a mental note to lubricate them. There was no white stuff on the ground at the moment, but if the temperature dropped a few more degrees, the roads would be slick with ice.

Olivia was ushered out first, and I mistakenly thought her gasp was in response to the harsh weather.

"Oh, my God." Toby rushed forward to wrap his arms against a shaking Olivia.

The windshield of the bride's Acura was covered in oozing metallic paint. The runny and hastily sprayed message matched the meaning of the words sprayed there:

*Gold Digger*

The perpetrator had taken the little wooden cradle and baby Jesus from the small crèche I'd placed on the front porch. The cradle rested on the hood of Olivia's car. A nasty gust of wind ripped across the yard, and the cradle threatened to topple off.

*Rock-a-bye baby, on the treetop. When the wind blows, the cradle will fall.*

We all shared a collective gasp as the cradle slid down the hood of the car and landed on the frozen grass. Thankfully the ceramic infant within was intact and safe.

But Olivia was not. She fainted dead away, caught by her fiancé. The glass angel in her hand crashed to the porch, its wing broken clean off.

# CHAPTER TWO

Toby carried Olivia inside the mansion, this time to the parlor. He gently settled her on the appropriately named fainting couch, as Rachel fetched a strong cup of tea from our office. It was the longest thirty seconds of my life as she lay in his arms, before her large lashes fluttered open.

"Who would have done that?" Olivia's voice was breathy and anguished. She sat up with a shudder, Toby's arms still protectively wrapped around her.

"I'm sure this has nothing to do with you personally, sweetheart." Alan March gripped his hands into fists and jammed them in his pockets. "Each new town we go to, we meet initial resistance. People fear change and progress. I'm sorry to say this isn't the first time a disgruntled person has tried to threaten or cow us." Alan's brown eyes flashed with anger behind his mild-mannered glasses. "I'm just sorry they decided to go after you."

I shook my head, trying to take it all in. The message sprayed on Olivia's windshield didn't even make sense. It was true that Toby Frank was considered wealthy, the son of a judge, his father once a surgeon as well, but now deceased. Toby no doubt was quite comfortable in his career as a surgeon. But Olivia herself had a lucrative career at the firm. "Gold digger" seemed an odd epithet to smear her car with.

No matter, a threat didn't have to make immediate sense to still be jarring and alarming. I dialed the number of my boyfriend's father, who also happened to be the chief of police. We traded some tense exchanges, and he assured me he'd be on his way.

"You've been under so much stress lately, Olivia." Goldie pressed the cup of tea into her daughter's hands. Olivia took a grateful gulp. Our eyes met. Olivia gave me a scared, if wavering smile. I returned it and gave her shoulder a squeeze. Then I stood back, assessing my best friend. I was more worried than I'd initially been.

The strain of wedding planning coupled with her final bid at making partner had taken a toll on Olivia. I was concerned because Olivia was known for having nerves of steel. She was a more than capable litigator. She'd been appointed second chair on cases faster than most young associates and then began helming her own cases as lead attorney. Nothing ever rattled her, but the sinister spray-painted message had accomplished just that. Before I gave the situation more thought, Truman Davies, Port Quincy's chief of police, arrived.

"Not the kindest welcome to town," he grumbled as he took off his sodden hat. He nodded his head toward the scene of the vandalized Acura visible through the front doors. I shivered and shut them against the disturbing scene and the almost-as-worrying weather.

"I know some are unhappy with the Marches' new housing tracts, but this takes it to another level." Truman furrowed his brows and squared his shoulders, his large frame nearly skimming the top of the door. Truman was a preview of what my boyfriend Garrett would look like in a few decades' time. I ushered Truman into the parlor, and he began a round of questioning.


An hour later, Olivia's car had been impounded for evidence. Truman finished his questioning of my visitors and examination of the frigid scene outside. The bride and her family retired to the aforementioned cabin, and Toby was called to work at the hospital.

Rachel and I bustled about getting our mother and stepdad all settled in. I set them up in one of the bedrooms in our third-floor apartment, opting to leave the rooms in the B and B portion of the mansion unoccupied. Ramona the pug sniffed joyfully around the third floor, her curly little tail quivering back and forth as much as its length would allow. My older cat, Whiskey, a sweet but sometimes aloof calico, gave Ramona a wide berth. Her daughter, Soda, an energetic orange puff ball, playfully batted at the pug before rolling over on her back in welcome. The two pets eagerly clattered down the back stairs after my family as we made our way to the main kitchen for a restorative cup of eggnog.

"Mallory dear, I need a favor." My mother set down her glass mug with its festive rim of holly berries and fixed a winning smile on her face. "I want you to put in a good word for me regarding the stager position at March Homes."

My sister snickered and set down her own mug of eggnog. My hand wavered upon hearing my mother's request, and I shook a measure of nutmeg over the kitchen island in surprise.

*Mom was never one to beat around the bush; I'll give her that.*

"You heard Goldie," I responded evenly. "March Homes already has a stager, Lacey Adams." And while I wanted my mom to be happy in her new life in Port Quincy, I wasn't so sure how I felt that she seemed to be gunning for Lacey's job.

"It sounds like Clementine wants to go in a new direction," my mother put in. "And with all of the developments the Marches have planned, they'll need more than one stager."

My stepdad Doug raised a brow. "You mentioned wanting to come out of retirement, dear, on a part-time basis. But a position with March Homes sounds like quite a commitment." A small cloud of concern seemed to dampen Doug's usually easygoing manner.

My mom waved her hand, dismissing all input. Her face was as serene as the light green she was clad in, from head to toe. My mom favored matching her outfits and today was no exception. Her mint sweater set picked up the mint pinstripes on her gray wool pants, further tied in with the light green moccasins on her feet. Light jade elephants dangled in her ears, complementing the similar beads around her neck. She liked to tie Doug's wardrobe in with her own, and today he sported a similar mint fleece henley. My parents were seamlessly matched and had a marriage that prioritized compromise and respect. But my mom's new obsession with gaining a full-time staging position with March Homes was news to Doug.

Gleams and schemes sparkled in my mother's lively eyes. "I already have a great rapport with Clementine. They must need more stagers if they're expanding!"

Rachel cast a skeptical glance at our mom. "But Goldie also runs March Homes, and she doesn't want to hire any more stagers."

Carole took a fortifying sip of eggnog and sighed at my sister, before turning to me. "I'm not asking you to get rid of their current stager or do anything irrational. All I would like is for you to reiterate my interest to Clementine and my skill set as a decorator." My mother set her glass mug down a bit more harshly than necessary, her version of a harrumph. I stifled a giggle.

"And if I were to gain a position with the Marches, it could lead to more business opportunities for you." My mother raised a brow, dangling an enticing proposition.

"I suppose so," I reluctantly agreed, although we'd already been able to secure some planning work with the Marches. I wasn't sure how my mom ingratiating herself with them would lead to even more business.

"Okay, Mom. I'll put in a good word for you." It was a promise I could keep. My mom was interested in working for March Homes, and they were extremely busy. Lacey, their current stager, had said as much. It couldn't hurt, and my mother had already made a somewhat successful pitch to Clementine.

"As it turns out, we do have a new engagement to plan for the March family," I admitted. "Or rather, an event moved up several months." I took a gulp of eggnog, wondering how my mom and stepdad would take the news that we were putting on a wedding the week we usually dedicated to holiday family togetherness. "Olivia's wedding has been moved up to December 23."

"What?" My mom let out a very indecorous yelp. Ramona trotted over to make sure she was all right. "But that's time I usually spend with you girls."

I traced the rim of my glass with my finger in a nervous movement. As soon as I'd assented to Olivia's request, I'd wondered how my mom would take the news. Putting on a wedding, even a small one, would encroach on our over-the-top holiday traditions. "I know. But Olivia and Toby seemed so keen to move up their wedding date."

"And what about Garrett?" A deeper frown furrowed the spot above the bridge of her nose. "I thought we'd be spending quite a bit of time with the Davies family this year. Shouldn't you have run these plans by him first?" My mother slyly cut her gaze to the fourth finger of my left hand and was treated to a view of my bare and unadorned finger. Rachel sent me an amused look and a wink.

"Garrett is my boyfriend, not my keeper." I tried to tamp out a testy tone in my voice. But a slight bit of worry crept between my shoulder blades. I'd been busier than ever this fall with weddings nearly every weekend at the B and B. My beau also had a busy caseload, and as a sole practitioner, all of the extra hours fell on his capable but harried shoulders. Garrett and I had fallen into an amiable but business-like schedule of just seeing each other on Sundays. I realized with a start that our relationship was beginning to look a lot like Olivia and Toby's workaholic setup.

"Earth to Mallory." Rachel snapped her long red acrylics before my nose, startling me out of my realization. "You didn't make plans with Garrett yet?" My sister seemed even more concerned than my engagement-obsessed mother. I squirmed under the lens of her careful scrutiny.

"Um, Garrett and I haven't discussed our Christmas plans," I demurred and cut my eyes from my sister's incredulous inquisitor gaze. Last Christmas my romance with Garrett had been relatively new. We'd spent the holiday separately, with our respective families. We got together the day after, spending it ice-skating with his lovely daughter, Summer. It had been the perfect arrangement, low-key and sweet. But the stakes seemed so much higher this year. I wondered with a start just why we hadn't discussed it. The nagging worry only grew. The beginnings of a headache formed behind my eyes.

"At least you have a boyfriend," Rachel grumbled. Her beaded earrings jangled their distaste along with her headshake. I breathed a sigh of relief. My sister's outburst seemed to have captured my mom and stepdad's attention, turning their focus from me.

"Don't be silly," I smoothly soothed. "You have so much fun, and you don't need to even think about settling down yet." Rachel was six years my junior, enjoying her mid-twenties with lots of easygoing dates and fun trips.

"Just because I'm younger and you're dawdling with deciding what to do with Garrett doesn't mean I haven't matured." Rachel threw her statement like a javelin, and I felt my mouth open and close. "What I really want to know is why you set Olivia up with Toby instead of me."

Not much rendered me speechless, but Rachel's verbal volley did.

"If I'd known you had any interest in Toby Frank, maybe I would have." I tried to tamp down the defensive note in my rejoinder. My head was spinning as I recalled thinking that from the moment I'd met the judge's son, I'd wanted to set him up with my best friend. It wasn't that I wouldn't have done the same for Rachel if she'd asked, but the thought hadn't crossed my mind.

My sister seemed to tap into the eerie sororal ESP we sometimes shared. "Why didn't you think of me with Toby? I could totally date a professional, too, you know." Rachel adopted a petulant pout, and only broke her glare to administer some pets to Ramona, who was panting at her feet. She picked up the pug and scuffed behind her little ears, to her doggie's delight.

"No one's saying you couldn't date a professional. You're a professional yourself." In addition to helming wedding planning gigs with me and helping to run the B and B, Rachel also had a burgeoning cake-baking side business. "Toby just isn't the kind of guy you usually date."

I distinctly recalled her one date with a doctor last fall, a cute but staid ophthalmologist, and Rachel's declaration that she would never want to date another physician again. "I remember you saying you didn't want to date someone who was looking to settle down."

"Well, that was last year." Rachel buried her nose in Ramona's holiday sweater. Carole and Doug looked at us girls with barely suppressed amusement.

"Tell you what. I know how you can make this right." Rachel wore a cunning look in her pretty almond-shaped green eyes. "Ask Toby to set me up with his most eligible doctor friends."

I threw my hands up in consternation. First my mom wanted me to put in a good word with Clementine March for a nonexistent stager job, and now my sister wanted me to facilitate her doctor chasing. The two women stared at me expectantly. Doug shook his head and sent me a shrug. I finished my mug of eggnog and let out an amused chuckle.

"Fine. Whatever makes you two happy."

My sister and mother exchanged triumphant smiles and clinked their mugs together. I couldn't help feeling I'd somehow been bamboozled.

\* \* \*

I left my sister to finish settling in our mom and Doug at the B and B. I had some last-minute threads to tie up for the Paws and Poinsettias auction and gala. Now that Olivia and Toby's wedding was moved up by a few hair-raising light years, I couldn't wait to throw a successful event for March Homes and place the current party on deck firmly in my rearview mirror. Then I could focus on crafting a beautiful day for my long-time friend, and not worry it would be somewhat of a rush job.

I grabbed a scraper from my trunk and brushed sleet from the front window of my ancient tan station wagon, a trusty 1970s steed I'd christened the Butterscotch Monster. I took in the festive atmosphere of Port Quincy as I made my way down slalom-like hills paved with yellow bricks. Thankfully, they were well salted in this nasty weather.

The cheery and idiosyncratic holiday light displays adorning most houses gave way to the old-fashioned ornaments and greenery of downtown. Each street lamp was festooned with winding red ribbons and lush evergreens, creating a fleet of candy canes marching down Main Street in striped precision. Wreaths bedecked with gold bells hung from wires suspended over traffic. The skinny deciduous trees dotting the sidewalks were twined with thousands of twinkling white lights, creating an icy winter wonderland. The citizens of Port Quincy braved the cold and sleet with upturned collars, tossle caps, and a hefty helping of holiday good cheer. They gathered under eaves with cups of coffee, the miniature jets of steam curling above their heads like smoke from Santa's pipe.

I pulled the Butterscotch Monster a few blocks away from the Candy Cane Lane Christmas-themed shop. The little store did a brisk year-round business but predictably was in overdrive during the month of December. I felt an infectious grin of childlike delight overtake my face as I took in the window display. An antique train set large enough to hold a toddler ferried all nine of Santa's reindeer, one per jewel-toned car. The reindeer were dressed for travel in turn-of-the-nineteenth-century garb. Some of the reindeer read period newspapers with spectacles perched on their noses while others knitted and waved at passersby. Santa helmed the train as the conductor, dressed in a striped engineer's outfit but still undeniably himself. I brushed past a gaggle of other shoppers and made my way inside. I was greeted with the scent of cinnamon and nutmeg emanating from a basket of glittery pinecones nestled by the door.

"Yoo-hoo! Mallory!" The owner, Nina Adams, waved from behind her perch at the cash register. She spoke to an assistant and handed off her duties to make her way over to the door.

"Just finishing off the last touches for Paws and Poinsettias?" Nina had to speak up over the chatter in her shop. It was a small space, and the dozen shoppers inside filled the space to nearly bursting. The shop was already cheerfully cluttered with a passel of intricate ornaments and decorations lining the shelves, bursting from barrels, and occupying themed displays. The store was almost a museum to holiday bric-a-brac, and I smiled thinking how fun it would be to visit, even when it wasn't December.

We made our way to the back of the shop, where

Nina ushered me into a small storeroom. I could hear the tones of Perry Como singing about a white Christmas more clearly without the customers' exclamations. Nina proffered a large box and beamed. She folded her plump hands together and brushed back a lock of her flyaway blonde curls.

"Thank you for putting these favors aside." I knelt to check the contents of the box. "These bells are the perfect touch to finish off the decorations." I'd waited with bated breath for the favors to top each place setting for Paws and Poinsettias. The tiny baubles featured a row of softly jingling sleigh bells on a red satin ribbon. Upon closer inspection, guests would see the sleigh bells themselves were molded in shapes of little cats and dogs.

"The purrrrfect touch." Nina laughed at her pun and gave a ribbon a shake, a delicate silver trill rippling through the air. Her rosy cheeks glowed with mirth. The storeowner was decked out in a reindeer sweater to match her front window display, complete with a blinking Rudolph nose.

"I can't wait!" I beamed and placed the bells in the box. "Thank you for your help. You and your daughter have as much to do with the success of Paws and Poinsettias as my sister and I."

Nina was the mother of Lacey Adams, the March Homes stager Goldie seemed to favor but Clementine did not. I'd had a lot to do for the Paws and Poinsettias auction and was happy to share some of the elaborate planning with the March family's own employee. There would be a pet fashion show, the auction itself, heavy hors d'oeuvres, and sparkling spirits befitting the holiday. It was useful to bounce ideas off Lacey since she knew what her employers favored when it came to decorations.

Well, that was what I'd thought before I'd heard Clementine trash Lacey's designs. I squirmed inside as I thought back to just an hour ago, when Clementine and Goldie were airing their company's dirty human resources laundry and sparring over whether Lacey's work was up to par or not. I was startled out of my thoughts as Nina turned around to pick up a carafe shaped like a snowman.

"Peppermint hot chocolate?"

"Don't mind if I do." The warm drink chased away the chill of my concerns, and I relaxed for the first time in days. But it was short-lived, as Nina seemed to pick up the vibe I was giving off about the March family.

"I'm so thrilled March Homes is moving into Port Quincy." Nina took a sip of her own cocoa. "Not everyone is happy that some of the undeveloped land will be turned into houses, but I'm happy my Lacey will be working closer to home. She has even put her townhouse in Pittsburgh on the market. She thinks March Homes will be developing in Port Quincy for the next three years, at least." Nina's cherub face dimmed a degree. "Not that moving back to Port Quincy will really ensure that I see Lacey more. The March family runs her ragged. She spends more time with Goldie March than with me and certainly more time with Goldie than Goldie's own daughter." She seemed to spit out the last pronouncement before blinking and tossing back the rest of her cocoa. I blanched at her censure of Olivia and rushed to defend my friend.

"Olivia is quite busy with her work. As is Goldie, it seems. I think Olivia and her mom will be spending more time together now that Olivia has moved up her wedding to the end of December." At least I hoped Olivia and her mom could grab a few minutes in the coming weeks to make some decisions regarding her rushed nuptials.

A barely perceptible cloud seemed to sweep over Nina's cheerful cherub face. I thought I'd imagined it. But then Nina's hand wavered, and the last bit of cocoa sloshed from her cup and doused her jaunty fur-lined moccasins. "Oh dear!" She tut-tutted looking for a tea towel in the back room and knelt to mop up her shoes. I rushed to wipe up the cocoa from the floor as well.

"I've been working so hard this December, I don't know where my mind is." She sighed and placed the tea towel on a metal shelf. "And if I'm being honest, I'd hoped Lacey could help out a bit with the store when she moves back to Port Quincy. I miss my daughter. People should slow down and spend more time with their families instead of being workaholics."

I squirmed anew, thinking of how I'd just taken on a wedding due to go off two days before Christmas. I wasn't sure how I'd break the news to my boyfriend, and my mom was only okay with it because she thought I could get her an elusive stager position. Lacey's position, in fact.

"Of course, this store wasn't even meant to be

mine." Nina's pretty round eyes grew wistful. "Candy Cane Lane originally belonged to my eldest daughter, Andrea." She nervously twisted a snowflake pendant around her index finger and then made the sign of the cross.

"I'm sorry." Something had obviously happened to Nina's other daughter, and I didn't want to pry.

"I'm sorry, too. But I still have my Lacey." Nina seemed to steel herself and changed course. "I do have to admit I'm surprised March Homes can even make a foray into Port Quincy. Half the land for the five developments is their own, from the hunting grounds they've owned forever. But the other half comes from the Gibson farms, and no one ever thought they'd sell."

"*Five* developments?" I nearly spit out my cocoa. I'd known the Marches were ambitious, but five new housing plans would change the face of Port Quincy.

"The March family doesn't do anything by half measures," Nina stated with some bitterness. "And the Gibson land was supposed to go to the family's son. The kid is a real hothead. He was furious when he found out his parents sold to March Homes."

*Furious enough to vandalize Olivia's car?*

I was sure Truman was on top of it but decided to run the theory by him later anyway.

Nina began to gossip anew when the door to the retail portion of the store opened. Her assistant beckoned her back, and I slipped out the rear door with my box of favors.

I headed to March Homes headquarters, lost in thought. Not everyone in Port Quincy wanted to welcome the March family. The temperature had dropped, and an icy gust of wind ripped through my wool coat. I wondered if Olivia's family would win everyone over with their holly jolly celebration—or come up cold.

# CHAPTER THREE

The next day dawned cold and clear. The chilly sleet was gone, and the sun blazed in a cloudless periwinkle-blue sky. Frost glittered on the blades of grass, and each inhalation tickled my nose with fresh, frigid air. Rachel and I loaded the Butterscotch Monster with the last few bits and bobs for Paws and Poinsettias.

We were happy to help the March family in their mission to ingratiate themselves with the people of Port Quincy. And not only would I be assisting Olivia's family, but I'd also be helping out some furry friends in need. The Paws and Poinsettias auction and evening of dancing and merrymaking would benefit the Port Quincy Animal Shelter. My sister had started nudging me in the spring to expand our event planning repertoire beyond weekend and Friday weddings, and I was now thrilled to plan new kinds of events.

"I never thought they'd finish in time." I scanned the street for a spot near March Homes's headquarters. Rachel let out a low whistle at the now-gleaming building. The March family had bought a dilapidated old eyesore of a building anchoring Main Street at the corner of Poplar. The edifice had once held a Gimbels department store, and according to locals, had been unoccupied since the 1980s. My friend, the contractor Jesse Flowers, and his crew had cleverly restored the building in quick fashion. And the development company quickly hired a fleet of employees to get to work on making the new developments a reality.

The swift hiring boom in construction had helped to win some fans of the company. Port Quincy was already going through a bit of a renaissance. A hundred years prior, the population had been three times the size it was now, filled with families and workers employed by the massive glass factory. When it closed, Port Quincy contracted. But it was growing again at a slow and sensible clip, bolstered by the giant hospital complex that kept expanding. The hospital was just outside the orbit of the bigger hospitals in Pittsburgh and was able to pick off prospective patients from nearby Ohio, West Virginia, and the tip of Maryland. Slowly more and more downtown buildings were being revitalized. The flourishing antique shops featured glass once made here, and I had a steady stream of brides from Pittsburgh and beyond. I was thrilled to be part of the mini boom.

I bit my lip as I maneuvered the boat of a car into a tight space. Rachel thankfully waited for me to cut the engine before she pulled my mind from my warm musings about my adopted hometown.

"Did you hear something last night?"

Our eyes met in the rearview mirror.

"It's an old house. I hear lots of things in my sleep." I didn't like where this was going.

Rachel shook her head, her giant marcasite chandelier earrings softly jingling. "I thought I heard someone on the back stairs." She took in my worried look and shrugged. "Then again, it could have been a dream."

We gathered steaming travel mugs of coffee and shouldered last-minute bags of items. I held the door open for my sister and smiled as she gasped at the decor. That was just the reaction I was looking for. Lacey and I had worked long and hard to create a dazzling display for Paws and Poinsettias.

I followed my sister in through the glass doors and let out a gasp myself. And promptly dropped my coffee, where the travel mug shattered on the marble floor.

"What in the heck is going on here?"

My voice rang out louder than I'd intended. The servers setting up the tables of glittering crystal and delicate china swiveled their heads to take in my coffee-splattered self. I hadn't dropped a mere slosh as Nina Adams had yesterday. My suede boots were soaked with peppermint latte. But I barely saw the surprised onlookers. I instead took in the former department store lobby, meticulously decorated over the last week, completely undone.

Where there had once been four stately pines anchoring each corner of the room, decorated in fanciful ornaments with animal themes, now there stood bright tinsel trees in turquoise, magenta, lavender, and green. The hundreds of red poinsettias I'd helped lovingly arrange had been replaced with cream, white, and light pink versions. The place settings of miniature gingerbread doghouses and whimsical cat condos were nowhere to be seen. Instead, each table bore a cut-glass bowl filled with glittery tropical fruit.

*Oh no she didn't.*

The color scheme and props had my mother written all over them. Rachel hadn't imagined a set of footsteps sneaking through the mansion in the wee hours.

"Isn't it marvelous?" Clementine March sidled up to me and wrapped a green-tipped manicured hand around my arm. I felt my mouth open and close, with no sound emanating from my throat. My mother's antics had rendered me speechless.

"I hope you like it." Mom emerged from the shadows, a sheepish yet proud smile settled on her face. She had the good sense to dampen her grin when she took in my and Rachel's expressions, and a slow blush climbed up her neck.

Clementine seemed to cotton on to the tension and gave my arm a squeeze. "You and Lacey did an admirable job, Mallory. But I was so taken with your mother's ideas yesterday that I decided to enlist her help at the eleventh hour." She bestowed my mother with a winning smile and dropped my arm to step back and further survey the room.

It was marginally less hurtful that my mom had undone all of my and Lacey's work at the official behest of March Homes. I grudgingly admitted in some distant part of my brain that the room looked great. I felt an alarming blend of appreciation, annoyance, and delight. But mostly annoyance.

Goldie appeared on the scene, her countenance far less cheery than her mother's. "I didn't
authorize this change, Mallory, just so you know."
Her announcement was couched as a whisper, but
came out more like a loud hiss.

"Mom, could we have a word?" I pasted what felt
like a pained smile on my face. My mother took a
step closer to Clementine, as if seeking protection.
Rachel nimbly pinched our mother's elbow and
nearly dragged her over to the magenta tinsel tree.

"Ouch! Rachel Marie Shepard, you don't need
to manhandle your mother."

"I think you're pretty familiar with manhan-
dling, Mom. Just look at what you did!" I did manage to keep my voice low, but just barely. I had a
flashback to my mother helping to redo my dio-
rama for drama class while I blissfully slept, unaware of her unauthorized changes. I'd been
furious at her overstepping then, as I was now. A
wave of realization crested and crashed over my
shoulder blades.

"You did this to audition for a staging position
at March Homes!"

*Bingo.*

My mother finally appeared properly chastened.
Her green eyes studiously fixed their gaze on the
floor.

"Mom, did you approach Clementine first with
this idea, or did she approach you?" Rachel demanded an answer with a tap of her silver stilettos
and a hand on her hip.

But before we could get to the heart of the matter, Lacey Adams tore into the room. I'd regretted

my over-the-top reaction of dropping my coffee in surprise, but I had nothing on Lacey. She glanced around the room and let out an actual screech, drawing all eyes her way.

"Who did this?" She scanned the high-ceilinged space and found me in her field of vision. "Mallory, I thought we were a team."

I blanched as Lacey made a beeline to where I stood. The servers had stopped pretending to set tables and stared in frank curiosity at the accusations flying around the room.

"I had nothing to do with these changes." I gestured helplessly around me and felt my mother take a step back.

"Well, who did then? This wasn't what we discussed." Lacey's pretty amber eyes were alight with fire and rage. I anticipated Lacey finding out the vigilante decorator's true identity and attempted to soften the blow.

"I guess we had a little help." I couldn't meet the stager's eyes.

*More like abject steamrolling.*

"Lacey, you need to control your temper. You're out of control. March Homes doesn't need to be associated with this kind of behavior." Clementine arrived to chastise Lacey, but the stager wouldn't be shushed.

"Did you have something to do with this, Clementine? Because Goldie, Mallory, and I worked tirelessly to plan this event. Why—"

"It was me." My mother finally owned up to her hand in the redecorating debacle and emerged from behind the magenta tree. "I'm so sorry,

Lacey. I was under the impression that my daughter Mallory had designed this event and wouldn't mind a bit of reconfiguring."

I felt a flash of exasperation. It wasn't okay to redo my plans even if I hadn't been working in concert with Lacey.

"That's even worse!" Lacey shook her head and narrowed her eyes at my mother. "You shouldn't have overridden your daughter. But I'm sure Clementine put you up to this, too."

Instead of seeming contrite, Clementine cast Lacey a haughty look, giving her all the confirmation the stager needed. Lacey flounced off, and the large room was silent for a moment before the servers resumed their amiable conversations. My mother seemed to deflate before me. Rachel looked torn between comforting her and telling her off for redoing our event planning. I was about to break my silence, my internal volcano of annoyance and frustration brimming to the top.

"Lacey doesn't have the chops to pull off something this daring." Clementine beamed and clasped her hands together. "Don't mind her, Carole. I think you did a marvelous job." Olivia's grandmother swanned off, leaving us three Shepard women alone once more.

"I really messed up." My mom dragged her eyes to meet mine with twin beads of tears gathering at the edges. "Clementine called me last night and said she desperately needed the decor for Paws and Poinsettias changed. I wouldn't have done it if I'd known she was doing it to upset that poor girl." My mother took a deep breath, the wreath pendant on her evergreen sweater set rising and falling. "Clementine said it hasn't been working out with Lacey lately anyway. But there will be so much work to do here. If I were to be hired, there'd be room for several stagers. I didn't mean to usurp her."

A plan seemed to be emerging. Clementine seemed hell-bent on driving Lacey out of her family company, without outright firing her. This seemed like an over-the-top and unnecessary coup to pull on the day of the Marches' entree into Port Quincy society. I wasn't sure I'd want my mom to work for such an unstable and over-the-top employer like Clementine.

"Are you sure you still want to work for the Marches?" I blurted out the question before I could stop myself. Seeing my mother's seemingly contrite tears momentarily stifled my urge to give her a piece of my mind for changing my decorations.

My mother cocked her head, her shoulder-length cut dyed to match Rachel's natural shade of honey caramel. "It was stressful running my own staging business when you girls were younger. You two understand now as businesswomen yourselves. Things can be unpredictable, with boom and bust times. I do want to come out of retirement and stay busy. But not be as stressed as when I was running my own show. You can understand, right? And I'm so sorry, Mallory. I realize I should have refused Clementine's request." My mother looked utterly miserable, the exact opposite of how she usually was during the holiday season.

"It's okay, Mom." I was still getting used to the changed room and tamped down the swirl of emotions coursing through my head. My sister and I had an event to put on in mere hours and still quite a bit of work to do. It was surreal walking through the newly-imagined and executed winter wonderland. I had to admit it looked great. I just couldn't shake the feeling that I'd been hood-winked. But there was no time to reflect. Rachel and I rolled up our sleeves and got to work.

Later that evening my sister, mother and I re-turned to Paws and Poinsettias freshly garbed in our evening wear to simultaneously work and enjoy the event. I'd been treated to a profuse string of apologies from my mother and had tried to set her mind at ease. I'm not sure what I would have done myself if I'd gotten a fire-drill call from Clementine March in the middle of the night, de-manding a decorating switcheroo.

We all oohed and aahed as we stepped through the glass doors. In addition to my mother's strik-ing decorating job, the left side of the room now held the final items on offer for the auction. There were tickets to shows at the local theater, baubles from Fournier's jewelry store, and certifi-cates to the local spa. The most fun feature was a display of outrageously adorable ugly Christmas sweaters for doggies and kitties of all sizes. I men-tally conjured up an image of Whiskey and Soda in one of the sparkly kitty tutus for sale and couldn't tamp down my grin. Not that I was sure my cats would ever consent to wear such items. They were safely tucked away at Thistle Park. Although they would have enjoyed seeing the other pets of Port

Quincy, I was on the clock and couldn't shepherd them at the same time.

Soon the large space was filled with a veritable who's who of pets and owners. The humans dined on savory hors d'oeuvres from Pellegrino's restaurant, and their furry companions gobbled treats crafted by local pet suppliers. It was a happy holiday menagerie of meows and barks and smiling owners.

The attendees wore a festive mix of evening wear, the women in scarlet and evergreen velvet gowns, silver-threaded sheaths and little black dresses. Their dates wore smart suits and tuxes. But outshining even their owners' sleek attire were the pets of Port Quincy, all dolled up as much as they would allow. The evening would kick off with a pet fashion show and behind the curtain of the temporary raised stage was a merry melee of dogs and cats sporting Scottish plaids, red bows, and adorably gaudy sweaters.

"Everyone loves my design!" My mother appeared at my side and beamed at the partygoers. Her former humble contrition had evaporated in a haze of pride. She clasped her hands together and went on. "Clementine is spreading the word that I decorated!"

My stepfather raised his eyebrows, and even Ramona the pug seemed to roll her bulging eyes. I burst out laughing, but Rachel glared at our mother. Doug could contain his laughter no longer and began as well, earning a sniff from my mother. Doug's laughter died when he spotted Jesse Flowers, the preternaturally tall contractor, who had restored my B and B as well as this building.

Once upon a time, before she'd met and married Doug, my mom had been in a relationship with Jesse. The affable contractor seemed torn about whether to acknowledge my mother and Doug's existence, or do an about-face. His fiancée Bev's dog decided for him, taking one look at Ramona and straining at his jingle bell leash.

"Elvis! Heel!" My friend and the owner of the Silver Bells Bridal shop was pulled along behind her basset hound. Elvis finally reached Ramona and an intense spate of sniffing ensued. My mother's bubble of happiness evaporated as she cut her gaze from Jesse to Bev, and she knelt to fuss over Ramona.

I knelt to pet Elvis, taking in his earthy, loamy basset hound scent of Cheetos mixed with gruyère. The sweet hound lifted his dolorous eyes to meet my gaze. But his stumpy tail motored fast enough to turn him into a doggy helicopter, revealing his true cheerful feelings and excitement. His owners laughed, and the ice broken, Jesse thrust out his mammoth hand to shake Doug's. The two men wandered off to catch the Pittsburgh Penguins score on the TV in the lobby, while my mother and Bev got to know each other. I breathed a sigh of relief.

"This is some event you put together." Ursula Frank appeared at my side, and I nearly didn't recognize the woman without her usual judge's robes. Toby's mother always looked like a sterner version of the goddess Demeter, with gray braids wound around her head in a heavy crown. Tonight she wore a striking red pantsuit, her ubiquitous reading glasses tied around her neck with a Pitt Panthers shoestring. The judge always made me a bit nervous, swishing around her courtroom like a tall tornado.

"This is Hemingway." The judge allowed me to pet the pretty Persian cat nestled in her arms. The snowy purring guy stretched out a paw to bat at my arm in a kitty hello. I squinted at his miniature toes, something different. "He's a polydactyl cat, just like the ones Hemingway the author owned. Hence his name." The judge seemed to soften as she discussed her kitty. I usually struggled to find similarities between the gruff jurist and her gentle son, but tonight, watching Ursula fawn over her cat, I could finally see the resemblance. "I wanted to apologize, too, for not being more involved in helping Toby and Olivia plan their wedding." The judge cracked a rare smile. "Thank you for moving the wedding up."

"It's my pleasure." I enjoyed speaking with the judge outside the formal confines of the court-house.

"Say hello to Garrett for me." And she was off, treating me to a glimpse of the Birkenstocks she always wore, even to this formal occasion. The judge had been my boyfriend Garrett's mentor in law school and continued to mentor him now.

A few minutes later the fashion show commenced. Rachel and I attempted to help pet owners wrangle their furry companions. There were doggies sniffing butts and barking out hellos and cats plaintively meowing.

"Despite this chaos, it's easier to work with these guys than the people whose weddings we put on," Rachel giggled.

I had to agree. "Sometimes it's like herding cats."

"Um, we're *literally* herding cats."

The first entrant was Alma Cunningham with her gorgeous Irish setter, Wilkes. Alma was a *Gone with the Wind* aficionado and had donned a gown similar to one of Scarlett O'Hara's dressing gowns in the film. Wilkes sported a leash woven with blinking Christmas lights and had consented to wear a green velvet topcoat. His gleaming auburn doggy coat rivaled any human model's in a hair dye commercial.

Next up was Alma's granddaughter, the wife of my once fiancé. Becca Cunningham proudly led her Maine Coon cat, Pickles, on a leash when the other cat entrants were carried or confined to cat strollers. The behemoth cat proudly strutted down the catwalk, soaking up the exuberant cries of "Work it, kitty!" I wasn't sure who looked prouder, Pickles or his owner Becca, in her daringly cut teal Badgley Mischka gown.

But the final entry produced the most oohs and aahs. My friend and one of my first brides, Whitney, sat in a wheeled sled dressed as an elf. She patiently moved the sled with her feet like Fred Flintstone, while her four-month-old son, Vance, sat ensconced in her lap dressed as the littlest Santa. Whitney's three Westies—Bruce, Fiona, and Maisie—nearly danced in front of the sleigh, each pup adorned with miniature reindeer antlers. The applause was unanimous, and Whitney and Vance were declared the winners.

The rest of the evening was fun and fancy-free. The silent auction commenced at one end of the room while denizens cut a rug at the other end on the dance floor.

"I know you've been busy with this event, and you probably haven't had a chance to speak to Toby yet about my future husband." Rachel materialized at my side, garnering constant looks in her gold lamé minidress complete with miniature crystal ornaments sewn all over the fabric. "So I've identified my own top prospects." She nodded her head toward a small group of men I recognized as Toby's groomsmen. "All doctors. All available. All eligible to become my partner!" And with that my sister dashed off, leaving me in a cloud of sweet jasmine perfume. Our cook at Thistle Park, Miles, looked crushed. He hugged his Dalmatian to his chest and turned away from my sister. The affable young man had held a torch for Rachel as long as he'd known her.

I stepped into the shadows and observed the event. I was ready to declare it a raging success. I shimmied down the Spanx helping to keep my black Dolce and Gabbana dress where it belonged. I caught site of Olivia discussing something with Toby. An acquaintance brought Olivia a flute of champagne, and she smiled her thanks. As the woman turned away, Olivia promptly poured the golden liquid into a potted plant. I blinked, unsure of what I'd just seen. But before I could ponder it further, I turned around to come face-to-face with my boyfriend, Garrett.

"Great job." He tilted my chin up and I realized we were right beneath a sprig of tropical-hued mistletoe my mother must have hung up. We met for a scorcher of a kiss.

"I had a little help." I let out a shaky laugh, not sure if I was unsteady from the lovely kiss or from reliving my mother's redecoration ploy. "You're looking mighty debonair."

It was true. My dashing boyfriend looked amazing, his lovely hazel eyes dancing with mirth, his tall frame filling out the shoulders of his tuxedo. The holiday lights glinted off his dark hair, and I still felt like swooning after over a year of dating as he tenderly brushed an errant curl from my forehead.

"You must help me find him immediately!" The voice of Judge Frank cut through the hazy glow of Garrett's embrace. Several heads swiveled to take in the judge glowering at an attendant.

"I guess I'd better put out this fire." I left my beau to help Ursula. She wrung her hands and darted her eyes left and right. "I placed Hemingway in his carrier. I was getting ready to leave. I turned to retrieve my coat, and in those mere seconds, someone picked up his carrier and ran off with my cat!" Her speech gained steam as she went, until the last few words were nearly a screech.

"Calm down, Ursula. I'm sure we can find Hemingway." Garrett smoothly stepped up to soothe his mentor. The two rushed to speak with Clementine and Alan March, who began to help the judge look for her cat.

And not a moment too soon, as their absence kept them from taking in Lacey. The stager appeared to have had too much to drink. She weaved unsteadily toward me, nearly tripping in her sky-high turquoise heels.

"Uh-oh." My mother sidled up to me and seemed to try to hide behind a potted palm. "I think Lacey's following me."

"Quick, duck behind there." I nudged my mother behind the bar, where the bartender seemed to have vanished. The last thing I needed was a drunken altercation between two vying stagers. But Lacey seemed to see just fine despite her inebriated state. She leaned over the bar, her stomach hanging over the edge, threatening to fall in.

"I see you, Carole Shepard. You don't need to hide from me." Her speech was slurred and several decibels too loud. I stepped in and placed a gentle hand on her arm.

"Would you like me to call you a cab, Lacey?" I wondered if her mother Nina would be able to pick her up.

"I still have business to attend to, Mallory." Lacey batted away my hand as if it were a pesky fly and attempted to focus on my mother. "I'd like some Hawaiian Punch. Neat."

My mother seemed to deflate with relief at not having to serve Lacey more alcohol. She gamely played bartender, pouring the tipsy stager a small cut glass tumbler full of electric blue Hawaiian Punch. Lacey seemed to reverently grab the glass and tottered away. I made to go after her to make sure she was all right, when my mother pulled me back.

"Have you officially put in a good word for me?" My mother's eyes were pleading.

I rolled my eyes and gestured around me. "I think your redecoration was audition enough. Besides, you need to cut it out. Lacey is the official stager, and it's not like they're advertising for a new one."

My mother proffered her cell phone as if presenting a royal flush, a gleam in her green eyes. The screen from March Homes's human resources department displayed a posting for a new head stager. The date of the advertisement was today.

"Oh, you have nothing to worry about." Clementine sidled up to my mother and gave her shoulders a squeeze. My mother beamed, until she saw Lacey return, Goldie March in tow.

"You lied! You said you weren't trying to replace me." Lacey's slurred speech ricocheted around the marble-clad room with alarming volume. Goldie shook her head, her ire directed at Clementine. "That's right, Lacey, we are not trying to replace you."

"Then what's this?" Lacey thrust a bejeweled phone into Goldie's face, nearly knocking into her nose.

Goldie winced as she took in the posting. "This is as much a surprise to me as it is to you. Be that as it may, you've had too much to drink, Lacey. I think it's time to go."

Lacey stared at Goldie with a dawning look of horror. She began to weep, then shouted at Clementine. The two March women helped escort Lacey out when the stager crumpled to the ground. Several onlookers gasped, and some of Toby's friends pushed to the front of the now-gathering crowd to help Lacey.

"She's having a seizure. Call 9-1-1."

# CHAPTER FOUR

"**S**he's gone." Truman stood at my door to deliver the bad news. His tall frame filled our front doorway as weak, winter sunlight filtered in behind him. It was twelve hours after the unceremonious end of Paws and Poinsettias. The gorgeous holiday decorations at Thistle Park seemed to mock his somber pronouncement.

Rachel wordlessly slung her arm around my shoulder. I knew my sister was as exhausted as I was. Lacey Adams had been in bad shape when the paramedics lifted her on the stretcher and screeched away, the ambulance lights flashing and sirens wailing. Guests at the auction has stuck around for another half hour, gossiping and exchanging worried tales of Lacey's inebriation before her apparent seizure and collapse. They'd finished their bids and tossed back their last glasses of champagne, the fizz evaporating like the good tidings for the evening.

The Marches and I decided to wrap up the

shindig early, and the evening gown and tux-clad attendants had slipped out into the night. We'd been worried sick. And now the hopeful feelings we'd felt percolating up at the sight of the retreating ambulance had been dashed to smithereens. What had been a furry and fun event was now indelibly mired in tragedy.

"What was the cause of death?" I stepped back to allow Truman to formally enter the hall.

"We don't know yet," Truman admitted. "But she did appear to have a seizure at Paws and Poinsettias. Her heart stopped in the ICU. They couldn't revive her." He looked even more pained than usual when imparting bad news. I gulped and let him go on. "According to Lacey's mother, she did have some health issues but absolutely no history of seizures."

Truman followed us down the series of hallways to the kitchen. He exchanged greetings with my mother and Doug, who were nursing cups of coffee at the table.

"So, do you expect foul play or not?" I blurted out the question as Truman accepted his own cup.

The chief ran a large hand through his thinning salt-and-pepper hair. "It's complicated, of course." He peered at my mother and Doug, seeming to weigh whether to share his theories with them. "There are plenty of people who were not fans of Lacey Adams."

I felt my mother's chair shift next to mine as she squirmed. She was one person who would perhaps benefit professionally from Lacey's demise. She stared dolefully into her coffee and was uncharacteristically quiet.

"There's the March family." I didn't name Clem-

entine specifically. "They were all concerned about
Lacey and of course worried for her last night. But
Clementine and Goldie did try to usher her out
right before she had her seizure." What I didn't
mention was that beneath the Marches' concern
for Lacey's condition, I'd detected a simmering
anger toward Lacey for ruining their resplendent,
splashy foray into the social world of Port Quincy.
"I don't think the March family was happy with the
way the event ended," I put in neutrally. "So that
would make it seem like they wouldn't have anything to do with harming Lacey, right?"

Truman nodded at the theory. "Although they
needn't worry about the negative publicity of
Lacey falling ill at their party. Mayhem and murder haven't staunched any of your business." The
chief spoke his words in a dry and rueful tone. I
felt a slow blush creep up my neck.

*It was true.*

I was busier than ever, despite some unfortunate things befalling my B and B over the last year
and a half. If anything, people perishing at my
events cultivated a lurid fascination in the denizens
of Port Quincy. My book of business hadn't suffered
at all.

"Lacey was about three thousand sheets to the
wind," Rachel helpfully offered. "I tried to offer
her a cab, and I know Mallory did, too."

"Yes, it could just be acute alcohol poisoning."
Truman gave my sister a shrewd look. "And the
toxicology report is being rushed as much as it can
be." He studied us all another moment. "I don't
like the insinuations I'm hearing from Nina
Adams, though."

I pictured the warm and bubbly Christmas store purveyor and felt a stab of pathos.

"How is she taking her daughter's death?"

"Not well. It was ten years ago that her eldest daughter, Andrea, disappeared."

*So that's what Nina had been alluding to.*

"While we can't prove of course that Andrea is dead, one has to assume after all these years it's true." Truman shook his head ruefully and pushed away his steaming cup of joe. "When I spoke to Nina early this morning, the first thing she said was, 'not again.' She seems to think these incidents with her daughters are connected. Although that's quite a leap."

"But maybe not a leap, if Lacey turns out to be murdered." My stepfather was listening in with the quiet analytical nature of the history professor he'd once been. He looked cowed when Truman sent him a glare.

"Which we don't know yet," Truman carefully reminded us. "And although it's unlikely that Andrea is alive, it's still possible. She disappeared without a shred of evidence of foul play. She'd been arguing with her mother and could have just run away."

But even Truman didn't look as if he believed that hopeful theory.

"In any event, we just need to be patient. The autopsy on Lacey is being performed as we speak."

I shivered, imagining the pretty, vivacious stager, now gone from this side of the earth. And through all of this musing, only one thing disturbed me more than the realization Lacey had died at an event I'd hosted. It was my mother's continued silence, more deafening to my ears than the kitschy cat clock ticking loudly away in the corner.

I refused to bring up the fact that my mom had basically begged for Lacey's job mere minutes before she'd collapsed. I took another sip of French roast and coughed as the hot liquid went down the wrong way.

*Mom made Lacey's last drink.*

I ignored Truman's eyes boring into me and slowly dragged mine to meet my mom's. I waited and waited for her to jump into the fray and clear the air, as well as her name. But she remained silent, if not agitated.

"Not her again." Truman rolled his eyes as his cell phone trilled out a text notification. He jabbed at the screen with large fingers and shook his head in consternation. "Judge Ursula Frank is used to people jumping when she so much as lifts a finger. I will not, however, open an investigation into the disappearance of her cat Hemingway when I have a possible murder on my hands."

We all giggled at the preposterousness of the judge, thankful the tense air had been cleared. I did hope the judge found her cat, though. I'd be worried beyond belief if anything happened to Whiskey or Soda.

"Do you have any idea who vandalized Olivia's car?" I thought I'd take advantage of Truman's sharing mood.

A dark cloud passed over his face. "We returned Olivia's car. We weren't able to lift any prints, and frankly, though the message was disturbing, a relatively harmless prank isn't worthy of a full-on investigation."

Truman bade us goodbye and slipped out the back door.

"At least Lacey didn't die here at Thistle Park." Rachel shook her head in sorrow as she stirred a lump of turbinado sugar into her coffee. Ramona had made her way to her lap and opened her doggie mouth in glee as my sister scratched behind her ears.

"Rachel!" I pinched my sister, who had the good graces to look marginally chagrined.

"Admit it, Mallory. You were thinking the same darn thing."

*Okay, so it's true.*

For some reason, a few of the events and happenings at my B and B had led to people perishing in the near past. I had to silently agree with my sister. It wasn't lost on me that Lacey had met her bad fate far from the grounds of my mansion. Still, she'd fallen ill somewhat on my watch, at an event she'd helped plan and one my sister and I officially ran. It didn't take away from the fact my heart went out to Lacey's mother.

"Penny for your thoughts, Mom?" Rachel pivoted and lasered her focus on our mother. Carole jumped in her chair and set her cup down with a start.

"I'm very sorry that poor girl passed away." My mom shook her head and pushed her cup away. "But I had nothing to do with it. It's a pity Clementine wasn't happy with Lacey's work when this happened. But I'm sure she's innocent, too."

I cocked my head in thought. It worried me a bit my mother was rushing to defend Clementine

March. The eccentric woman seemed poised to be my mother's patron of staging career comebacks, and I wondered if the possibility of working for March Homes was creating a premature and dangerous alliance.

My mother's cell phone blasted out Justin Bieber's version of "The Christmas Song." We all jumped with a laugh as she peered at the screen, pushing up the electric blue reading glasses that matched today's snowflake sweater set.

"It's Clementine." My mom couldn't tamp down the frisson of excitement in her voice. She slipped into the dining room to take the call. Rachel, Doug, and I exchanged glances as my mother's voice became more and more obsequious and animated. She nearly bounded into the kitchen mere minutes later on her electric blue moccasins.

"Clementine would like me to formally interview for the stager position!" My mother's face fell when she took in the panoply of frowns on our faces.

"Isn't that a little . . . rushed?" I said carefully.

"Yeah, Mom. Lacey's body isn't even cold." Rachel tsked and popped a cardamom cookie soldier neatly into her mouth.

"I'd be careful, my love." Doug's brow was furrowed as he counseled my mom.

"You are all just being sticks in the mud. That job was posted on the March Homes website *before* Lacey had her unfortunate accident."

*Yeah, like a whole five minutes before.*

My mother dismissed our concerns and retrieved Ramona from Rachel. She swept from the room with her pug, Doug chasing after her.

"This doesn't look good." I gathered up coffee cups and ferried them to the sink.

"Thank goodness that call from Clementine didn't come while Truman was questioning us." Rachel trailed her gaze up the back stairs. "I don't think Mom realizes how this could seem."

The optics were terrible. If Truman followed the natural order of the past few days' events, and if it turned out Lacey's death was at someone else's hand, my mom would soon be suspect numero uno.

Rachel squirmed in her chair and echoed my concerns. "It's almost as if Mom is being set up."

I added to my sister's anxiety. "Did you know Mom made Lacey a drink?" My voice was small and meek.

"She *what*? She has to tell Truman. Like right now."

The chief would flip his lid if he knew my mom wasn't being immediately forthright.

"I'll do no such thing, young ladies, and I resent the implication." Our mother alighted on the last back stair. She must have returned to listen in. My sister and I froze. Carole's moccasins made for the perfect sleuthing shoes, her footfalls nearly silent as she crept around the mansion. "Whose side are you girls on? Blood is thicker than water, you know." My mother's face was a mixture of hurt and anger. "Is your allegiance to your family, or to Garrett and his?"

I felt as if I'd been slapped. "I don't like your insinuation, Mom. I just think you need to tell Truman you made Lacey her last drink on this earth before he finds out himself and wonders why you actively kept that information from him."

But it was too late. My mother flounced up the stairs, and this time, we heard every angry footfall.

Rachel shrugged and bit into another cookie figure. I retreated to my office. I wasn't keen on involving myself with Olivia's messy family any longer. But I had an upcoming toy drive to facilitate for them, and of course, Olivia and Toby's moved-up wedding.

A nagging thought percolated up in my brain as I tried to switch into planner mode. I closed my eyes and recalled Olivia pouring out her drink into a potted plant.

*Almost as if she knew it was poisoned.*

An hour later, I tried to put my mother's machinations out of my mind. I ushered Olivia into the library for an impromptu meeting about her rapidly approaching nuptials.

"I can't believe Lacey is gone." My friend blew her heavy sable bangs off her forehead in a gust of exasperation. She hugged her middle, then waved off the cup of strong tea I offered her. She gazed at a copse of trees outside the window, seemingly lost in thought. "She was so close to my mom." She shivered. I handed her a cozy crochet shawl I sometimes slung over my own shoulders when I worked in the window seat in the library. Olivia managed a small smile as she drew the brightly patterned shawl around her. The buttery yellow walls and roaring fire did little to warm our spirits after reflecting on Lacey's death.

I broached the next subject as delicately as I could. "It certainly wasn't the impression your parents and grandparents wanted to make. I could understand if you and Toby wanted to postpone the wedding in light of what happened with Lacey."

"No!" Olivia sat up straighter, the shawl slipping down her shoulders. She seemed to have realized she'd nearly shouted her answer and modulated her voice. "What happened to Lacey was terrible." She gazed at her engagement ring and seemed to steel herself. "But Toby and I are still going to wed at the end of the month."

Her answer brooked no discussion. We were going to have a wedding two days before Christmas. I squeezed my friend's hand and gave her a gentle smile. Olivia seemed to melt with relief.

"I'm glad you understand, Mallory."

I really didn't understand the rush to wed. But if that's what my friend wanted, I would do my very best to make it happen. The vision of Olivia hastily and surreptitiously pouring out her drink into the plant, mere minutes before Lacey crumpled to the ground, kept rearing its head. But now didn't seem the time to play grand inquisitor. I turned to wedding planning instead.

"Then let's get started." I placed my tablet before Olivia on the striped ottoman. "I wanted to show you some ideas we can pull off in—" I paused to gulp, "ten days' time."

Olivia peered at the screen and nodded. "My mother wanted to give me wedding homework last night. It was the only thing that took her mind off of Lacey's death." Olivia shuddered again and slid her finger over the Pinterest board I'd compiled for her approval. The first representative board showed a traditional red December wedding. Olivia stared at the screen, her pretty dark eyes impassive.

"Okay, let's look at the next one." I brought up a pale blue winter wonderland of an idea board, complete with white branches and sparkly accouterments.

Olivia gave a wan smile and nodded. "This could work."

I shook my head. "But you're not excited about it. I want you to fall in love with your wedding, even if it is being put together fast."

"What about a simple forest green?" Olivia peered at the oval emerald on her hand. "This was the ring Toby's dad gave to Ursula. The green seems fitting with the season. Would it be too cliché?"

"Not at all!" I breathed a sigh of relief and scrolled over to the last Pinterest idea board. "This might be a winner. For this theme, I chose a silver and evergreen palate. We could weave in small angel elements to tie in the theme with your ornament." I gestured to the tree topper Olivia had retrieved from her purse and placed on the ottoman before us. I observed a kind of hairline fracture where the angel's wing had been glued back on. "There will be glass angel candelabras at each table. I found a little storefront on Etsy that has ten in stock. Just say the word, and I'll order them within the hour."

Olivia nodded, warming to the idea. "Your choices

are lovely. I'll just go with whatever you've selected. You know my taste. And frankly, I just want to get married."

I nodded, appreciative that my friend was being so honest, but a little miffed too that she didn't really seem to care about the minutiae of her wedding details. Then again, maybe she had her priorities in the right place. She was coming up for partner and her family was attempting to win over the town of Port Quincy amidst the death of its stager. I loved planning weddings and crafting memorable details, but there had been times when I wondered if some of my brides were more interested in an intricate and showy ceremony than spending the rest of their lives with the partners they were marrying.

"There is one thing." Olivia brightened. "I want to honor my dad in some way." She grew wistful. "The women in my family can be a bit . . . strong-willed. My dad is more sentimental, and he has a Christmas tradition we hold each year." She smiled in seeming reminiscence. "Christmas Day itself is a March family affair, with Christmas crackers and all the usual dishes. But the evening before Christmas, my dad cooks a traditional Czech Christmas Eve meal. There are twelve dishes, ones his mother and grandmother taught him how to make."

"What a beautiful idea." I warmed to the tribute to her father and thought it would be a lovely, personal touch to the rushed nuptials, in addition to the subtle angel theme.

"Mom and Grandma will flip out, of course." Olivia giggled. "Let's just keep the menu under wraps until the big day."

"It's a deal." Olivia and I high-fived with glee at deciding on a menu for her wedding. But my friend's joy was short lived as her cell phone pinged out an email notice. She frowned as she scrolled through the message and mumbled something about a case she was working on.

I observed the deep circles resting beneath Olivia's eyes and her petite frame that looked more slender than usual. Her appearance corroborated the inordinate amount of stress she was under. I would overlook her lack of interest in picking each detail of her big day and give my friend a much-needed break.

"What I'm really worried about are the logistics of things after we marry," Olivia admitted. "Toby and I haven't really discussed where we'll live, work, and start our married life."

*Then why the rush down the aisle?*

I pushed my pushy thoughts away and focused on my friend in need.

"Toby can't move from Port Quincy since he's so frequently on call."

"You're not tied to Russell Carey. You could leave and try to find a position closer to Port Quincy."

I floated the idea, knowing it was already a loser.

Olivia twisted her pretty face into a frown. "I could do that. And perhaps I should. Different jobs come up in a lifetime but not the love of your life. Then again, I've been working so hard. I'm on the precipice of making partner. I can't just cast that aside."

We sat in amiable if not sad silence for a moment when the doorbell gave its sonorous clang. I beamed as I let my boyfriend Garrett in and he joined Olivia in the library.

"I don't want to interrupt." He smiled as I waved off his concern. "I finished a case this morning. The jury decided in our favor." He beamed and bestowed me with a fleeting kiss. He loved his work and getting wins for his clients. The contrast between him and Olivia couldn't be more stark.

"It sounds like you truly love your job." Her eyes were wistful as she took in my beaming and energetic boyfriend.

"It isn't what I set out to do. I thought I wanted to get a clerkship and teach initially. But transferring from Harvard to Pitt and becoming a small-town attorney was the best thing that ever happened to me." Garrett alluded to his decision to come home to raise his infant daughter, Summer, fourteen years ago.

"What kind of caseload do you have?" Olivia asked questions in more than just a polite way. I wondered what she was thinking.

"It's too busy, to be frank." Garrett's exuberance dimmed a notch. "It's a good problem to have. But I'm spending too much time away from my daughter and from you, Mallory." He turned to me with an apology in his lovely hazel eyes.

It was true. We'd both been too busy for months. Garrett had new clients and old ones to attend to. His business was booming. As was mine. The assistant I'd hired had returned to school, and I hadn't yet replaced her. Garrett's natural down time was on the weekends, but even those were becoming clogged up with extra time spent back at his office. I was tied up most Fridays and Saturdays putting on weddings and events. That left Sunday. Garrett and I had fallen into the routine of attending his family Sunday dinner. I got to see Garrett and chat with Summer as well as Truman and his wife, Lorraine. But for the last few weeks, that was our only contact. I'd been looking forward to the month of December, a time when I'd refused to book any weddings. Well, except for Olivia's moved-up affair.

A kernel of an idea seemed to percolate as Garrett regarded Olivia. "I've been considering taking on a partner these last few months. I'm at a tipping point where I need to start turning more work away or finding someone else to join my practice."

His half-suggestion, half-invitation hung like a pendulum in the air.

And Olivia grabbed it.

"As it so happens, I've been wondering how I could practice here in Port Quincy." Her former exhaustion seemed to evaporate with excitement as she pondered Garrett's idea. "I have experience running my own trials, although in a different county, and sometimes in federal court. But I have had experience with smaller trials and cases with my pro bono work."

"You'd figure out the differences between practicing in Pittsburgh and Port Quincy pretty quickly." Garrett began to pace around the room. "This could really work!"

His enthusiasm was infectious. I'd been lamenting how to help Olivia out and ease her mind, and my boyfriend had conjured up a solution that would benefit all three of us. Olivia could relocate to Port Quincy to start her married life, Garrett would have immense pressure taken off of him with work, and I would get to spend more time with him and Summer.

"I could also bring a pretty big book of business to the table." Olivia cocked her head in thought. "I'm sure I could handle the legal work for my family's company in Port Quincy. They've been groaning about maintaining counsel from Pittsburgh to handle their issues here."

Garrett nodded. "I have no conflicts of interest that I know of. I don't currently represent anyone with claims against March Homes. And while I don't do a lot of transactional work, it would be a good direction to expand in."

"And I already know a bit about your practice. I think my skills as a litigator will mesh well with the needs of your current clients." Olivia looked more content than I'd seen her in a while. "Now I'll just need to explain to everyone why I'm walking away from the firm when I'm so close to making partner." A flicker of doubt marred her happy expression.

"Are you sure you can walk away from that accomplishment?" Garrett grew serious.

Olivia took a deep breath. "If I'm being honest, I'm not enjoying it anymore. The thrill of the chase is gone. What I do enjoy, however, is working on my smaller cases. This will be a great career move." She spoke in calm, steady tones. "For both of us."

Two of my favorite people beamed at each other. It was the start of a beautiful professional partnership that had blossomed right here in my library.

Garrett turned to me. "I just stopped in to say hello and gained a business partner. Not bad." The three of us laughed.

"I actually need to get back to Pittsburgh." Olivia glanced ruefully at her pinging cell phone. "But it'll be easier to work this month knowing it's my last at the firm."

Olivia left with a happier heart. Garrett and I saw her off before stealing another kiss beneath the mistletoe in the front hall. What started off as a small embrace evolved into a five-alarm scorcher.

"Do you know what this means?" Garrett peered into my eyes, his smoldering and serious. "We'll get to spend a lot more time together."

I blinked up with a slow smile. "Now I just have to do my part and hire another assistant."

"Okay, you two. Move it somewhere else." Rachel made her way down the stairs with a playful smile. "What brings you here, Garrett?"

"I just gained a business partner." He filled my sister in on Olivia joining his practice. He and Rachel exchanged high fives.

"This is a wonderful holiday season." I reflected on all of the changes happening, bringing those I loved closer to me. "Mom and Doug have moved back, Olivia will be in Port Quincy, and Garrett and I will have more time to see each other."

Things were back to normal. It would be a busy December but one filled with new beginnings and reconnecting with loved ones. My heart was filled with cheer.

Then the flashback of Lacey collapsing at Paws and Poinsettias edged its way into the frontiers of my conscience. I shivered at the recollection and chased away the chill with another cup of hot cocoa.

That evening I shared the good news of Olivia and Garrett's new business partnership with my stepfather. There was only one person missing from the celebration. My mother hadn't returned from what must have been a marathon interview with March Homes for their inauspicious stager position.

"What's taking her so long?" Rachel testily shoved her fork into her lasagna. Her cutlery screeched across the plate. I had to admit the fuzzy feelings I'd felt were evaporating fast. If March Homes would monopolize my mother's time so much just for an interview, what would it be like working for them?

Doug echoed my concerns. "Your mother had planned on doing some staging after we relocated. I wasn't imagining her starting a new full-time position."

"Did you and Mom discuss her plans?" I didn't want to delve into the minutiae of my parents' marriage, but Doug seemed downright downcast.

"This opportunity came out of nowhere." He set down his fork, his lasagna untouched. "I just want your mother to be prudent. I wasn't there at Paws and Poinsettias. But just hearing how things went down, it doesn't seem right."

"Mom needs to be careful." We all resumed dinner in silence. I heard galloping paws overhead and broke into a smile. My cats were asserting their dominance and letting Ramona know they ruled the roost. The pug was happy to comply, spending her days basking in a patch of sun on the third floor. Soda had been successful in engaging the dog in a daily game of chase, though. But for the most part the pug had ceded control of our little animal kingdom at Thistle Park.

"I got the job!" My mother sailed in the back door followed by a whoosh of chilly air. She took off her electric blue wool coat before she realized she'd been met with only wan praise. "What's with all of you? You're supposed to be happy for me!"

I stood and served my mom a steaming helping of lasagna. She usually ate like a bird, but tonight she tucked into the food with gusto. She set down her fork and tried to allay our concerns. "Now I know you're all a bit spooked by the demise of their other stager—"

"At an event you took over from her!" Rachel interrupted.

"Just be careful, honey." Doug cast a doleful look at our mother.

"Not you, too! I'd expect this from the girls, but I thought you'd be supportive." My mother set down her water glass with a clatter. Doug rubbed her shoulders and murmured his support.

It was weird being concerned for my mom rather than the other way around. She had been overprotective when we were kids; she was a true helicopter mom. Even when we'd been latchkey kids she'd managed to find out what we were doing each second of the day.

"I'm happy you got the job, Mom," I said evenly. "What I'm specifically worried about now is how it'll look to Truman."

My mom had resumed her munching and waved a breadstick in dismissal of my concerns. "I have nothing to worry about. I'm completely innocent."

"We know that," Rachel agreed. "But it looks like you bumped off Lacey to get her job." She shrugged as our mother sputtered.

"I'll admit it was a little uncouth how Clementine basically had me audition for the position before they tried to nudge Lacey out."

Rachel's cell sang out a cheery ditty, and she disappeared into the dining room to take the call. The rest of my family ate in silence again, pondering my mother's new position. The optics looked horrible. There would be no way to hide from Truman that my mom had gotten Lacey's job a mere twenty-four hours after she'd perished.

*And right after Mom made her a drink.*

"I did it! I have a date with a doctor!" Rachel returned to the table. She glowed with excitement and filled us in on her upcoming date with one of Toby's groomsmen, the thoughtful man who'd attended to Lacey, a surgeon named Evan.

I offered my sister an encouraging smile. "I'm glad something good came out of Paws and Poinsettias."

# CHAPTER FIVE

The next day my mother was as nervous as a kindergartner on the first day of school. Doug and Ramona looked on fondly as she donned a smart business suit and accessories, all in a purple palette. Ramona watched her leave from her third-floor window seat perch. Then she seemed to give a doggie shrug and curled up under a Christmas tree for a nap. Doug puttered off to read about Revolutionary War reenactments. He was looking for hobbies to resurrect now that my mother would be occupied with her new job.

Rachel and I had studied the advent calendar in our small third-floor kitchen. It was another tradition my mother had instilled. I swallowed the lovely German chocolate like a bitter little pill. It was December 11.

"We only have twelve days to make Olivia and Toby's wedding happen." Rachel popped her piece of chocolate into her mouth and gave a vicious crunch.

"And we have yet to see the proposed venue."

But it was something I would remedy that afternoon. I received an email from a harried Olivia with the truncated guest list. Now that the happy couple had rapidly reduced the guest list to a more manageable fifty, I could breathe a sigh of relief. The wedding really wouldn't be that hard to pull off. I did need to see the space Rachel and I would be working with. I left Rachel preparing for her date with the doctor and headed off to the Marches' cabin two miles west of town. The sun was setting ahead of me. The sky was a deep cobalt in the rearview mirror and a vivid sherbet canvas up ahead. The wedding was scheduled for around this hour, and it would be neat to see what kind of light I'd be working with.

The turn off to the March hunting property was marked with a large wreath tied to a fence, the bow jaunty and burnt orange, the color of the company logo. I was glad they'd placed the decoration; otherwise, I would have missed the turnoff. There was plenty of undeveloped land surrounding Port Quincy, most of it apparently owned by the March family and the Gibsons. I made a mental note to further jazz up the entrance to the secluded parcel come wedding day. It didn't look like anyone lived on the lot, which was crowded with evergreen and deciduous trees. I couldn't make out a single structure as I plunged the Butterscotch Monster down an unlit gravel road.

I felt like Hansel and Gretel on the way to the witch's cabin under a black sky overhead, only snatches of which I could see though the towering foliage. "I should have brought some bread crumbs," I joked aloud to myself. The trip into this forest was getting downright creepy. I wended my way further in, and a mile later I saw a glimmer ahead. It was a real light at the end of the tunnel of branches and trees.

"Holy moly!" Before me rose a magnificent edifice crafted in warm wood. The rustic yet refined structure held turrets, multiple stone chimneys, and row upon row of gleaming windows. It was like the cabin on the maple syrup bottle, infused with a healthy dose of steroids.

Olivia beamed from the front porch of the building. "You found it!"

"I was getting a bit worried there, honestly." I had no idea the place existed before today. "And this is a castle, not a cabin."

"Everyone has that reaction." Olivia chuckled. "You feel like you're plunging into the wooded abyss, and then you see the cabin."

"Is it new?" The structure was so pristine, the rough-hewn logs and boards giving off a distinct, fresh-cut lumber smell.

"Nearly. Dad designed it and had it built in the spring. This is the site of Grandpa Rudy and Grandma Clementine's original cabin. It was considerably smaller and had been on this site for thirty years. But Dad wanted a showpiece retreat to bring people to now that we'll have a greater presence in Port Quincy. Come inside." Olivia ushered me into a giant great room with a warm fire glowing in the two-story fireplace. I relaxed as the warmth enveloped me. The inside was as impressive as the outside, and I took in the space with interest.

*This design has Mom all over it.*

I beamed as I took in tropical holiday splendor, much like that of the redesigned Paws and Poinsettias theme. My mom had waved her fairy wand. Glittery wreaths of turquoise, magenta, and lime ornaments hung in each window. Melon-colored polka dot ribbons were twined through the evergreen garlands leading up the wide staircase. And the towering tree in front of the floor-to-ceiling window was adorned with pineapples, flamingoes, and little palm trees.

"Your mother did this yesterday as her official audition to become a stager." Olivia gestured around her. "My grandmother is ecstatic. Carole designed it with elements of the Florida they both love. There's plenty of evergreen from the natural pine garlands, and the other silver elements she selected will fit in well for our wedding day."

I scanned the room once more. "You and Toby could be married in front of the fireplace or next to the giant tree." My decorating work for Olivia's wedding was basically finished. I'd ordered the angel candelabra centerpieces yesterday. While they wouldn't fit in with the tropical flair of my mother's decorations here, they wouldn't clash, either. My work was done before it was begun. I let out a sigh of relief.

Olivia beamed. "It'll be perfect."

*But is Goldie just as happy with it?*

Olivia's mother entered the room and seemed to wordlessly answer my unspoken question. Her eyes darted around the room as her lips thinned in a pursed grimace. "Lacey had already decorated this space to my specifications."

I could nearly feel Olivia's hackles rise next to me, the tension rolling off her petite shoulders in palpable waves. I wouldn't want to be reminded of the deceased stager, either.

"But your mother, Mallory, did a compelling re-design as her project to gain the new stager's posi-tion." While not exactly a ringing endorsement, Goldie grudgingly acknowledged my mother. "She's here, you know."

"Mom's here?" I followed Goldie into an im-pressive command center of a home office. The rest of Olivia's family sat and stood at various sta-tions. A few other employees buzzed around copiers, scanners, and a fax machine. My mother was looking over blueprints attached to an easel. Her purple reading glasses perched atop her head perfectly matched her pantsuit. A pencil resided behind her ear. She was all business.

"Hi, Mom." I didn't want to interrupt her, but I was so proud. She'd retired with great fanfare five years ago when she sold her business in Pitts-burgh, and she and my stepdad left for Florida. But I'd had a sneaking suspicion she'd regretted the move the moment after she'd left. She seemed fulfilled and excited in her new job.

"Mallory, dear!" She set down her pencil and sketchbook and gave me a quick hug. "So nice to see you here."

"You did a lovely job as always decorating this cabin."

My mom accepted my praise with a smile. "I de-signed it with Clementine. It is meant to invoke the Gulf we both love."

Olivia appeared at my elbow. "My family is so happy to have you on board, Carole."

I relaxed. Truman had to know my mom didn't have a hand in Lacey's death. She was obviously thrilled to be working here, but the two didn't have to be tied together.

It was now five o'clock, and the office workers filtered out. My mother gathered her purple purse and sent me a friendly wave and a wink as she announced she was going to finish up some of her work for another hour at March headquarters downtown. I was glad she was gone when I heard Clementine's next comment.

"I'm sorry Paws and Poinsettias ended the way it did. Lacey was always looking for attention." Clementine grumbled her complaint from across the room. I felt my mouth open and close, no words coming out. I was appalled at her insinuation that Lacey had become ill as a way to garner attention.

Goldie glowered at her mother but didn't take the bait regarding her former mentee and stager. "Be that as it may, we still have a way to redeem ourselves in the eyes of the town."

"Ah yes, the toy drive." Rudy hoisted his giant frame from the plaid couch he'd been sitting on. "It's in a little less than a week." He was the perfect person to be discussing Christmas toys. I did a double take at his outfit of brown corduroy pants with black boots peeking out of the bottom cuffs. He wore a white fisherman's sweater topped with red suspenders. His long white beard was gleaming. He appeared just as I imagined the real Santa would on a casual day off.

"Lacey was supposed to run the toy drive." Alan

made his way over from his desk, a folder in his hands. He stopped expectantly before me. "I know you're busy with my daughter's wedding plans. But could you take on the toy drive?"

I gulped as all assembled peered at me with expectant expressions.

"Um, sure." I tried to tamp down the uncertainty I heard in my voice. "I'd love to!"

"You're a gem." Alan deposited the thick folder of details in my outstretched hands and beamed at his family.

"We want the town to be on board," Goldie worried. "Winning over prospective buyers of our homes is the very first step. It's more important than the designs of the homes and housing developments themselves."

"But it has to be organic," Clementine reminded her daughter. "I've single-handedly made many inroads with the women and men who take my yoga class."

It was true. My sister was smitten with the fiery businesswoman and grandmother, all from taking one of her classes at Bodies in Motion.

"Which is why your toy drive will be a success and recoup some of the good will we lost with the way Paws and Poinsettias ended." Clementine slung an arm around her worried daughter, and Goldie seemed to relax.

"And we should give credit where credit is due." Goldie grew solemn. "The toy drive wasn't actually my idea—it was Lacey's."

Clementine dropped her arm from her daughter's shoulders like a hot coal. The deceased stager was the ghost of Christmas past who kept making an appearance in our conversations, whether Clementine liked it or not.

"This is quite a home office." I tried to fill the awkward space of dead air that stretched before us.

"We worked here all summer while we were renovating the building downtown," Goldie explained. "And now that it is a crime scene, we relocated back to the cabin." She sighed and took in the recently humming workspace. "But I really don't like mixing business with pleasure."

"There wasn't a place for an office when we had the original cabin." Clementine seemed to volley her reminder at Alan. She stared at her son-in-law when she made her statement.

Alan winced and then squared his narrow shoulders. "That old thing? It was no place to entertain prospective business contacts." He glanced around him at a space both light and airy, with its oversized windows stretching fifteen feet high. "This is a triumph for March Homes."

"I would have stopped construction of this albatross if I'd known in time," Clementine grumbled next to me. I don't think anyone else heard her. But her voice grew loud enough for all to hear. "We should have kept it a simple, rustic retreat."

*Ruh-roh.*

Alan waved off her complaint with a flick of his slender fingers. "What's done is done, Clementine. Every once in a while I do get to make a decision as part of the executive board of March Homes."

So, this was the kind of steamrolling of her dad that Olivia had alluded to when discussing her proposed wedding menu. But it seemed like Alan got his way occasionally. And judging by this log cabin mansion, he'd gotten it big.

"Guess what I had taken out of storage?" Goldie's usually calm and prim countenance was alight with mirth. "The family wedding dress!" She smoothly swept the consternation between her mother and her husband under the rug and wheeled out a dress form from behind a screen.

"It's lovely!" Olivia breathed out. She stepped forward and gingerly extended a satin sleeve of the gown.

Rudy grew misty-eyed and extracted a red, plaid handkerchief from his back pocket. He dabbed at his twinkling jet eyes and blew his nose loudly on the large square of fabric. "Don't mind me. I just can't believe my little grandbaby is getting married!"

Clementine and Goldie were considerably taller and bigger boned than the petite Olivia. The gown would need to be cut down quite a bit. I bit my lip and wondered whether Bev Mitchell, owner of the Silver Bells Bridal shop and a skilled seamstress, would have time to take on the job. It was already mid-December, and Bev had her own wedding to plan for this summer. It would be a lovely gown if we could find someone to alter it in time. The dress was a creamy satin that had mellowed and aged into a deep ivory color over the decades. It featured a scalloped neckline with lace trim at the bottom. Olivia would look lovely if Bev could take in the waist, shorten the bodice, raise the hem, and augment the voluminous dress to perfectly fit the bride's tiny frame.

"I can't wait to wear it and to marry right here."

Olivia's eyes shone in anticipation, and for once, her family seemed at peace and unified in the goal of giving her a lovely day.

My friend seemed to steel herself and took a deep breath. "And I'll be spending more time in Port Quincy soon, too. Not just for the holiday." Olivia's voice wavered as she took in her father's frown. I wondered not for the first time where the fierce litigator I knew my friend to be had gone. But the approval of family was a powerful thing, and Olivia seemed keen to have it.

"What do you mean, sweetheart?" Alan tented his thin fingers under his nose and peered at his daughter expectantly through his wire rims.

Olivia carried on, seeming even more cautious than before. "I'm going to join Garrett Davies's practice here in town. I'm so excited to relocate and be with my husband." She turned to me with a fond gaze. "And old friends. And family." She seemed at peace with her announcement, no longer seeking her parents' permission, but laying out her intentions.

"No, no, no." Alan paced in an agitated manner before his daughter. "You need to keep your eye on the prize, Olivia. Your partnership is almost within reach. It would be ludicrous to quit right before the finish line."

Olivia's winning smile quavered, but to her credit, she didn't falter.

"No, Dad." Her voice was firm with conviction. "I've thought this through. This is what I want."

A pin could drop in the formerly bustling home office.

Alan nodded, but his eyes narrowed. "I just

don't want you to get distracted, Olivia. Your mother and I are happy for your marriage." He stopped to grab Goldie's hand in a physically united front. "We just want to make sure you really want to speed up your wedding. You need to protect yourself and your career." He took a deep breath and seemed to weigh his next statement. "What if it doesn't work out with Toby?"

*Say what?! Does he know something we don't?*

Olivia appeared as if she'd been physically slapped by her father's words. Her response was testy. "Love is more important than some kind of business arrangement."

Alan dropped his wife's hand and dug his fists in his pockets.

"I thought you'd be excited." Olivia shook her head in a bitter manner. "I imagined I could take on the legal work for March Homes in Port Quincy."

Alan and Goldie exchanged a pregnant glance. I detected an odd range of emotions on Alan's face, one of them fear. But I may have imagined it, as his expression turned tender and kind. "I would love for you to be part of the family business, Olivia. But you've just worked so hard for this partnership. I wouldn't want you to walk away from it yet. You can marry Toby at the end of the month, make partner in January, and then reassess."

I was growing annoyed at Alan's attempts to control his grown daughter's life. And something else was itching in the recesses of my brain.

*Why doesn't he want Olivia to do work for March Homes?*

It seemed odd. Alan should be thrilled his daughter wanted to maintain her practice and also get a foothold in the family business. I would have guessed he'd have thought it was a clever solution.

"Besides," Alan sneered, "do you even want to practice law in a small town?"

I bristled silently next to my friend, trying to send her invisible psychic support.

But Alan wasn't finished. "What kind of cases does this man even do?"

I did something I tried never to do and waded into the fray of a disagreement between a bride and her parent. Not to mention defending the professional honor of my beau.

"Garrett is my boyfriend. He tries matters both big and small. He defends men and women in criminal court, wins contract disputes between businesses, and irons out knotty divorces and custody issues that change the course of families. What he does isn't just small potatoes. It affects people's lives. Olivia would be lucky to join such a thriving, varied practice, and Garrett would be lucky to have her as his partner in his expanding business."

My chest heaved after my impassioned speech. Alan blinked as if seeing me for the first time. He studied Olivia's face for a moment.

"If this is true, that you're really considering leaving Russell Carey, your mother and I have to rethink the restructuring of your inheritance."

Olivia blanched. I wondered how she'd address the callous volley. Her response surprised me. She arched a perfectly shaped black brow and crossed her arms. "I know Grandma and Grandpa play that game, but it won't work with me. I don't need my inheritance."

*Check and mate.*

Alan swallowed and took a step back. Olivia peered into the faces of her mother and grandparents, looking for what I didn't know.

"Perhaps you shouldn't wear the March dress," Goldie suggested with a wounded expression. Her allegiance was with Alan, and she wanted that fact to be known.

Olivia finally did look hurt. "I won't, then."

Clementine screeched from her silent perch on a loveseat. "What do you mean, Olivia? Your mother is just being emotional. Three generations of March women have worn this gown. Of course you'll wear the dress."

"No thank you, Grandma." Olivia drew on some inner reserve of strength. "I'll make my own path."

The bride turned on her heel and walked out the door, leaving me as bewildered as the family she left behind in her wake.

"Let's get the heck out of here." Olivia was waiting for me on the front porch of the cabin, her chest rising and falling with each intake of breath. We climbed into the Butterscotch Monster, and I enlisted the high beams against the cloying darkness. I forged through the dark forest of the Marches' secluded property with my heart still pounding. The dark swath of trees surrounding my station wagon and the claustrophobic feeling of being in an evergreen tunnel didn't help my racing heart. I couldn't wait to get home, take a hot bath, and then spend the evening with my sometimes crazy but not vindictive family.

"The police returned my Acura, and they scrubbed the paint off the windshield." Olivia stared out at the pitch-black window. "But I can't bring myself to drive it. I've been using a rental car." I'd nearly forgotten the vindictive message sprayed in gold paint on her windshield a mere three days ago. So much had happened since then. I walked with Olivia into Toby's loft downtown. I settled her on the comfy suede couch with a mug of steaming peppermint tea, and her laptop open to some discovery requests.

"Thanks, Mallory. And please excuse my family. They're not normally like this."

*Yeah right.*

"I'm not privy to everything that goes on with their business, but I don't think this project in Port Quincy is going as seamlessly as that of their former developments."

I pondered what Olivia could have meant as I made my way back to Thistle Park—and was greeted by the sight of Truman's police cruiser in the drive.

*Out of the frying pan and into the fire.*

The chief was already sitting at the kitchen table addressing my sister. Rachel wore a worried expression atop her green-and-white striped minidress and red tights.

"I was just telling your sister about Lacey's toxicology results." Truman beckoned me to take a seat. The local radio was blasting Chipmunks Christmas music. I snapped off the dial for this macabre conversation. The cheery, ultra-falsetto voices seemed discordant with what might be depressing news.

"As I was telling your sister, it was no accident. Lacey Adams was poisoned."

My heart skipped a beat in morbid anticipation.

"How?" I asked Truman.

He shook his head, already baffled by what he was about to say. "By drinking antifreeze mixed with Hawaiian blue punch and blueberry vodka."

My heart beat in my rib cage like an agitated bird. I recalled my mother's shaking fingers unscrewing the top of a bottle of electric blue juice, Lacey glowering above her atop the bar. Luckily, Truman hadn't yet noticed my panicked expression. He'd stood to help himself to a mug.

"I'm so sorry. I'm being a terrible hostess." I shooed him away from the kitchen counter after I plucked the mug from his hands. I filled it with steaming French roast. Rachel must have made a fresh pot in the retro percolator that matched the kitchen's aesthetics. I was happy to busy myself with the coffee. I took as long as possible positioning the mug on a jaunty holly berry print napkin, the better to compose myself before I turned around.

It was no use. My hands shook as I placed the mug before Truman. The pretty napkin soaked up the coffee spill.

"I'm rattled, too," Truman reassured me.

I nodded, but didn't tell him what I was thinking. I'd just remembered Olivia pouring out her drink into a plant at Paws and Poinsettias, seemingly unnoticed by anyone but me. Did she know there was poison in her champagne flute, too? Had my friend been tipped off, or was she on high alert?

*Or did she poison Lacey herself?*

I shook my head against the deafening crash of nonsense flittering through my head, willed myself to stay calm, and focused in on Truman's presence.

"She had no other drink or food in her system," Truman continued. "And we searched the scene meticulously. There was no sign of antifreeze anywhere. Someone probably brought it in a flask or bottle. Perhaps someone close enough to Lacey to hold her drink or converse with her and pour it in."

Another detail itched in the back of my head, but I couldn't dredge it up amidst my worry for my mother.

"Lacey was well liked, so it could have been anyone chatting with her." I heard my voice come out normally enough and breathed a small sigh of relief.

"It's true," the chief agreed.

If he knew for a fact my mother had made the last drink Lacey consumed, with at least one of the more innocuous ingredients matching the contents of the poisonous stew in her system, it wouldn't be a great leap to assume she'd also added the antifreeze, too.

"Maybe it was suicide," Rachel said. "The March family wasn't happy with her performance, right?" Rachel sat back, satisfied to offer some information. "Ouch!"

*Oops.*

I'd kicked her under the table a bit harder than I'd intended. Truman gave me a knowing glare. It wasn't that I wanted to actively conceal information from Truman. But I was concerned about the possible blowback for our mother. I wanted to get our stories straight before talking to Truman. Then again, over the years I had somewhat informally deputized myself in some of his cases. It had been a dangerous place to be in.

"Just what are you talking about, Rachel?" Truman narrowed his hazel eyes at my sister.

"Um, nothing." Rachel exchanged an uh-oh glance with me. But it was too late.

"It's not a big deal," I rushed in. "It seemed like Goldie liked Lacey's work and Clementine did not."

I conveniently left out the teensy-weensy detail of my mother pulling an all-nighter to systematically undo every decoration Lacey and I had lovingly placed for Paws and Poinsettias in exchange for her and Clementine's own plan. It was getting hard keeping straight all of the information I was withholding from Truman. But it turns out I didn't need to spill these beans.

"I gathered that," Truman nodded. "What interests me is that the March family tried to deny it. Even Clementine stated that she was just fine with Lacey, but she needn't have bothered. Clementine March's acting performance when she's not telling the truth is about as subtle as that crazy hairdo of hers." He smiled ruefully, seeming to recall Clementine's green-tipped spiky hair.

"That doesn't make them look innocent," I eagerly said. I couldn't believe I was not so subtly throwing my friend's family under the suspect bus. But it was all in an effort to protect my mother. I decided to advance another theory.

"Lacey was supposed to be spearheading the toy drive in another week. The March family would have wanted to keep her on for that, right?"

Truman arched a bushy gray brow. "And just what is going to happen with the toy drive?"

"Um, I'm taking over the planning of it." I plucked the folder Alan had handed me and placed it before Truman. He rifled through the stack of papers for a moment. Then he gave me a sharp and thorough once-over.

"I suppose March Homes will be looking for a new stager now. They'll be lining up at the door to fill that position, even after what happened to Lacey."

His statement hung in the air for far too long.

*Oh crap, he doesn't know.*

Truman observed my sister and me studiously avoiding his eyes.

"Spill it, you two."

*You can't protect her forever.*

"They have a new stager." I nearly whispered the response.

"And?" Truman let out a hot gust of air, his annoyance no longer hidden.

"It's our mom." Rachel dragged her eyes miserably from the table to meet Truman's.

"Holy heck." Truman dropped his professional manner and gave us sorrowful looks. "That wasn't what I was expecting you to say." A flash of frustration darkened his face, then dissipated. "I'm annoyed you didn't tell me outright. I would have found out soon enough anyway. But I understand why you didn't say anything."

I relaxed by a millimeter and sent Truman a grateful look.

"Now, where is she?" Truman stood, his chair scraping the black-and-white tile in a harsh grate.

"She's at her first day of work. She was at the Marches' home office today, and then she left to finish up at the downtown building. Please, please don't go find her with your guns blazing." I heard the pleading tone in my voice and hoped Truman did, too.

He sighed and dropped back in his chair. "Okay. I'll wait a little bit to question her." He shook his head as if he'd been tricked. "I'm just doing this for you two, though. And don't you dare give your mother a heads-up." He glowered at Rachel as she sheepishly placed her sequin-encrusted phone on the kitchen table. She needn't have bothered.

Mom sailed in the door, followed by an exuberant Doug. She was high on the heady fumes of a job well done at her new and fancy career. She nearly skipped into the kitchen in her purple suede pumps. She stopped short when she saw Truman. Doug didn't get the memo and bumped into my mother, nearly catapulting her into the kitchen.

"Truman. What a lovely surprise!" My mother gathered her wits about her and surveyed the scene. She seemed to figure out that this wasn't a mere social call. That didn't stop her from trying to turn it into one.

"I had a magnificent day working for March Homes. Maybe an old dog can learn new tricks.

Goldie and Clementine are most definitely keeping me on my toes." She bent to pick up Ramona, who had materialized at her feet with her tiny pug tongue lolling about. Mom's smile cooled when she realized Truman wasn't reciprocating her friendly vibe.

"Um, Mom," Rachel began. She stopped short when Truman sent her a murderous gaze.

"Did you make Lacey Adams a drink at Paws and Poinsettias?" Truman asked his question in an even tone.

*Uh-oh.*

I felt like kicking myself. Truman always found out everything about everyone. The thought that Rachel and I were successfully keeping the information secret about our mother making Lacey's last drink now seemed preposterous. Paws and Poinsettias had been crawling with people in addition to pets. One of the other hundreds of people Truman questioned must have tipped him off.

My mother bristled. "That poor girl was totally inebriated. I guess the bartender must have stepped out." She paused and held her head high, her purple reading glasses slipping a degree in her carefully coiffed hair. "I did Lacey a favor and poured her a drink when she demanded it."

Truman said nothing. He was employing a tactic he'd unfortunately used many times on yours truly. He would pose a question, then allow the answering party to prattle on, filling up the space with their deepest, darkest secrets. Which my mom did in spades.

"And it was funny, she just wanted a blue Hawaiian punch. No alcohol."

"So you gave her alcohol anyway." Truman stated it like a fact.

"I did no such thing! It wasn't my business why she wanted a nonalcoholic drink. And besides, the poor thing was already so drunk. I wish I had given her a cab ride home and a cold shower."

"Your prints will be on the bottle of punch," Truman warned. "I'd like to confirm it as soon as possible."

The room grew very still. Ramona let out a contented sigh and snuggled closer to my mother, unaware of the tense situation.

My mother winced. Then her eyes grew very large and afraid. "You don't need to take my prints. I just admitted that I did indeed make Lacey a drink."

*This is going very badly.*

My mother was freely using language of guilt, playing right into Truman's hands. Doug nearly bounced on the balls of his feet next to my mother, no doubt wanting to end this questioning post haste.

"You can't possibly believe Carole had anything to do with Lacey Adams's death." Doug ended his statement with a little laugh that strangled in his throat.

"I'll need to question you further, Mrs. Shepard."

*Ohmigod.*

My mother had just gone from Carole to Mrs. Shepard. Alarm bells were clanging on DEFCON one in my head. Truman was downright scary in his professional impassivity. This was no longer a social call, indeed.

"But you *are* questioning me. What more do you want?" My mother's voice was high pitched.

Truman turned it down a notch and sent her a look of pity. "I meant downtown."

My mother shook her head, her amethyst drop earrings pelting her cheeks with force. "Not today I just want to take a long, hot bath after my first day of work." When she saw that he was serious, she placed Ramona on the floor and skittered away from us. Her hands shook as she assembled the start of a tea service. "I'll make you a cup of something else and you can finish your questioning here. How about a nice cup of gingerbread tea? It's much less harsh than the French roast the girls drink." Her attempts at steamrolling appeared to work as Truman made no moves. He allowed her to bustle about for a few moments. Truman's icy demeanor melted a notch.

"Carole." The kindness that had returned to Truman's voice made my mother stop her frenzied ministrations. "We really do need to finish this questioning downtown. Now."

My mother dropped a cup, a lovely Spode number embossed with a Christmas tree filled with woodland creatures. It broke in two at her feet. She barely noticed.

"And as a courtesy, I'm letting you know an attorney can attend, too."

I was simultaneously cheered and frightened. He hadn't formally read my mother her Miranda rights. This was just a questioning session. But with the police, it was never just a questioning session. My former attorney antennae were quivering. My mom was in deeper doo-doo than I thought, more than just the pug variety.

"I'll go, Mom. I haven't practiced in a while, but I still have my license." I knelt at her feet and rescued the broken cup.

Mom looked down at me as if waking from a trance.

"I don't *need* an attorney, as I've done nothing wrong!" She violently whipped her blue wool coat from the back of her chair. "I can't wait to put this behind me. Truman, come along." My mother flounced down the hall, with the chief of police in her wake.

Rachel, Doug, and I pressed our faces against the cold glass windows in the parlor. The scene before us was downright disturbing. Truman opened the door of his cruiser, and my mother climbed in. At least for now she was ensconced in the passenger seat, not the back where suspected criminals were separated from law enforcement by a metal grille. She looked stoic in her profile. At the last second her head swiveled around, her bob dyed to match Rachel's hair fanning around her face. She looked utterly terrified but offered a weak wave. I didn't know I'd been holding my breath until the red taillights disappeared in the thick fog at the end of the long drive.

"It'll be alright. She didn't do anything! It *has* to be alright." Rachel brushed away a stream of tears coursing down her face. I slung an arm around my sister, and Doug did the same.

*Oh, dear God.*

The detail that had escaped me earlier finally

freed itself from the recesses of my thoughts. The day my mother arrived from the airport, she'd stepped into Thistle Park and soon plucked a half-empty jug of antifreeze from Doug's hands. The very substance used to poison Lacey.

I hoped my sister was still right.

# CHAPTER SIX

The next day dawned cold and damp. The fog that had rolled in as my mother rolled off to the police station had yet to dissipate. If anything, it was thicker and more opaque. It mirrored my read on the current crime situation in Port Quincy. Which once again maddeningly involved my family and friends.

I was exhausted from Truman's brief questioning in the kitchen yesterday and knew I hadn't even borne the brunt of it. That cheery duty had befallen my poor mother. I'd lain awake until I'd heard my mom's weary footfalls on the back stair. I had heard her murmuring to Doug. I'd glanced at my watch and realized she'd been with Truman getting grilled until eleven o'clock.

I joined my parents and sister for breakfast. Doug got out the holiday blend of coffee after my mom's declaration yesterday that she was tired of French roast.

"I'm sorry I even tried to make that heathen a

cup of tea yesterday," my mother tsked. She squinted at the shattered Spode cup before her and applied a clear trail of Super Glue. My mother seemed to be her usual spitfire self despite her late-night questioning. It could have just been latent adrenaline. Beneath her show of normalcy I detected a humming bundle of nerves.

"So what did Truman ask you?" Rachel tied the sash of her robe tighter around her curvy frame. The fabric was silk and featured an endless loop of penguins skating around a sheet of ice. I couldn't help but think we were all skating on our own thin sheet.

"Oh, this and that." My mother was frustratingly enigmatic. "He just wanted to go over a few details. We basically discussed what you'd already heard at the kitchen table."

*Yeah, right.*

I exchanged a glance with my sister. Doug caught my eye and gave a barely perceptible shake of his head. I shrugged, and we wordlessly agreed to drop it.

"Enough of that!" My mother clapped her hands together, and Ramona sat up straighter. My mother tossed her a tiny sliver of bacon, and the pug happily lapped it up. "Let's turn to happier topics. I love my new job. And because of the scope of the five developments, the Marches have given me permission to hire an assistant stager and decorator."

"That's awesome, Mom." And it would have been, under any other circumstances. And while I still adored my friend Olivia, I was beginning to regret my other entanglements with the March family.

Doug cleared his throat. "And I'll be teaching a class at Quincy College this summer on the Revolutionary War."

"You're both un-retiring!" I raised my coffee cup and beckoned my family to clink theirs together in an impromptu toast. "How does it feel?"

Doug chuckled. "Until class starts in late May, I'll just be holding down the fort here while your mom runs herself ragged with her new staging job." Doug attempted to sound cheery, but his statement came out a bit accusatory.

"Now, now, dear. I know it'll be a big commitment working as a stager again full time. But we'll still have plenty of time together." My mother rubbed my stepfather's back and sought to ease his concerns.

Doug used the moment as an opportunity to pounce. "Why don't you really tell us what Truman asked you last night? You were there for nearly three hours."

My mother dropped her hand and took a step back. "I said I was done talking about that."

"I was an attorney, Mom. It might be helpful to hear what he asked you."

*And then we'll know if we need to hire counsel for you.*

My mother shook her head. When she saw the three of us aligned in a row, not taking no for an answer, she threw her hands up.

"Fine. It was no idle chit-chat, I can tell you that." She blushed and took a fortifying slug of coffee. "Truman has a way of turning everything around. He's a sneaky, sleuth-y, silver-tongued son-of-a-gun!" She set her cup down and nearly crumpled. This time she allowed Doug to put his arm around her.

"We talked about everything and nothing. He kept hammering home the same points, then attacking from a slightly different angle." She squirmed at the memory.

"Um, that is his job, Mom." Rachel tried to be gentle in her reminder and slight defense of Truman, but my mother shot her a dagger glare.

My heart sunk into my stomach. It was initially hard to defend Truman, but my sister was right. He was just doing his job. But couldn't he see my mother wouldn't hurt a fly? I also realized my mother could be a bit hyperbolic. Her recounting of what had happened with Truman was probably quite embellished. I did wonder what she'd told the chief. I could have kicked myself; I should have just insisted on going with her to the questioning— scratch that—interrogation. But then I'd be persona non grata with Truman because I would have just told my mom to immediately shut it.

"And I would have thought," my mom began, casting me a wounded look, "that Truman would cut me some slack. He's almost family, you know."

I opened my mouth to rejoinder and then thought better of it.

"Don't you see, Mallory? If you had married Garrett by now, Truman wouldn't be treating me this way." My mother crossed her arms in front of her and raised one brow.

*Say what?!*

"Don't be ridiculous, Mom." I brushed off her crazy claim. But a nagging kernel of truth rested in my mom's claim. I was happy with things the way they were with Garrett. That is, until I realized lately that we'd barely been spending any time together. I'd cast a side-eye at my friend for starting a marriage as a workaholic wedding another workaholic. I wondered how Olivia's marriage would fare if she only saw her husband on weekends. I knew some couples made that arrangement work but knew it would never be for me. Except I was now in just such a relationship. I barely saw Garrett and his sweet daughter Summer save for Sunday night dinners and the occasional coffee break.

"Earth to Mallory." Rachel snapped her fingers in front of my nose. I dimly saw her magenta acrylics flash before my eyes. My sister pivoted and bestowed my mother and Doug with a winning smile. "And you don't have to wait around for Mallory to wed. I bet I'll beat her down the aisle first!"

My mother sent my sister an amused look. "Don't be silly, Rachel Shepard."

A crimson blush graced my sister's cheekbones. "And why not? I have a date with Evan. He's the third-most eligible bachelor in Port Quincy, right behind Garrett and Toby." She smoothed her penguin robe. "Maybe it's time I settled down and started a family."

My mother's face grew truly alarmed. "Is there something you're not telling me, Rachel?"

My sister giggled now that she had our attention. "It's just that I've matured in recent months. Just because Mallory doesn't ever want to get married doesn't mean that I can't start seriously looking."

Her speech sobered me. I'd fought off the silent expectations of the town of Port Quincy around my one-year anniversary with Garrett. Everyone expected a diamond to appear on my left hand,

and I was secretly pleased that we were progressing in our relationship at our own speed. But things weren't going in the right direction. I barely saw my beau. It was mid-December and we hadn't discussed spending the holiday together. I blushed when I realized I would have to admit I'd agreed to throw Olivia's wedding a mere two days before Christmas. I wanted to spend the holiday with Garrett. I wanted things to change. Starting right now.

"Plus," Rachel continued, oblivious to my silent epiphany, "just because you don't care that your biological clock is ticking away, I care about mine. I think I'd like to start a family sooner rather than later."

This declaration made my mother's eyes bug out of her head.

"What did you just say?" I stared at my sister, a thought percolating up in my head.

"Just that I'd like to start a family. Not everyone is married to his or her career, Mallory."

"She's pregnant." I whispered the revelation to all assembled.

"Oh dear." My mother crumpled against the counter, where Doug thankfully propped her up. He fanned her face with a recipe card, while I rushed to correct her.

"No, not Rachel, Mom. Olivia."

I thought back to Olivia's curious action of pouring a flute of champagne into the potted plant at Paws and Poinsettias. And pondered her rush to move up her wedding. And recalled her crushing exhaustion and her displeasure at the fish dish she'd once been so excited about. A bubble of relief rose in my chest. If Olivia had poured out her drink to avoid giving away news of her pregnancy, she probably had nothing to do with Lacey's poisoning. I felt elated on one hand, but a bit chastened at ever having suspected my dear friend of murder.

"Thank goodness. You're not ready for that, Rachel Marie Shepard. Not for a long time." My mother laid her hand over her heart, trying to recover. My sister sent her a wounded look and flounced up the stairs.

My mother and sister carefully avoided each other as they got ready for the day. Mom left for work in her rental car. Doug retired to the library to read a new biography on Benjamin Franklin. And I feverishly texted Garrett with the suggestion of an impromptu lunch date.

I was going to spend more time with the love of my life. Now that Olivia was going to join his practice, Garrett would be able to spend more time with his daughter Summer and with yours truly. I beamed at the prospect. I'd been dragging my feet replacing the assistant I'd lost. It was time to hire a more permanent member to the wedding planning team. My relationship depended on it.

I was honestly surprised he had a half hour free for lunch. I usually declined when he suggested a noontime meal, and he did too when the invitation was mine, so we'd stopped asking each other. He really did need Olivia to join his practice. She'd held off on giving her official notice at my old firm, but she was slowly extricating herself from her commitments. Today, for example, she was back in Port

Quincy. She'd taken the day off from work to help me take an inventory for the toy drive and to do some quick wedding dress shopping. She'd stood firm on her decision not to wear the March wedding dress. It was probably for the best, as it would be too late to alter the antique gown. Olivia would just have to find something off the rack that fit.

My heart was full as I parked the Butterscotch Monster on Spruce Street. I was elated at the thought of my best friend and boyfriend working together. And I couldn't wait to gently broach the subject regarding my hunch. The holiday would be triply exciting if it were true Olivia was going to have a baby.

A group of carolers sang "Silver Bells" in four-part harmony. The pretty window displays revealed themselves as I passed each window, the veil of fog from last night slowly dissipating. I was content and finally feeling good about this December.

"I have big news." Garrett clasped my hands in his after I slung off my coat and slid into the yellow vinyl booth at the Greasy Spoon Diner.

"Yes?" My voice was breathy. I couldn't wait to share with him the realization I'd had about our relationship, and how I was committed to spending more time with him and his family.

"Judge Frank is going to retire."

"Oh." I smiled at the bit of gossip and wondered why we held hands for such a mundane piece of news. "That's great for her. She's been such a wonderful mentor."

Garrett nodded, a sparkle lighting up his hazel eyes. "Her retirement also impacts the trial law practicum she teaches at Pitt."

I'd known Garrett had met the judge when she was teaching him in the very same class in law school. He'd booked the course, earning the highest grade in the class. When he started practicing in Port Quincy, the judge continued on in her role as his mentor. I knew he had the highest respect for Toby's mother and offered her unparalleled deference.

"Ursula wants to spend more time with Toby and Olivia. She wanted me to offer you her apologies. She wanted to be more involved in the planning of the wedding."

I nodded. "She said as much at Paws and Poinsettias. Has she found her cat, Hemingway?" I glanced outside at the chilly December weather. Save for a few evenings of sleet, the weather hadn't yet dipped below freezing. I worried about the pretty Persian and hoped he'd been reunited with the judge.

"Not yet, unfortunately. Ursula is beside herself." He chuckled. "She said losing her cat was a wake-up call that she needed to spend more time with those she loves."

I smiled at the sentiment. I'd just come to a similar realization and wanted to hear Garrett's news so I could share my epiphany with him.

"She has asked me to take over her class." Garrett's face lit up in a way it hadn't in months.

"That's fantastic!" I leaned across the sparkly Formica tabletop to grace Garrett with a kiss. "You've always wanted to teach."

It was true. Garrett had started out his legal career with teaching in mind before he'd transferred schools and returned to Western Pennsylvania to take care of Summer. It would be a sweet bookend to end up in the classroom after all.

"The class meets one day a week, right?" That wouldn't be so bad. With Olivia joining his practice, it wouldn't change much to have him driving home late one evening after teaching in Pittsburgh.

"I met with the dean, and the opportunity has morphed into so much more." Garrett let go of my hands and took a sip of iced tea. His hazel eyes twinkled. He seemed rueful, nervous, and excited.

"Oh?" Little alarm bells began to trill in my head. The menu I'd picked up slithered from my grasp. I knelt to retrieve it from the floor.

"Don't worry. I'll ask the server for a new one." Garrett seemed impatient to continue. "The law school has offered me a position running their newly proposed criminal defense clinic!"

"That's amazing, sweetheart." I heard the edge of doubt in my words, but Garrett didn't seem to pick up on it. "That's a pretty big commitment."

I recalled the environmental clinic I'd participated in at Georgetown for a semester. It had been an intensive experience.

"I'd get to design the clinic before we launched. I could begin in January, with the inaugural semester beginning in the fall."

"Could you plan the clinic from here?" My voice was small and pleading.

Garrett's gaze turned soft. "Summer and I would be relocating to Pittsburgh."

"You ready to order, hon?" A harried server arrived, letting me off the hook. It didn't matter. I was rendered speechless.

"I'll have a cup of coffee and the shepherd's pie." Garrett filled the silence as the server turned expectantly to me.

"Um, the same," I mumbled, barely cognizant of what I'd ordered.

"I know it's sudden." Garrett clasped my hands again. His were warm and capable but mine had suddenly gone cold. "But we'd still see each other on the weekends, just like now."

I withdrew my hands. "You mean Sunday night dinner."

His buoyant mood cooled a few degrees. "We're so busy, Mallory. I've wanted to spend more time together. We just have to make it more of a priority."

A little sly stab of pain hit my middle. Mere minutes ago, I'd been on the precipice of suggesting we spend more time together to strengthen our relationship and deepen our commitment. And now Garrett was moving away.

"What about the proposed partnership practicing with Olivia?" I blurted out. Now that she had her heart set on permanently relocating to Port Quincy, my friend's heart would be broken if she knew Garrett was rescinding his offer.

"I haven't accepted yet. I wanted to float this idea with you." Garrett's hazel eyes filled with tenderness and concern. A small feather of hope drifted up from my middle. "Besides, if I were to direct the clinic in Pittsburgh, I'd be happy to hand over my whole practice to Olivia."

The feather of hope vaporized in a pop of despair. I grabbed the ice water before me and choked down half the tall glass in an effort to choke back the tears I felt forming.

"Hey, that's why we're discussing this." Garrett reached across the table and tucked his finger under my chin. "Right now this is just an idea. I haven't accepted yet. I wanted to hear what you have to say."

But I didn't trust myself to say anything just yet. I wanted to scream that Garrett should stay in Port Quincy. But he was so giddy at the prospect of running the new law clinic. The stars in his eyes were so bright. It wouldn't be fair to immediately demand he remain in Port Quincy.

"It's a lot to think about," I ended lamely. I pushed my food around on my plate for fifteen minutes before choking down a few bites. What was normally a delicious dish tasted like sand and ash in my mouth.

"Does Summer know?" I wondered what Garrett's wonderful daughter thought of his potential plans.

Garrett slowly nodded. "She knows it's a possibility. But nothing is set in stone."

We walked back to his office through the fog in what should have been companionable silence. But my heart was thumping in my chest. The idea of Garrett moving away was heavier than the opaque atmosphere.

Just six months ago I'd pushed to keep our relationship low key. And now maybe Garrett was moving on to greener pastures professionally, at least.

He held the door open for me when we reached the lobby. His office resided in a once-shabby art deco office building. Garrett had chipped in some funds for the owner of the building to repaint. The space was now a lovely bright cream and mustard yellow. I felt the cool chill ebb from my bones as I adjusted to the arid, forced air in the lobby.

"I'm not going to just up and leave, Mallory." Garrett gathered me in his arms and gave me an intent and tender gaze. "If we can find a way to make it work, I'm game to take the position. But if not, I want to prioritize us."

The cloud of doubt lifted, and I turned up my face to meet Garrett with a kiss. As our lips met, an electric spark from the dry air shocked me. We laughed and ran the soles of our feet on the carpet to diffuse further sparks and try the kiss again. This time we made our own sparks.

"I'll see you again soon," Garrett promised when we finally pulled apart.

"Of that you can be sure."

I nearly skipped from the lobby. I was riding high, impervious to the drizzle and fog that awaited me outside, just beyond Garrett's embrace.


Though I was electrified by the kiss I'd shared with Garrett, I needed to ground my priorities and turn to earth bound matters. The toy drive I'd inherited was due to go off in a mere five days. I opened my bag and patted the thick folder of papers Alan had handed me regarding the event and headed back to March Homes headquarters.

Someone had mercifully removed the yellow crime scene tape. The lobby was scrubbed of all vestiges of Paws and Poinsettias save for the poinsettias themselves. The riotous bloom of pink and cream plants were clustered in pretty islands on windowsills and coffee tables in the lobby. Someone had found the red poinsettias Lacey and I had used before my mother redid our design and the scarlet plants were woven through the design.

"Mallory, dear, so good to see you." Goldie crossed the lobby and took my hands in hers. "Lacey did a good job with the toy drive, as it was her baby, so I don't think you'll need to do too much to bring the project to fruition."

I nodded and retrieved the folder from my bag. "Lacey had planned on having the reception for the toy drive right here in the lobby." I glanced around the room. It was as if the murder had never taken place in the now cool light of day. But everyone in town knew better.

"We were going to have a splashy ceremony before we distributed the toys." Goldie raised her hand to her chin. "But that doesn't seem right after what happened. Tell you what. It'll be more altruistic to just count the toys, match them up with families' requests, and deliver them."

I felt a sigh of relief whoosh from my lungs. "Fantastic. I emailed the list of volunteers last night and everyone is still on board to help."

Goldie cocked her head in thought. "My dad loves to play Santa, as you can imagine. Perhaps we can still get a few photos of Rudy and Clementine in their Mr. and Mrs. Claus getups distributing toys."

I nodded my assent and reflected on how obsessed Goldie was about her family's image. The important thing was to collect the toys and distribute them to children who might not have any toys under the tree, but Goldie also wanted her publicity photo.

"I'm sorry I'm late." Rachel whooshed through the glass doors and found Goldie and me in the lobby. "Your mother is the most challenging yoga instructor I've ever had." She turned her head to the left, seeming to try to stretch her neck. "Man, is Clementine limber."

"My mother is always at the cutting edge of each exercise regime currently in fashion," Goldie drily responded.

"Well, now that we're all here, let's do a quick inventory of all of the toys businesses have dropped off so far." I retrieved the printed spreadsheet Lacey had compiled from the folder.

"Are there more toys than there were a few days ago?" Rachel got out a pen and notepad, ready to inventory.

"Lots more." Goldie beamed. "The hardware store and several businesses from the mall dropped off a huge load of toys for the boys and girls of Port Quincy."

Rachel and I followed Goldie's retreating form to the refurbished brass elevator in the corner of the lobby. Goldie inserted a key into a slot amidst the elevator buttons. No one could reach the bottom level of the former department store without the key.

The shiny doors slid open. I blinked in disbelief. There had been hundreds of toys, including dolls, plush stuffed animals, board games, and bikes when I'd set up the lobby for Paws and Poinsettias. The room had looked like Santa's work-shop, and I'd giggled at the time imagining Rudy at home in the space.

But there was literally nothing to laugh at.

"Where are all the toys?" Goldie turned in a panicked circle in the now empty, cavernous base-ment. She was like Cindy Lou Who on Christmas Day, after the Grinch had absconded with all of Whoville's Toys.

"Let's call Truman."

# CHAPTER SEVEN

"This is a despicable and heartless crime." Truman shook his head in disgust at the empty basement. He seemed more perturbed by the stolen toy drive proceeds than he was by Lacey's death.

"Things really aren't going well for them, are they?" Rachel nodded toward the March family. Goldie was distraught. Olivia had arrived on the scene. She'd journeyed from Pittsburgh to quickly select a bridal gown from the stock at my friend Bev's store. Our appointment was in half an hour, but it may as well have been in a million years. Olivia's attention and concern was with her family and their most recent setback. She soothed her mother as she gave her statement about when she'd last visited the basement.

"I think I've figured it out." Goldie jabbed her finger in the air to punctuate her statement. "Some-one wants us to leave Port Quincy. Someone who is furious we are developing land he thinks is rightfully his."

"Let me guess. You're going to suggest Greg Gibson." Truman tried to tamp down a thread of amusement woven amidst the thin-set line of his mouth. "I read the legal paper today, too. I know he's suing his parents for selling their land to your company."

Goldie threw her hands in the air. "Then you know he's the one! Who else could be so upset as to steal from the hands of innocent children?" She gestured around the now-empty basement. "And I know he's behind the spray paint on Olivia's car."

Truman blinked impassively, which seemed to irritate Goldie even more. "Mrs. March, Greg Gibson is resorting to seeking redress of his claims in court. There's no evidence he vandalized your daughter's car." He held up his hand. "But of course I will be looking into the matter, all the same."

Goldie was momentarily chastened. A loud ping from Olivia's cell phone made her jump.

"Excuse me, Mom." Olivia stepped away from her mother and hurriedly scanned the screen of her phone. Dark storm clouds gathered in her eyes.

"It's the Fisher case." Olivia bit her lip and closed her eyes. "I swear, they're making me run the gauntlet right at the end before they bestow the hallowed title of partner." She jabbed at the screen and tossed the phone deep into her cavernous purse. Her eyes scanned my face before she spoke again. "Garrett told me about possibly taking the clinic gig."

I gulped and nodded. "He thinks it can work

only seeing each other on weekends." I gave a bitter laugh. "Which is what our relationship has already descended to as of late."

A slow blush graced Olivia's high cheekbones.

*Nice one, Mallory. Extract your foot from your mouth.*

"I mean, there's nothing wrong with only seeing your significant other on weekends—"

Olivia cut me off with a genuinely joyous laugh. I felt myself deflate with relief. "I know what you mean, Mallory. That's why I was so excited and eager to join Garrett's practice. I'd have more control over my own practice, I'd have a five-minute commute, and most importantly, I'd see Toby each and every day." Her pretty dark eyes grew wistful. "I'm not sure I want to jump in and take over Garrett's whole practice if he goes. And," she bestowed a gentle look, "he did say he wanted to discuss it with you. I think he'd give up the opportunity to stay here permanently, Mallory."

I nodded, a lump of misery forming in my throat. "That's the thing. I'd never forgive myself if I held him back."

It was true. Of course I didn't want Garrett to move to Pittsburgh. He'd guaranteed we'd see each other on the weekends, but with the unique hours of a wedding planner, that would only mean spending Sundays with Garrett, Summer, and his family. And although it was the way things were at present, I now knew I wanted more.

Olivia and I stood in sad silence. We were each in our own kind of limbo, professionally and romantically. Thankfully Rachel snapped us back to reality.

"Sorry to interrupt, ladies. But your dress fitting

is in five minutes." Rachel held up her sparkly rose gold Michael Kors watch and gave it an impatient tap.

"Mom will kill me." Olivia glanced at her mother, then seemed to shiver at her word choice. Lacey had collapsed one floor above us just three days ago. "But I can't make it."

"I love you like a sister, but you'll need to break the news to your mom." I didn't want to be on the receiving end of an already distraught Goldie's anger.

Olivia dug around her purse and came up with a foil-lined bag filled with gingersnaps. "Want one?"

Rachel and I shook our heads as we watched Olivia cram the cookie into her mouth. I guess my mother wasn't the only one in town who reduced her daughter to stress eating.

*Gingersnaps.*

I scanned Olivia's outfit choice for the day. She was clad in a loose burgundy knit dress over black leggings and boots. The dress featured a subtle empire waist. To top it off, she wore a pretty holly berry-patterned scarf that hung over her midsection.

"I have a crazy idea." Olivia seemed oblivious to my quick once-over and a smirk gathered on her face. "We're nearly the same size, Mallory. Could you try on some dresses for me and select them?"

I shook my head. "Oh no, no way, no how." I flicked my eyes over Olivia's figure again. Even with the pregnancy I assumed she was concealing, she was finer boned than I was.

"We're both just a hair over five feet." Olivia

nodded, warming to the idea despite my protestations.

"I'm an eight. You're a what, four or six?" I rested my eyes expectantly on Olivia's midsection. "I mean . . ."

Olivia glanced at her belly, then at me. "The jig's up, huh?" A sheepish grin spread over her face.

"I'm so happy for you!" I gave Olivia a fierce hug and remembered just in time that we were still in the basement with Truman and Goldie, though a good twenty feet away. I toned down my voice and they were none the wiser.

"When are you due?" Happiness sparkled in my sister's eyes as she gave Olivia a hug.

"Mid-June. I really don't think my parents or grandparents have a clue." She frowned. "They're all surprisingly old-fashioned, though, even Clementine. Especially Clementine." She let out a gust of air. "Thus, the moved-up wedding date."

It all made sense now that Olivia's pregnancy was confirmed. The wedding, the wish for a shorter commute, and the reticence at making partner.

"So you'll do it? You'll try on some dresses for me, and pick the one you think will look best?" Olivia's eyes were alight with mirth and hope. I couldn't deny her.

"Of course."

I wasn't sure who was more excited at the prospect of me trying on wedding dresses, Olivia or my sister. The bride dashed off to break the news to Goldie that she had to run.

Faith Hendricks, Truman's partner, showed up minutes later. Truman asked me a brief series of questions, then released us to continue processing the scene.

"I knew she was up the duff!" Rachel nearly crowed her guess when the elevator doors safely shut us in. "And I can't wait to take pictures of you trying on gowns." She slipped her sequined purple cell phone from her bag and primed the camera feature. I grabbed the phone and dumped it back into her bag as the doors of the elevator opened and we crossed the lobby.

"Uh-uh."

"But what if we want to send some pictures to Olivia to help her decide?" Rachel wasn't taking no for an answer.

"Over my dead body." I glanced down the moment I said it, and Rachel and I realized we were crossing the threshold of the March building right where Lacey fell. Our laughter died in our throats.

We walked in tense silence three blocks east to my friend Bev Mitchell's bridal shop. Her window display was all decked out for the holidays. Cotton batting snow infused with iridescent pastel glitter lined the bottom of the display. A dress form wearing an impossibly heavily beaded gown of seed pearls in snowflake patterns held center stage in the middle of the display, seated in a silver sleigh. A dress form clad in a gray tuxedo sat beside the bride. Hundreds of blue, lavender, and mint snowflakes rained down on the scene on an invisible fishing line. Interspersed among the snowflakes were tiny silver bells, in a nod to the shop's name. The gorgeous tableau distracted us from our worries a bit as we pushed open the doors to the Silver Bells dress shop.

"Hello, Mallory and Rachel!" Bev pulled my sister and me into a hug by way of greeting. The dress storeowner was all dressed up for the holiday season in a red velvet tunic and red plaid leggings. Her towering blonde beehive featured glittery red holly berries. A ruby candy cane adorned her necklace. She scanned behind us, expectant.

"And where is the bride?"

"Unfortunately, it's no surprise Olivia couldn't make it." Clementine held the door open for Goldie and the two March women marched in. "I wish my dear grandchild would try to find a new career here in Port Quincy. That law firm will be the end of her."

I wondered if Clementine knew anything about Garrett possibly rescinding his offer. My fingers reflexively reached for the citrine pendant I wore around my neck. I'd often twist the modest stone around my fingers when I was anxious, like a worry stone or talisman.

"It's gone." I blurted out my revelation as my fingers fluttered against my naked collarbone.

"Your necklace?" Rachel frowned and peered at me. "The one Garrett gave you?"

I gulped and nodded. "I know it was still on when we had lunch a few hours ago at the Greasy Spoon. I'll text him." I didn't expect a response, as Garrett was so undeniably busy these days. Somehow the thought of losing the necklace he'd given me last Christmas was like a bad omen. I couldn't keep a hold on the man I was in love with nor the things he'd given me.

"Don't fret, Mallory. It'll turn up."

"Let's get this show on the road." Clementine

clapped her hands together, the bright green tips of her reverse French manicure gleaming in the shop's lights. "Trying on dresses for Olivia is a novel solution, Mallory." She graced me with a warm smile. "I think this just might work."

*Phew.*

I was glad Clementine seemed to have gotten over the fact that Olivia wasn't wearing the family wedding gown.

Bev's eyebrows shot up upon hearing the plan, and then she shook her head and chuckled. Her eyes seemed to bore into me. "This'll be so fun, Mallory. I've waited ages to get you into my store to try on a gown rather than just help brides select theirs. I thought you trying on gowns would be under somewhat different circumstances, but I'll take what I can get."

I felt my heart accelerate, but then I relaxed. I didn't want word to spread around town that I was trying on wedding dresses for myself. I especially didn't want Garrett to know. But Bev Mitchell was the reigning queen bee of gossip. All tall tales and tidbits of news started and ended in this very store. Fortunately, Bev would set them straight and let everyone know I was just serving as Olivia's stunt double.

"Now, let's see. This would be lovely for a late December wedding." Bev flicked her plump fingers over a rack of white and cream confections, selecting a slinky mermaid with a flared train. I took in the clingy midsection and shook my head.

"Um, I have it on good authority that this isn't the cut Olivia wants."

Bev frowned and return the gown to the rack.

*Bullet dodged.*

"Okay. How about this?" She held up a frothy number with lace sleeves and a wide velvet sash. It was vaguely reminiscent of Duchess Kate Middleton's wedding dress, as many of the dresses these days seemed to be. I cocked my head and studied the dress. With the wide, almost cummerbund-like sash, it could work.

"What're you waiting for?" Rachel egged me on as I disappeared into the dressing room.

Minutes later I stepped out, my heart thumping. Wearing the dress was much like being enveloped by a clingy boa constrictor. And it wasn't the fit. The dress would probably not need many alterations should Olivia's family decide it was the one. But the fleeting vision I caught of myself in the triptych mirror almost made me gasp. I'd just declared a mere six months ago to Garrett that I wasn't sure I was the marrying type. It took the threat of him leaving to start to change my mind.

"Wow. You look amazing." Rachel took a slow circle around me on the raised dais. "You should put this gown on hold. For later." She waggled her eyebrows and broke the spell of my concern. I burst out laughing.

"It's nice." Goldie was noncommittal.

"It's not the one." Clementine twisted a green tip of her spiky hair. "It's pretty. But that dress is wearing *you*, my dear, not the other way around." She nodded to herself. "Olivia will have more presence."

I smirked as I shimmied out of the gown. I hadn't ever been able to imagine wedding gown shopping for myself. But now I could imagine my own mother's unfiltered comments and broke out into a grin.

On and on the farce went. I tried on every gown that would give Olivia a fighting chance of hiding the beginnings of a bump.

I predicted Bev's last choice would be the winner and hoped the women would like it. It was a silvery-white gown, done in a heavy, winter floral-patterned brocade with cap sleeves. The slightly raised waist was very subtle, accented with a single row of silver sequins. It seemed like a sleek design choice rather than a tool for camouflage. I almost teared up in the dressing room picturing Olivia in the dress.

*And if I'm being honest, myself. With Garrett beside me.*

I pushed away a single bead of moisture from each corner of my eyes and pushed open the door. The peanut gallery was silent.

Finally Goldie spoke. "That's the one." She seemed to study the forgiving waistline a nanosecond too long.

Even Clementine had to grudgingly agree. "Yes, this one will do."

Bev nodded, rendered silent for once. She plucked a simple veil from a display and affixed it at the bottom of my messy bun of sandy curls.

Rachel stopped taking pictures and stared at me in thought.

The pretty trill of silver bells affixed to the front door of the store announced a new arrival. Garrett strode in, swinging my citrine pendant as he whistled and made his way into the shop.

Our eyes met, and time stood still.

"Mallory." Garrett's voice was husky and serious. He strode across the room, no longer swinging the pendant. He stood before me and swallowed. There was a strange look in his hazel eyes. It was a mix of love and wonderment, nervousness and indecision.

No, I was just reading too much into this silly situation.

*Projecting is more like it.*

But he refused to break the spell. He gently fumbled with the delicate clasp of the pendant and tenderly affixed it around my neck. He leaned in until his lips were a millimeter from my ear.

"I've been thinking of this moment. Maybe I'm making a mistake even considering Pittsburgh." He pulled back and looked me in the eye, but still spoke softly enough that only I could hear. "Maybe we need to speed this up."

I stepped out of his heavy orbit, stumbling over the too-long hem of the gorgeous gown. I tumbled down, but Garrett caught me. He pulled me in for a smoldering kiss, not caring who was witnessing it. Goldie, Clementine, and Rachel cheered.

"Oh, thank God." Truman's voice boomed through the shop. Garrett and I parted, and I felt a hot blush climb up my neck to stain my cheeks.

Garrett laughed, a delightfully silvery sound. He kissed my cheek and tenderly rubbed his thumb over the edge of my face. "I've got to go. See you later, my love."

He left with the silver bells chiming. I stepped down from the dais and grabbed the nearest flute of champagne Bev had poured for Clementine and downed it in one frantic gulp.

"So he's staying in Port Quincy. Good work, Mallory." Truman clapped me on the back a little too hard, and a spray of champagne flew out.

"Watch it! This is the dress we're getting for Olivia." I hurried into the dressing room, the spell officially broken. I shimmied out of the gown and tucked it safely into Bev's arms for Goldie and Clementine to purchase. But Truman wasn't letting me off the hook.

"So this gambit isn't about you and my son?" The jowls in his face fell as Rachel filled him in.

"Nope," I confirmed. "I was trying on dresses for Olivia."

"Dammit." Truman thumped his fist against a case filled with pretty crystal tiaras and baubles. The jewelry jumped, and he sheepishly took away his hand. "I don't want my son moving to Pittsburgh, Mallory. Or Summer, for that matter." He narrowed his eyes. "It's poop or get off the pot time for you two, I'm afraid."

Rachel started to laugh, but it was no laughing matter for me. The subtle holiday string music piped into Bev's store seemed to fade away with a rush of blood to my head. I heard the pounding of a far-off ocean in my ears. I gulped and fingered the necklace Garrett had so tenderly returned.

I regretted insisting that we keep our relationship so casual, slow, and steady last spring. I'd lamely assumed time would march on unchanged and that we could safely reside in the gentle rut we'd carved out for ourselves. But now I wanted more.

*Maybe marriage is for me.*

I didn't just want the pageantry of a well-planned

wedding, just as I always wanted much more for the brides and grooms I helped to wed. I took for granted Garrett's permanence. I wanted love, family, and a declaration. A promise between two people, and with his daughter Summer, three people. I was ready to take the leap.

And I felt the undeniable urge to hyperventilate.

"Don't worry, Mallory." Truman watched me cycle through a complicated set of emotions. His eyes crinkled as he smiled. "I have a plan."

Garrett's sort-of declaration was as close to a proposal as I'd ever had.

*Um, except for your actual proposal from Keith.*

Oops. I'd just conveniently blocked my entire relationship with Keith Pierce from my brain. A twist of fate had brought me to Port Quincy. I'd inherited Thistle Park from Keith's grandmother, Sylvia, after she amended her will. Keith had turned out to be a cheating creep, but Sylvia was amazing. Her bequest had kicked off my new career and my new life here.

I couldn't help but think Olivia would be happy in my adopted hometown, too. I figured she would grow to love Port Quincy just as much as I had. That is, if she still had a chance to move here.

I drove the Butterscotch Monster four blocks east and cut the engine behind the Bloomery flower shop. Toby lived in the loft apartment above, and I knew Olivia had retired there this afternoon to remotely be at her boss's beck and call.

"I heard from Mom and Grandma that you

found the dress!" Olivia met me at the door with a big grin. Her infectious excitement almost distracted me from seeing the dark circles under her eyes. Still, she also had a pregnant glow. She ushered me into the living room of the spacious apartment, with its river view of the roiling Monongahela beyond.

"Thanks for trying on the dresses, Mallory." Toby rose to greet me as well. He removed the garment bag with the magnificent dress and carefully slung it over a dining room chair. "I did hear through the grapevine before Olivia filled me in that you were spotted trying on dresses for yourself."

"It figures," I grumbled. "I wonder who else in town believes that rumor?"

Olivia's eyes sparkled with mischief. "And what if they do?"

I wondered dimly if I'd been had. Though Olivia's wedding was only a few weeks away, we didn't need to find her a dress today. Maybe my best friend had nudged me along to a realization I didn't even know I needed to have.

Olivia sank onto the plush eggplant-colored velvet couch and gestured for me to sit down. "I made a pot of chamomile tea, and there are some shortbread cookies, too." She leaned back and closed her eyes. "My OB said now that I'm nearing the end of the first trimester, I should be getting a burst of energy." Her long lashes fluttered open. "So where is it? I need it now!"

Toby sat next to his bride and wrapped his arm around her shoulder. "You work too hard, Liv." He was concerned, without a bit of censure in his tone.

"I'll agree for once." Olivia sighed. "I don't even want that darn partnership anymore. Some whipper-snapper associate caught me napping at my desk yesterday. They're going to figure out I'm pregnant and maybe try to delay making me partner."

I felt my eyes nearly bug out of my head. "They can't do that. That's gender and pregnancy discrimination."

Olivia gave a bitter laugh. "Think back, Mallory, to when you were at the firm. They've done it before."

I wracked my brain and realized it was true. There had been several women over the years who were pregnant while they were senior associates and had their partnerships unofficially delayed until the firm could judge how productive they'd be when they returned to work.

"You really wanted to join Garrett's practice." Toby rubbed Olivia's back.

"She still can," I blurted out. "He hasn't made a decision yet."

The couple blinked at the fierceness of my tone.

"I just want you to be safe and happy, Liv. And this little peanut, too." He gazed fondly at his fiancée. "A two-hour commute is nuts."

"Well, even if Garrett does end up taking the offer to run the clinic…" Olivia carefully avoided my gaze, "I would've thought my parents would be ecstatic to have me finally join the family real estate development business as their in-house counsel." She looked at me, bewilderment clouding her eyes. "But you heard him, Mallory. My dad doesn't want me working for March Homes."

It had been odd. Alan would rather his daughter stay in a situation he knew no longer made her happy than join the family fold.

"At least he doesn't know I'm pregnant." Olivia smiled at her secret. "We'll let everyone know the day we return from our honeymoon."

"Mmm, I don't know about that. Your mom was studying the cuts of the gowns I said you'd like. She may have cottoned on."

"No way." Olivia batted away my concerns and stood. "I want to see the dress!"

I carefully unzipped the silvery brocade concoction and held it aloft in front of Olivia.

"Ooh, it's lovely." She ran her slender fingers over the raised brocade pattern of holly and vines, the delicate silver thread a subtle contrast to the diamond-white fabric. "I'll go try it on!"

She disappeared into the bedroom for a few minutes, then reappeared with tears in her eyes.

"It's magnificent."

The gown looked lovely on Olivia, but different than when I'd tried it on. She spun around in a slow circle, catching sight of herself in the large mirror hanging over the couch.

"What's wrong, Liv?" Toby noticed first that Olivia's tears weren't exactly happy.

"This dress is so pretty. But it's not me. I think we all made a mistake, my family and I, bickering over where I'm going to work and live, and what dress I'm going to wear." She took a deep breath. "I want to thank you for literally going dress shopping for me, Mallory. But I should wear the family dress."

My heart melted at the sentiment, and I crossed the room to envelope my friend in a hug.

"I'm going to call my mother."

I listened on in amusement as Olivia discussed her change of heart. I could hear Clementine's forceful voice join the call as well. Olivia finally set her phone down and outlined her plan.

"My parents and Clementine are still working downtown." Her lips turned up in a knowing smile. "Talk about workaholics. But Rudy is at the cabin. Grandpa likes to leave each day at five, no matter what." Her gaze grew wistful. "I'd like to try on the family dress, tonight. Then we can get started on finding a seamstress willing to cut it down in time for the twenty-third."

"It sounds like a plan."

Ten minutes later, I left Toby's loft downtown with a beaming bride. We wended our way west of town and down the long, forest drive to the cabin. But this time, the night sky wasn't pitch black. There was an eerie glow.

"Please hurry, Mallory." Olivia frowned and strained the length of her seatbelt peering out through the front windshield. The air filtering through the car began to smell of smoke.

"Oh, dear God."

We'd finally reached the clearing where the resplendent cabin rose from the ground. The entire left side was engulfed in flames. A massive pillar of smoke billowed overhead. Though it was a wooden structure, it was burning more than seemed natural. The whole edifice would be gone soon, incinerated like a cheap pile of tinder.

I saw in the glow of the fire a pretty iridescent sheen in the puddles before the house.

*Gasoline.*

This was no accident.

"Grandpa Rudy!" Olivia scrabbled to get out of the station wagon, but I held her back.

"No, it's not safe. I'm sorry, Olivia." I spluttered out my warning and held fast to my friend's hand. She wriggled out of my grasp and made her way to the glowing cabin.

The front door flung open, and out crawled Rudy. I couldn't help even in this bizarre and tragic situation to reflect on the fact he could be Santa's doppelgänger. Soot streaked his rosy red cheeks, as if he'd just alighted down a chimney to tuck some toys under a tree. His formerly snowy beard was caked with the stuff. He stood on shaky knees, a big bear of a man, and tumbled down the half flight of front steps.

Olivia and I grabbed Rudy under his arms and dragged him thirty feet away from the cabin, which now resembled a live coal more than a residence. Sirens wailed in the distance. We stared in mute horror at the night sky, lit up in shades of orange, red, and yellow.

# CHAPTER EIGHT

"He's going to be all right." Truman's words about Rudy March, resident Father Christmas, were a welcome contrast to when he'd announced Lacey's death. A weak ray of early morning sunshine escaped through a blanket of leaden clouds and seemed to illuminate Truman.

I felt a ripple of relief ricochet around the front hall. My mother, sister, and stepfather embraced at hearing the good news. I knew none of us had slept much. It had been a late night, filled with worry and fear.

I'd watched Olivia board a wailing ambulance with Rudy on a stretcher. The bearded man had an oxygen mask pressed to his face as the doors had clanged closed. The fire marshal arrived next on the scene and roughly pulled me to my feet.

"You need to get out of here, now." His voice brooked no wiggle room. I'd shaken off my fear and run to the Butterscotch Monster. I'd reversed down the drive. A glance at the rearview mirror showed me the look of horror and fascination etched upon my features. A safe fifty feet from the burning structure, I'd turned my station wagon around to make my way down the narrow path to civilization. A sickening whoosh resounded behind me, and I turned to see the entire grand cabin collapse in on itself. As I floored it out of there, I felt the heat chase me in a gust. I worried about the Butterscotch Monster's retro-wooden panels and tan paint job, then doubled up with hysterical laughter. I was so shaken; I was concerned with my car's aesthetics instead of the close call I'd nearly been in. I'd made it out of the woods on the narrow path just as three more fire trucks blared their way through.

I shuddered now in the calm peacefulness of the front hall, recalling an evening I wouldn't soon forget.

"All of the Marches are at the hospital." Truman glanced at me. "They wanted to know if they could move into your B and B." He took in my shocked face. "Temporarily, of course."

I recovered and slowly nodded. "Yes! They're all welcome here."

It would be unexpected, but not an imposition. And after all they'd been through, the March family needed some hospitality extended their way. Their castle of a cabin had gone up in flames, and they'd just broken ground on their new housing developments. I was sure Olivia's parents and grandmother would feel more at home at Thistle Park than at the hotels located downtown.

"I'll make our morning coffee." My mother was downright cool in her interaction with Truman. I couldn't blame her after the grilling she'd received from the chief. Still, she walked around a free woman, with no suspicion currently hanging over her. At least that I was aware of.

Truman waited until my family left for the kitchen.

"In here." He held open the door to my office and ushered me inside.

"I want to know what you saw."

I recounted Olivia's decision to wear the famed March wedding gown after all. "Goldie and Clementine suggested she head over to the cabin to try it on."

Truman twisted up his face in thought. "They said this while they were still working downtown?"

It was a bit odd. They'd pushed Olivia to go get the dress right then, instead of waiting until all the March women were assembled to ooh and aah. I shrugged. "They knew Rudy was supposed to be there."

Truman made some notes. "I know Olivia's version of events. Now let's hear yours."

I wearily recounted holding my friend back from plunging into the fire. Truman nodded when I told of Rudy crawling from the door and tumbling down the stairs.

"Oh! And there was some shiny rainbow stuff in the puddles. Like gasoline on the ground after it rains."

"Yes. This was definitely arson." Truman cocked his head in thought. "After Lacey's death, the March family moved most of their business records to the cabin office. According to Goldie, most of their recent documents are backed up in the cloud. But their older records are gone."

*How convenient.*

Truman glanced at the open door and rose to shut it.

"I spoke with Nina Adams."

"How is she doing?" The poor woman had lost two of her daughters, one to a disappearance, and now Lacey. Her funeral had been yesterday.

"Lacey was in dire need of a kidney transplant." Truman let the tidbit hang in the air.

I took the bait. "Then why did she drink so much at Paws and Poinsettias?" I would've thought drinking alcohol was contraindicated in a person needing a new kidney.

"Maybe she was so distraught that the Marches wanted to replace her that she thought she would go out with a bang."

"I'm not sure." I frowned. "She asked my mom for a regular Hawaiian blue punch with no alcohol." I hated to even bring my mother back into this conversation.

"But she was already totally inebriated by then." He frowned. "Maybe not by choice."

"If the Marches wanted to fire Lacey, they could have done so. They didn't need to slip her a mickey and poison her with antifreeze!"

*Tread lightly, Mallory.*

I remembered just in time that I needed to keep it under wraps that my mother had waltzed into the B and B just days ago with a giant bottle of half-empty antifreeze. I squirmed in my poofy chintz chair, just imagining how apoplectic Truman would be if he knew I was concealing that little fact.

"And if the March family was unhappy with Lacey,

then you definitely don't need to suspect my mom."
My feeling of guilt led me to prattle on.

Truman studied me carefully over tented fingers. "Who said anything about suspecting your mother?" He blinked and grew even more serious. "Something's not right, here, Mallory. If I were Carole, I'd watch out."

A shiver skipped down my spine. On one hand, I was cheered. If Truman wanted to protect my mother, he truly didn't think she had anything to do with Lacey's death. But the fact that he thought she could be in trouble was not okay.

"There are the perfect motive, means, and opportunity to accuse your mother," he continued.

"But you just said—"

Truman held up his hand. "Carole desperately wanted to work as a stager for March Homes." He held up one finger. "She undid all of Lacey's work the eve of Paws and Poinsettias." He held up a second finger. "She happened to be at the bar and poured Lacey her last drink."

"It's a setup," I whispered. "But who, and why, and how?"

Truman rubbed his lined forehead. "I don't know. Just watch out for your mother, okay? She won't give me the time of day."

My mind floated back to Olivia. It seemed like such a simple explanation now, that she'd poured out her drink that evening because she was pregnant. But Truman should know, so he could decide. I wrestled with revealing a piece of information that would undoubtedly lead my friend back into Truman's laser beam of inquisition. I opened my mouth to spill the beans when the doorbell clanged.

I heard my mother fussing over Goldie and Alan March. I stood to greet them in the hall.

"Thank you, Mallory." Goldie sported deep purple circles under her eyes. For the first time ever, I saw her chignon in an unkempt state. Alan seemed to prop up his wife. I took their coats and sent them to the kitchen for a restorative breakfast I knew Rachel and Doug were whipping up.

My mother turned to Truman with a cold glare in her pretty green eyes. I supposed she was still angry with the chief for the questioning he'd put her through. She had no idea he was concerned with her welfare and had tasked me with warning her.

"Carole," Truman began.

"You can leave now, Truman." My mother stood ramrod straight, formidable even in her floral flannel dressing gown.

The chief sent me a sheepish gaze and let himself out.

The rest of December was going to be a doozy. *Fa-la-la-la-uh-oh.*

I spent the rest of the morning settling Goldie and Alan into their rooms at Thistle Park. Another room was prepped for Clementine, as soon as she returned from the hospital. Truman had assured me Rudy would be on the mend soon, released as early as that evening.

With a more hopeful heart, I headed back to Silver Bells to return the resplendent brocade gown. Despite the March family wedding gown having gone up in smoke, Olivia still didn't feel at home in the gown I'd tried on in the dress shop. I returned the dress with a hint of wistfulness. As I handed Bev the garment bag, the vision of myself in the dress and the feeling I'd had kissing Garrett flooded back in a blizzard of emotion. I left the store feeling more confused than ever. And ran smack into Judge Ursula Frank.

"Oh! I'm so sorry, judge. I'm not sure where my mind is these days."

The judge reached out to steady me and gave a commiserative nod. "Toby told me about Rudy and the cabin. It's just awful." She wore a camel-colored cashmere coat over her black robes. Her crown of braids was tightly coiled around her head. But despite the frigid weather, she still sported her ubiquitous Birkenstocks. In the summer, her trademark sandals revealed her long, pale toes. Today her feet were clad in a pair of jaunty holiday socks. Snoopy and Woodstock frolicked near a doghouse, while Charlie Brown decorated a shabby tree.

"I just want Olivia and her family to be safe," the judge said. "I can't understand why people don't settle their differences in the orderly world of the courts."

"I can imagine some people are upset about all of the new developments but not enough to try to kill Rudy over it." I noticed a sheaf of thick card stock in neon shades of orange, yellow, and pink tucked under the judge's arm.

"It should be unfathomable. But unfortunately I can think of a few people who would fit the bill."

I gulped and raised an eyebrow.

The judge leaned in conspiratorially. "Greg Gibson is suing his own parents regarding the sale of their land to March Homes. He doesn't have much of a case, but he will get his day in court." Her dark gray eyes flashed with anger. "He is simply an inveterate hothead. His first appearance in my chambers earned him contempt when he said I'd better decide the case the right way."

I gulped. I would never want to cross the formidable judge, and declaring how she should decide a case was not the way to endear oneself to her.

"When I set him in his place, he muttered under his breath that he would make me pay if I did not. That's when I handed down the contempt order." She waved the neon papers under my nose. The colorful fliers featured an adorable picture of Hemingway next to a Christmas tree, with the judge's plea and offer of a hefty reward for his return or information on the kitty's whereabouts. "I have to wonder if Mr. Gibson had a part in my dear Hemingway's disappearance."

I patted the judge on the arm. "I'm so sorry you haven't found your cat. I couldn't imagine the stress."

I wasn't prepared for the judge's next actions. She burst into tears, her pillar of strength persona melted away in a puddle of lost pet grief.

"There, there." I patted Ursula on the back and gently steered her two doors down. "Maybe a nice cup of cocoa or tea would make you feel better." The judge allowed me to take the pile of fliers from her. I opened the door to Pellegrino's restaurant and ushered the sniffling jurist inside.

Five minutes later we were sitting in a deep, dark wood booth. A pretty, lacquered red pot of peppermint tea steamed between us. The judge had reclaimed some of her stern strength and regally nodded at the movers and shakers of Port Quincy who sent her smiles and waves in deference. I thought it would look odd that we were dining together, but then again, this could just be construed as a planning session with the mother of the groom.

A server took our order but not before the judge convinced her to tape a flier about Hemingway to the hostess podium at the entrance of the restaurant. The college-aged server had accepted the neon orange flier with a smirk, but from the corner of my eye I observed her dutifully taping up the card stock.

"Hemingway isn't the only thing on my mind." The judge sipped her tea and let out a sigh. She cocked her head and seemed to be considering me. "I can trust Garrett to be discreet about any matter. I suppose I can ask the same of you."

I gulped and nodded. Come to think of it, Garrett had never spilled the beans about one iota of the judge's business.

"March Homes may not be the most squeaky-clean establishment." The judge winced as she made her statement. "I worry about their reputation tarnishing my son's."

I set my cup of tea onto the table before my shaking hand belied my nervousness. "Go on." We were silent as the server returned with our soups.

Ursula frowned and set down her soup spoon as soon as she'd left us alone. "Let's just say I'd hoped Olivia would stay at Russell Carey, make partner, and not involve herself in her family's business.

Come to think of it, I'd be happy if she didn't even relocate to Port Quincy. She needs to keep them at arm's length."

I was stunned into silence. The mother of the groom didn't want his soon-to-be bride to move to his hometown? A stray thought bubbled up from the recesses of my memory. Olivia's own father, Alan, had been remiss about Olivia joining the family business. He'd been pushing Olivia to stay at her firm and not become counsel for March Homes.

"It seems that no one wants Olivia to have a presence in Port Quincy. Except for your son, of course." I nearly clapped my hand against my mouth. I hadn't meant to spit out my thoughts, they'd just sailed out unbidden.

Judge Frank shook her head, the braids anchored firmly into a heavy halo. "No, no, no. Make no mistake, I love Olivia. She is like a daughter to me. I'll admit I was a bit shocked at the pace of the engagement, but I truly believe my son has found his soul mate. It's just her family . . ." The judge trailed off.

I was this close to demanding the judge to spill it, whatever it was. The woman was usually direct to a fault, but today all I could get from her was a series of confusing riddles. I bit into a warm, crusty roll in frustration.

"I've even thought of warning Garrett about taking on Olivia as a partner and bringing in March Homes as a client." The judge took another sip of peppermint tea and brightened. "But now that he'll be helming the clinic at Pitt, I don't need to worry about overstepping there."

I coughed, a morsel of roll going down the wrong pipe. "I was under the impression he was just *considering* taking the clinic offer." Little alarm bells were clanging somewhere in my conscience.

"Oh, you have nothing to worry about, dear." The judge bestowed me with a warm smile, the first one I'd seen from her since literally running into her nearly an hour ago.

*Phew.*

"You are both careerists, like I was with my husband. Your relationship will manage just fine with Garrett in Pittsburgh and you in Port Quincy." The judge let out a chuckle after taking in my astonished face. "You can have it all, Mallory. My husband was head of the surgery department at the hospital, and I had my law practice and then ascended to the bench. But we still managed to raise Toby and have a little time for each other."

*But I don't want just a little time with Garrett.*

My heart began to accelerate unbidden. Did the judge know something about Garrett's decision-making status that I didn't?

But Judge Frank had returned to the seemingly juicier topic at hand. Her former mirth dimmed. "I've been on the bench for thirty years. And before that I practiced on both sides, as a prosecutor and a defense attorney. I have my hunches. And I have some big ones about the March family." She sat back and glanced at her purple Swatch watch. "Then again, rumors can be just that. Completely unfounded. And ultimately, I do believe in innocence until proven guilty."

I wanted to press her further before she left our impromptu lunch. "Does Olivia have any idea you suspect improprieties with her family's business?" I kept my voice even. It only seemed fair to try to protect my friend. The judge was looking out for her son, of course, and seemed to love Olivia, but I wasn't sure Olivia was getting a fair shake.

"I've dropped a few hints," the judge admitted. "I can't just come out and accuse my future daughter-in-law's family of shady business deals when it might not even be true, now can I?" She shook her head. "No, I've just encouraged her to claim the partnership she's worked so hard for. That way she and my son can continue to grow in their careers, her family can expand their business, and we'll see where the chips fall."

I shivered. Olivia seemed to be functioning as an unwitting chess piece in a complicated game played by her grandparents, her parents, and her fiancé's mother. I wasn't sure how it all fit together, but it wasn't right.

"I've said too much." Ursula Frank briefly colored. "I really shouldn't have aired my concerns. And I do take solace in the fact that Olivia is her own person. She's not a chip off the old block." The judge carefully folded her cloth napkin and placed the pretty fabric with its candy cane pattern atop the table.

"I guess not," I softly agreed. The piped in muzak changed from an instrumental version of the hallelujah chorus to a string composition of "Away in a Manger." The judge broke out in a wistful smile.

"I don't want you to get the wrong idea, Mallory. Olivia is a very special person to me. She really is incredible, as incredible as the story of how she came to be adopted by Goldie and Alan." She included me in her smile and gestured upward toward the ceiling.

I frowned, not understanding.

"Oh, come on. 'Away in a Manger.'" The judge's eyebrows fell in a realization I wasn't in on some secret. Her smile fell. "You don't know? Oh dear." She blushed anew and muttered something unintelligible, seeming to beat a hasty retreat.

Thankfully for her, Garrett rescued her from having to provide an explanation.

"Two of my favorite people." Garrett smiled and joined me in the booth. The judge beamed at her protégé, seeming nearly as proud of Garrett as she was of her own son, Toby.

"We should have a toast before I go." The judge made to wave down our server. "We can celebrate your acceptance of the clinic position, Garrett."

He must have felt me stiffen. I felt a strained smile slide from my face.

"I haven't accepted, Ursula," Garrett gently informed the judge.

"Well, see to it that you do." The judge bestowed us with a smile that dimmed when she picked up her Hemingway fliers. She swanned out of the restaurant, leaving me confused in her wake.

"I'll have a piece of pecan pie and a cup of coffee, please." Garrett put in his order and gently slung his arm around me. He made no move to relocate to the other side of the booth. "Ursula is jumping the gun a bit. I haven't accepted the clinic offer."

*Yeah, not yet.*

It was telling enough that he hadn't rejected it, either. The proposition to move nearly two hours away was still very much on the table.

"It is ultimately your decision, Garrett. Yours and Summer's, too."

Garrett turned to face me, a bit awkwardly in the booth side we shared. "No way. It's your decision, too. I've been a bit distracted. But seeing you in that wedding dress . . ." He trailed off, his voice growing husky. I leaned in for a quick kiss when an "ahem" startled us apart.

"Your pies." The server gave us a cheeky smirk as she set down two slices of pecan and a piping hot silver carafe of coffee. Now that the moment was ruined, I decided to plunge in with what I'd just learned.

"The judge has some concerns about Olivia joining your practice." My voice sounded small and miserable.

Garrett dropped his arm from my shoulder and his brows creased together. "What kind of concerns?"

I reiterated the nebulous and largely unfounded hunches of the judge, based on rumor and feelings alone. But Garrett didn't seem to think her wishy-washy claims were unsubstantial.

He rubbed his chin, the start of a sexy five o'clock shadow beginning there. "This changes things."

*Ruh-roh.*

I cursed my need to be transparent.

"I've worked so hard on building this practice from nothing. And it sounds like Olivia isn't aware of anything untoward her family's business is involved in. Nevertheless, I wouldn't want to jeopardize all I've built if Ursula thinks there are reasons to be concerned."

"Maybe you should talk to Olivia first." I hastily tried to walk back the beans I'd unceremoniously spilled all over the floor. "I think Judge Frank is just a little emotional right now, what with her son getting married and trying to find Hemingway."

But Garrett shook his head. "I was excited to work with Olivia, but if that even happened now, she definitely couldn't bring any of her family's business to the table." A realization stole over his handsome features. "I'll admit, Ursula has been pushing pretty hard for me to take the clinic position. Now I know why."

I began to grow desperate. The music had changed to a treacly version of "I saw Mommy Kissing Santa Claus," and I wanted to silence the speakers to get a moment to think. "Maybe the judge is wrong."

Garrett appeared particularly affronted. "Oh no, her judgment is usually spot on."

"Well then, if there's any truth to these random rumors about March Homes, then maybe I need to loop my mother in, too."

Garrett frowned and pushed away his piece of pie. "She's a grown-up, Mallory. And this seems like a delicate situation. I'm sure your mom is going to be just fine. She's just working as a stager for them, right?"

I bristled at his brush off of my concerns. "Yes, but if you're worried enough to rescind your offer to Olivia, then I'm allowed to be worried about my mother working for March Homes, too."

We ate the rest of our slices of pie in testy silence. I rarely argued with Garrett. We had our differences, like most couples, but something seemed different. A finely rumbling current of discord had been planted, sending out subtle little seismic shocks. We exited Pellegrino's together, the warm spark in the booth extinguished. I offered Garrett a hasty goodbye, and he bestowed a perfunctory kiss atop my head. I stared at his retreating figure as he made his way back to his office.

I'd imagined my friend Olivia as a chess piece, moving across the board with no control over her actions.

*And something tells me she's not the only one.*

# CHAPTER NINE

I made a beeline to see my friend that evening. I wanted to see the gown Olivia had texted me about and also pick her brain about her family's company. My quest took me up to Pittsburgh and Olivia's apartment atop Mount Washington. I couldn't tamp down my grin as I caught a glittering glimpse of the city below. A tree of lights punctuated the point where the Monongahela and Allegheny Rivers met to form the Ohio. Skyscrapers of glass and steel gleamed beyond, and their lights reflected off the rivers' waters. I felt a pang of regret and realized though I'd made a wonderful new life for myself, I did miss the city. Maybe I was wrong to want Garrett to give up a chance to live here with his daughter. It hadn't been a quick trip up from Port Quincy, but it also hadn't been impossible.

I stepped into the lobby of Olivia's condo with a sinking feeling of déjà vu. I hoped this impromptu dress reveal didn't presage some crisis with fire and mayhem like the last one did.

"Come in." Olivia opened the door clad in a fuzzy red robe with a pattern of Scottie dogs roaming all over. "This is one time I'm happy to live so far apart from my fiancé. I can try on the dress without him getting a peek."

I settled in on the couch to await for Olivia's return. She didn't disappoint.

"Ta-da!" She was a vision in winter splendor in a simple cream satin gown with tight-fitting long sleeves and a pretty bateau neckline. The plain yet rich fabric was unadorned, save for a thin line of champagne sequins just below the bust. The dress would be forgiving, yet not automatically reveal her pregnancy. She'd placed a pretty, pearl-beaded headband atop her lustrous dark hair, but sported no veil.

"This dress is you, Liv." I clapped my hands together and circled my friend. "I'm glad you were able to find it up here on such short notice."

Olivia's joy dimmed a degree. "I did want to wear my family's dress in the end. But what's more important is that Grandpa Rudy is okay."

I nodded my assent. The jolly old man was finally out of the hospital. He was settled into the yellow bedroom at Thistle Park where Clementine was lovingly caring for him. I didn't want to press Olivia any further, but the strange meal I'd shared with her soon-to-be mother-in-law was replaying in my head.

"Did Truman share any ideas about who would want to burn down the cabin?"

Olivia twisted her face into a frown. "Not beyond the obvious possible culprits. Townsfolk who aren't happy about all of the houses my parents plan to build in Port Quincy." She sighed and flounced down on the couch next to me, still wearing her wedding gown. "To be honest, I don't know if I'd want the drama of working for March Homes if I were to pair up with Garrett."

I took the opening and ran with it. "So you'll be taking the partnership here?"

"Oh, no." Olivia shook her head, sending the beaded pearl headband slipping down her bangs. She pushed it back into place. "I know my life should be in Port Quincy now. I'm tired of making the drive. I'm tired of this rat race. I want to be with Toby and actually see him each day." She beamed and rested her hand on her still rather flat belly. "I'm even beginning to think of Port Quincy as home. Isn't that funny?" Her dark brown eyes sparkled. "Who would've thought us two city girls, meeting as summer associates, would both eventually end up in sleepy little Port Quincy?"

I smiled at my friend while inwardly squirming.

*She doesn't know Garrett seems to be on the precipice of leaving Port Quincy.*

If Garrett handed over his entire practice to Olivia, it would take some time to get up to speed, especially with a new baby in tow. I realized enough was enough. I was going to tell Olivia about Garrett's probable acceptance of the clinic offer, so she had enough time to change her plans if necessary.

"And I think I need to take a bit of a break from my family, even if I do end up practicing with Garrett." Olivia spoke before I could croak out my warning. "I'm still hurt my dad didn't want me to take over legal duties for their company in Port

Quincy. He must have his reasons, but he isn't sharing them with me." She frowned and stood, pacing the hardwood floors in her wedding gown. The floor-to-ceiling glass windows fronting the city below were an interesting backdrop. "My parents are definitely of the helicopter variety," she mused. "Maybe it's because they adopted me so late in life or because I'm an only child." She nervously picked up the angel tree topper from the fireplace mantel. I noticed she'd glued the angel's wing back on. "I came to them under . . . unusual circumstances, and looking back, they raised me as if they were always waiting for the other shoe to drop."

I tried not to be nebby, but the long day got to me. "Judge Frank mentioned something about it."

Olivia turned around, a flash of anger in her eyes. "She's not as discreet of a woman as I'd expect in her position on the bench." A flush of pretty crimson climbed from her throat to dot both cheeks with color. "It's a pretty incredible story but not hers to tell." Olivia stared down at the city and wheeled around. "I was left as a days-old infant in the manger display at the Port Quincy Lutheran Church." She blinked, seeming to try to remember the event, though of course it would have been impossible. "My family would leave Pittsburgh Christmas Eve, head down to their old cabin in Port Quincy, and attend church that evening. My mom heard me crying in the manger and picked me up. I was placed in their care as a foster child and then they adopted me. And the rest is history."

"That's a pretty amazing story." The judge had

been right. But so had Olivia. It wasn't Ursula's story to tell, even to hint about. I'd known Olivia for over five years, and she'd kept the story a private piece of her identity.

Olivia sank back into the couch, thoroughly exhausted now. A knock at the door startled us, but not so much as the rumbling of the lock as a key was inserted.

"It must be Toby. I've got to get out of this dress before he sees me!" Olivia sprang to life and left me standing in the living room.

"Hi, Mallory." Toby graced me with a warm smile as he looked beyond me to catch a glimpse of his fiancée. He carried a cone of pretty pink roses in one hand and a brown bag concealing what smelled like one delicious pizza.

"What a lovely surprise!" Olivia must have shimmied out of her wedding gown in record time. She cast a fond glance at the gorgeous, lush roses, but her eyes really lit up upon spotting the pizza.

"I got you Campiti's." He mentioned a tiny pizzeria in the Dormont neighborhood I'd eaten at a time or two.

"My favorite." Olivia relieved Toby of the pizza. "The way to a pregnant woman's heart is to remember her particular cravings. Thank you, sweetheart." The two shared a sweet kiss.

I stayed for a slice, and Olivia and I made hasty plans for a tiny bridal shower to be held in three days' time. Goldie and Clementine insisted, and I could squeeze it in one afternoon. My heart melted as I listened to Toby talk about their little family-to-be with the arrival of their son or daughter due in the summer.

I thought of having my own family someday as I slid across the frigid, worn leather of the Butterscotch Monster. I shook my head at my presumption as I turned the key. The engine coughed and sputtered in the cold. Nothing seemed certain anymore. When I reached Port Quincy, I took a detour past the Lutheran Church. The pretty crèche out front had a fresh coat of paint, but the wood and craftsmanship of the figures featuring Mary, Joseph, the three wise men, and baby Jesus looked quite old. Old enough to have been the same set in front of the church when Olivia was abandoned Christmas Eve, then found. I stared at the wooden cradle surrounding the wooden infant, a bed big enough to hold a real baby. I shivered at the thought of Olivia lying in the manger, waiting to be discovered.

My shivers accelerated as I recalled the message on the hood of her car, the small cradle from my own nativity sliding off and into the snow. Someone else knew about Olivia's history, and they weren't playing nice. My friend's sudden fainting spell now made all too much sense.

The next day my sister and I headed to March Homes headquarters downtown. I carried a list of toys to be gathered at record speed for the toy drive. Word had traveled fast around town about the purloined presents, and the people of Port Quincy had rallied with good cheer. Many of the toys had been replaced, and some families' wish lists were nearly complete. I had spent the morning inventorying the toys collected from various businesses, and now it was time to present the list to the March family to make up the rest.

"Into the lion's den." My sister seemed to hold her breath as she laid her hand on the brass handle of the lobby's front door. She wore gloves with the fingertips cut off, the better to show off her sparkly silver-and-red striped acrylics.

"And Mom's the last to know." I'd filled my sister in on the judge's misgivings about March Homes in a roundabout way. Rachel had agreed we should let Carole know she was working for a company that might not be on the up-and-up.

"I'm sure she'll love this visit." Rachel chuckled without mirth as we made our way to the shiny brass elevator. We stepped out into a bank of offices hugging the walls of the second floor, with a busy hive of workers in a series of cubicles in the center. It was decorated with the same joy as the lobby below, but not as plentifully.

"Girls, girls! I'm so excited to show you my office." My mother bustled forward from the back row of offices and linked arms with my sister and me. She was clad monochromatically per usual, today's hue a pretty burgundy.

"It's lovely." She'd led us to a corner room in the back. The walls were a pleasing heavy cream, and she'd hung festive ribbon wreaths of silver and gold in the windows. I could see a pretty silhouette of Port Quincy through the old-fashioned panes. Her desk was a clean expanse of blonde wood. Blueprints, fabric swatches, and tile samples were piled neatly on an ample side worktable. I viewed pictures of Doug and my mom relaxing on their dock in Florida, a framed picture of Ramona, and photographs of Rachel and me.

*Gulp.*

Mom had really settled in. It didn't look like she'd want to leave her new job anytime soon.

"They're really taking care of you," I mused. "Are they in the office?"

I craned my head out my mom's open doorway. The other large offices in the back appeared quiet and dim.

"All the engineers and construction managers are onsite. Alan and Goldie are onsite, too."

And I knew Clementine had just left to shuttle Rudy to a follow-up doctor's appointment.

"Ouch!" I gave a tiny yelp as my sister pinched my side with her shiny acrylics. "Okay, okay. Um, Mom?"

"Yes, dear?" My mother had migrated to the worktable and taken her burgundy reading glasses from their perch on her forehead. She looked down at a swatch of gray silk and juxtaposed it with a slate tile.

"Rachel and I are concerned about you."

This made her stop and listen. The reading glasses returned to her head, and she crossed her arms and squinted at my sister and me. "Now what could you two be talking about?"

"These people are cray." Rachel stated our concerns in her typically blunt manner.

"Excuse me?" Our mom frowned.

"I think she means the March family seems to be up to something hinky. The—" I stopped myself before I mentioned the judge by name—"er, certain townspeople have hunches about how they run their business. And we don't want you to get caught up in anything."

A dim echo of Garrett's warning to basically mind my own beeswax flashed through my conscience. I batted it away.

My mother arched one artfully lined brow. A tiny vein on her forehead stood out.

*Uh-oh.*

I knew the signs and was worried my mom was about to have a conniption. But she decided instead to recede into mere annoyance.

"Lots of people are unhappy with the Marches' plans for Port Quincy. That doesn't mean there's anything untoward going on here." She gestured to her office and those beyond. "I have seen nothing strange. Just a hardworking family trying to expand their business and bring more progress and opportunity to this town."

"But—" Rachel opened her mouth and was silenced by my mom holding her hand up.

"Tell me, ladies. What exactly are these rumors? What specific claims do people have against March Homes?"

*Huh.*

I wracked my brain revisiting lunch with Judge Frank. She'd been aggravatingly unspecific in her complaints against Olivia's family's business. The more I thought about it, her actions could have just been an elaborate smear campaign.

"You see? You have nothing." My mother angrily slapped the tile sample down, and I winced as it connected with the wooden table.

"That's where you come in, Mom." Rachel

cheerily broke in. "We want you to do a teensy-weensy bit of snooping."

My mother whirled around almost fast enough to appear a blur.

"Under no circumstances, Rachel Marie Shepard, will I be snooping on the March family!"

"Oh, please. You're the best snooper in town, Mom." Rachel smirked. "You spent my entire middle school and high school existence snooping on me!"

It was true. My mom knew Rachel had been a wild child. Snooping had headed off some of Rachel's more daring but less-than-stellar ideas.

"Only to prevent all the trouble I knew you were trying to get into." My mother's eyes softened and she shook her head with a chuckle. "You girls are just worried about me. It's very sweet. But I'm having the time of my life here!" Her kind visage dimmed a degree. "I know you're not trying to jeopardize my job. But that's what could happen if I entertained your Nancy Drew fantasy. And besides." She gave me a soul-searching look. "I thought you'd have more allegiance to your friend, Mallory. Olivia has so much going on in her life with her impending marriage and now the fire and Rudy's recuperation."

I gulped. No one could serve up a heaping helping of guilt and introspection like my mom.

"I think it's because of Olivia that I want to know," I said. "And to protect you."

"Well, I don't need protecting." My mother moved to sit down in the impressive leather chair behind her wide desk. She crossed her hands in front of her in a settled manner.

"Rudy probably didn't think he needed protecting either. He was napping in a chair when someone lit the cabin on fire." I nearly whispered the facts.

My mother's superior face fell. "That brand-new wooden palace up in smoke." She shuddered and seemed to doubt herself.

"Brand new?" Rachel had only heard about the cabin from my description. It had looked recently built when I'd arrived and my mind scrambled to recall what Olivia had said about it.

"Yes, look." Our mother led us out of her office and into the hallway. She pointed to a series of framed photographs. The first three depicted outside shots of a tiny specimen of a cabin, the kind that would grace a cozy maple syrup label. Shots that were presumably of the inside of the structure followed next, with an impossibly young Clementine and Rudy, a child Goldie, and later Goldie and Alan with baby Olivia. The final series of photos showed the construction of the wooden castle I'd seen and the end result in all its splendor.

My mom looked up and down the hallway and seemed to consider something. She bit her lip and decided to go for it.

"Alan does have a little problem with extravagant spending. Clementine and Rudy don't think he pulls his weight. I heard he wanted to put an addition onto the original cabin, but Clementine and Rudy wouldn't allow it. So he went against their wishes, had it razed to the ground, and erected that huge wooden castle on the same spot. He revealed it late this spring." She shook her head. "That poor man is henpecked. He claimed he redid the cabin for Goldie, but no one cared.

Clementine and Rudy were furious at the amount he spent—almost more so than the fact he tore down the original family cabin."

"So there *is* trouble at the palace!" Rachel nearly crowed at succeeding in getting our mom to spill the beans once and for all.

"Oh, you two!" My mother turned on her heel and returned to her office. "That's just family squabbles. It has nothing to do with their business." The frown lines deepened between her eyes. "I'm grateful for this job. I don't need the money, thankfully, but I was frankly pretty bored in my early retirement."

It was true. My mom's well-meaning but incessant inquiries and uninvited suggestions about my and Rachel's lives had kicked up a notch after she'd retired. This past week had been blessedly free of nudges to speed up my relationship with Garrett, cut my hair, or lose five pounds. I'd been worried about fending off my mom's sweet but nosy comments, and instead, she'd been too busy to meddle.

"Just be careful, that's all," I mumbled, ready to leave it at that.

"And don't forget you're still a suspect." Rachel wasn't as keen to drop it.

"I know how to handle myself! Truman didn't arrest me, I must've done fine on my own, missy." My mother glared at Rachel and included me in her dark look. Oh well, if Rachel was going to wade back in, I could, too.

"Just think of what happened at the party thrown right in this building, one floor below." I winced at the memory of Lacey collapsing. "Someone tried to set you up, Mom, and we don't know who."

"A party *you* hosted, let's not forget." Ire flashed in her pretty green eyes.

A gentle cough sounded in the doorway. The three of us Shepard women jumped. My mother quickly rearranged her expression to one of calculated pleasantness and genuine relief.

"Oh, I thought we were alone. No matter. Justine, I'd like you to meet my lovely daughters." My mom lingered over the word lovely, as if to remind us to behave.

"Nice to meet you." The woman before me was small and dark and delicate boned, almost like a sparrow.

"I'm your mother's assistant stager, Justine Bowman." Justine beamed and shook my hand. She had a pretty heart-shaped face, one that almost looked familiar.

"What brings you to March Homes?"

"We've taken over the toy drive," I said smoothly. "Almost every item has been gathered for the children's wish lists." I brought the printout of items amassed and showed it to Justine.

"That's phenomenal." Her pretty whiskey-colored eyes sparkled. "The kids will love this."

"Do you have kids yourself?" Rachel continued our small talk with the pleasant woman.

Justine's eyes shuttered, then took on a wistful look. "No, I don't."

My mother walked us to the elevator.

"Be good, girls."

Her statement wasn't a simple goodbye, it was a command.

\* \* \*

That night I aimed to redeem myself and have a nice evening with my boyfriend. I hadn't been so worried when we'd parted ways yesterday because I knew we could make up at dinner. I nearly bounced up the steps to the neat brick ranch house where Garrett lived with Truman, his mother Lorraine, and his daughter Summer.

"Hi, Mallory." Summer flung upon the door and gave me a hug.

"Hi, sweetie." It astounded me to no end that I now had to look up to peer at Summer. She was fourteen and growing like a weed. Garrett and Truman were preternaturally tall, and Summer's mom Adrienne was willowy and no slouch in the stature department. I was five foot nothing, so it shouldn't have come as a surprise.

"Grandma made a Christmas dinner dry run so she could try out a new stuffing." Summer nearly pulled me into the formal dining room.

"It smells heavenly." The table was set with the normal floral dishes the Davieses always used, but there was a fancy turkey with festive sides.

"Summer spilled the beans." Lorraine, Truman's wife, bustled out from the kitchen carrying a large baking pan. "And it's all for this." She set down the hearty looking dish of stuffing on a trivet. It was dotted with cranberries and almonds.

I helped Lorraine ferry a few more dishes to the table and grinned when Garrett arrived home from work to give me a tender kiss before he took his seat. The misgivings I'd felt yesterday on the sidewalk began to melt away. I took a bite of the stuffing that was being auditioned and closed my eyes in satisfaction. It was a mélange of savory sage and thyme, sausage and cornbread, with the unexpected sweet kick of cranberries.

"I think this is a winner." Truman nodded to his wife.

"Well, *you* found the recipe." Lorraine winked at the chief. I smiled at their rapport. I could only hope to have a marriage so fun and harmonious someday.

"So, Mallory. If Dad and I move to Pittsburgh, will you be coming with us?" Summer's elfin face was filled with a confusing mixture of mirth, trepidation, and downright curiosity.

*Thank goodness I don't have anything in my mouth.*

I stammered and fell silent. Garrett sent his daughter an exasperated look.

"Is there something you haven't told us?" Lorraine beamed and stared openly at my left hand. I felt a furious blush consume my face.

"No. Not that I'm aware of." I turned to my beau, who looked pretty miserable. "Is there something you haven't told *me*? Are you officially moving to Pittsburgh?"

Garrett cleared his throat. "No. I've been exploring with the dean whether I could have earlier hours for the clinic, so I could be home here in Port Quincy at a reasonable time." His face softened. "For you, Summer, and Mallory, and everyone."

Truman and Lorraine shared a look of relief.

"But the dean thought it would be best for the clinic to keep normal hours." And just like that, the helium balloon Garrett had handed his parents was viciously popped. "Summer has been pressing me for a decision." Garrett glanced at his watch and stood. "I need to get back to work for another hour or more. I'm sorry, everyone." He seemed genuinely contrite as he ducked out. He gave me another kiss and smiled fondly at Summer.

"That went great." Summer frowned miserably and picked at the rest of her stellar stuffing. Her frown hid her magenta braces. Lorraine tsked and bustled back into the kitchen.

"It's time for the nuclear option." Truman raised one bushy brow at his granddaughter, and Summer perked up.

"Tell her the plan, Grandpa."

*What?*

Tiny alarm bells began to sound in my head.

"Mallory, we'll be frank. No one wants Garrett to take that offer teaching up in Pittsburgh. Summer and I have devised a way to keep him in Port Quincy. And we need your help."

"Whoa, whoa, whoa! What about following your dreams and autonomy and all that?" I didn't want to be a roadblock to Garrett's decisions.

"But what about me?" Summer appeared truly flummoxed. "I just started ninth grade. I love it here. All of my friends are in Port Quincy."

"And I don't think we'd really see much of Garrett," Truman truthfully put in. "So it's time for you to take one for the team, Mallory."

*Uh-oh.*

"What do you have in mind?" This had better be good.

"You'll propose to Dad!" Summer crowed out their solution with teenage exuberance.

"It's about time, Mallory." Truman was smug about his solution and sat back as if to rake in all my adulation.

"I hate to break it to you two, but absolutely not." I stood and scraped my walnut dining chair against the floor. "This is ridiculous."

"Oh, come on." Truman stood and gently placed his hand on mine. "I thought this would appeal to your sense of feminism." He blanched as I retracted my hand. "I know you're the one for my son."

Lorraine reentered the dining room with her eyes shining with mirth. "I told these two schemers you wouldn't go for it." She took in my mouth opening and closing in shock. "Though it is a clever idea."

"It's too late to just wait for Dad to make a decision." Summer sounded downright scared. "What if he really wants to move? What in the *h-e-*double hockey sticks will I do?"

"Summer!" Lorraine scolded her granddaughter for her language and resumed her dinner. She was more affronted by Summer starting to spell out the word *hell* than she was by the personal hell I was currently in.

"What's up with you guys?" Garrett popped his head back into the dining room, and we all jumped. "I forgot a file." He retrieved the redweld folder from a credenza and carefully studied our nervous movements. I bent over to pick up the fork that had slipped from my hand and clattered to the ground.

"N-nothing." Truman stuttered for the first time I'd ever heard.

"Okay. Have a good night." Garrett frowned as he left again, sensing something was up. We waited until the front door of the ranch clicked closed, and all of us collapsed into a fit of nervous laughter.

Dinner continued, the tension broken. It was a fun meal, but I wasn't entirely present. My mind strayed to thoughts of marrying and having my own children. I remembered how hot and bothered everyone had been to see Garrett and me get engaged in the spring and summer, about a year after we'd met and started dating. We'd decided to slow things down and go at our own pace. But now the pressure was turned back up for a different reason.

My cell phone beeped out a text alert, and I sheepishly checked it under the tablecloth. "This is Justine. I wanted to tell you some things about March Homes. Meet me now at the Greasy Spoon?"

I gave the excuse of needing to work on the toy drive and ducked out of dinner just as Lorraine started to serve her huckleberry pie. I usually loved dining with the Davies family, but tonight, I couldn't wait to leave.

I escaped from the pressure-cooker environment of the Davies household largely unscathed. But my mind was swirling with ideas and not a small amount of panic as I guided the Butterscotch Monster back downtown. My stomach grumbled in protest. After my initial forkful of stuffing, I hadn't been able to consume another bite of Lorraine's gourmet Christmas dinner tryout.

I scanned the interior of the Greasy Spoon, but Justine wasn't present. No matter. I didn't think she was punking me, but I could eat either way. Instead of picking something sensible like a salad, I opted for a double-stuffed BLT, chicken noodle soup, and a slice of apple pie.

"Thanks for meeting me, Mallory." Justine's appearance made me jump. The slim woman slid into the yellow vinyl booth opposite me and ordered a black coffee and a slice of gourmet fruitcake. The Greasy Spoon had gone all out with kitschy decorations. I slid the miniature pink tinsel tree that doubled as a ketchup and saltshaker holder back toward the window so I could focus on Justine.

"I couldn't help but overhear your conversation with Carole." She sheepishly set her cup of coffee down and blinked. "But I do think there are some interesting anomalies going on at March Homes."

"Go on." I finished my delicious soup, the liquid warming and fortifying.

"I haven't worked for your mother long, but she's wonderful. I wouldn't want her to get into anything sticky." She seemed to consider how much to tell me. "Alan likes to spend money lavishly. It wasn't just the cabin."

I snorted. "The cabin itself would be enough." And now it was gone, up in a fiery inferno.

"Alan incurs many business expenses that are questionable. Clementine chews him out, and Goldie tries to smooth it over. I've already seen this happen several times in the week I've worked for March Homes. You didn't peek into his office while you were there. He redecorated it to the tune of twenty thousand dollars, a sizable chunk of the renovation budget for the whole headquarters squandered on one little room."

I felt my eyes bug out in my head.

"Clementine made him absorb some of the costs. One of the accountants told me he bought a Lexus to use as a work vehicle but really intended it for personal use. Clementine made him return it, so Goldie bought it back for his birthday."

"Okay, but Alan's overstepping and misuse of funds doesn't necessarily make their whole business hinky, does it?" I took a satisfying bite of my sandwich and leaned back into the booth.

Justine took a big breath. "There's more. Our passwords for the internal system work for the accounting software, too." The woman bit her lip as twin spots of pink graced her high cheekbones. "I did a bit of snooping myself after you and your sister left today. March Homes has made a cash payment of three thousand dollars each and every month for the past year. It's mailed to a post office box here in Port Quincy."

"How is it documented?" A post office box was weird but not necessarily a concern.

"It's entered generically as 'charity.' But I went a step further and looked at March Homes's tax returns. They didn't itemize this donation." Now Justine's blush had overtaken her full force.

"It could be hush money," I mused. "And they just brokered the deal to buy the land for their housing developments three months ago. They've had land here in the family for years, according to Olivia, but they just used it for hunting and their Christmas Eve and morning celebrations."

"Right. So why make a payment of three thousand anonymously each month? And I could only access the last year of accounting records. Who knows how long they've made this payment?"

We chewed and sipped in pensive silence for several minutes.

"Fresh coffee, ladies?" Our server reappeared. I'd left my purse too close to the edge of the booth and it tumbled to the ground.

"Oh!" I gasped as Olivia's glass and ceramic angel made another tumble to the floor. Thankfully, the repaired wing held. I gratefully placed the tree topper on the table.

Justine laid her fork down on her plate and picked up the piece. "This is so pretty. Where did you get this?" Her tone was even and unaccusing, her pretty whiskey-colored eyes filled with genuine curiosity.

"It belongs to Olivia."

"It's a common piece." Justine flipped the piece over and traced the seam of the repaired wing. "I come from a family of glassmakers." A soft glow of pride graced her delicate face. "My father was the head glassmaker at the McGavitt factory before it shut down in the seventies." Her gaze grew wistful, seeming to stare into the past.

We chatted amiably for a few minutes about the legacy of the glass factory. Thistle Park was built by the owners, and the woman who had bequeathed me the house had been the last person helming the glass company.

Justine bestowed a kind smile on me. "I think I should go. Thanks for listening to my concerns about March Homes. I've met their daughter,

Olivia, and her fiancé, Toby. Such nice young people. I wouldn't want them to get caught up in anything."

Once again, someone seemed to be vouching that Olivia had no idea whatever her family was into.

"And I'm so grateful to your mom. Carole beat me out fair and square for the staging position. But then she lobbied for me to be hired and at a higher starting salary than I'd negotiated. I want her to be above reproach."

"And you don't think she is?" A knot formed in the pit of my stomach, right before I took my last bite of pie.

"It does look like someone wants her to seem guilty, doesn't it?"

"She didn't do anything to Lacey." I set down my fork and stared beseechingly at Justine.

"I know that, but who would go to the trouble to cast doubt on your mom?"

"You didn't see anything else in the business records to give a clue?"

Justine shook her head sadly.

A crazy idea began to percolate in my head.

"I wish I knew what we needed to look for." I clapped my hand over my mouth. I hadn't meant to voice the beginning of a preposterous plan.

But Justine nodded, slowly warming to the bad idea. "It wouldn't hurt to go back in and take a peek at the physical records. I'm kind of upset I looked at the financials digitally. I don't think anyone will notice, but I can't be sure. But as for the physical records, I know some went up in flames in the cabin fire, but there are plenty in accounting."

*No, no, no!*

The more sane part of my brain put its foot down. But the curious side of me got the upper hand.

"I suppose we could just take a little peek."

"And if Carole finds out, I'll tell her it was my idea."

"No way, Justine. I don't want my mom to fire you. I'll tell her it was my idea." Which it technically was.

Justine and I agreed to meet in an hour's time at March Headquarters. I justified this silly mission by thinking of those I loved. Truman hadn't charged or arrested my mother, but she wasn't off the hook yet. And Olivia was trying to decide what to do with her life. The judge's hints at impropriety almost seemed like an invitation to snoop. A lot hung in the balance.

*What have I gotten myself into?*

# CHAPTER TEN

An hour later I found myself staring up at the back of March Homes headquarters. Rachel rubbed her hands next to me, as much to ward off the cold as from excitement.

"This is so much fun!" My sister nearly whooped and I clapped a mittened hand over her mouth.

"Shh. The point of this mission is to look for things without getting caught." I saw the condensation appear in front of me as I spoke. It was a frigid evening, the temperature dipping down into the teens. Rachel and I had dressed in our reconnaissance outfits, hastily assembled black garb.

Our mother had been pretty suspicious as we attempted to slip out of the third floor apartment. We'd told her we were going to buy her and Doug Christmas presents, but she didn't believe us. Doug had sent us a mirthful look over his glasses and returned to his biography of Benjamin Franklin.

So here we were, freezing our butts off, dressed head to toe in black.

"Hi, girls." Justine giggled as she took in our outfits. She was still dressed in what she'd had on when we'd met at the diner. I suddenly felt ridiculous.

"Um, hi."

She inserted a thick key into the lock and ushered us into the building. We were in the basement where the toys had been stored and made our way across the empty chamber to the elevators. All three of us seemed to breathe a collective sigh as we made it to the office floor of the building seemingly unscathed.

"I'm glad the building isn't outfitted in some fancy modern security system," I noted.

"What are you doing?" Rachel hissed at Justine as the woman flicked on a switch, flooding the space with light.

"Oops. Snooping 101—don't turn on the lights." Justine sounded cowed as she turned them back off.

"Here." My sister rummaged around her large, tasseled black leather bag and handed out three flashlights. "You're welcome, ladies."

I started giggling as I turned on the beam and moved to the accounting files. We looked like some modern-day Watergate snoopers. I didn't want to get caught, but the preposterousness of the situation got the better of me.

We spent a frustrating hour digging through financial files.

"It would just make it so much easier if we knew what we were looking for," Rachel lamented. I had to agree with her.

"Maybe it's time to call it a night." Justine

wearily rubbed her eyes, unwittingly smearing a trail of mascara.

"Let's just take a peek in the owners' offices before we go," I suggested.

"Ah, this is so sweet." We started with Goldie's office. She'd had it painted a neutral gray. Shots of Olivia, Alan, and Goldie covered the walls. On her desk was a pile of bridal magazines and a sweet note from Olivia on top.

"She is making an effort to tend to her wedding." I smiled at the note. "There isn't much time, and Olivia knows her mom is a bit disappointed that things are rushed."

"What's this?" Rachel held up a slender silver key on a length of red velvet ribbon. We tore through the rest of the office, poking the little slip of metal into several slots, to no avail.

"How about this?" Justine found a small wooden box behind a big-potted ficus.

*It fits.*

The slip of silver turned effortlessly in the box. Out fell a small leather book.

"Bingo." The book was a rudimentary ledger, detailing a single three thousand dollar payment, made once per month for nearly thirty years.

"Thirty years?!" Rachel made to grab the delicate leather book when I tucked it back into the box.

"Okay, that was something we definitely were not meant to see. Justine, what was the post office box address again?" We plugged the numbers into Google but came up with nothing.

"I doubt the post office would reveal who owns that box."

We moved on to Alan's office to see what juicy secrets it might contain.

"Nada." My sister shut the final drawer on his big desk and shook her head. "Not much paperwork in here at all."

"I guess he keeps it all in the cloud," Justine mused. "Or he has nothing to hide."

I peeked into his trash can on a whim and plucked out a napkin.

"Ew." Rachel was a bit of a germaphobe and let me know she disapproved of my action.

"Um, I think you'll have an even stronger reaction after you read this." I spread the napkin on Alan's desk, and the three of us shined our flashlights on the smeared paper.

It appeared to be a brainstorm about who may have killed Lacey.

"Mom is at the top of the list!" Rachel recoiled in horror.

"These may not be his musings about who killed Lacey—this may be his plan to frame Mom." Clementine was also on the list, in the number two slot. I was furious. I had an appointment to bake with Alan the next day, and now I wasn't so sure I could spend the afternoon with the man who seemed to be trying to frame my mother.

"Who is number three?" Justine squinted in the near darkness.

"I can't tell. It just looks like a smear of ketchup." That was the trouble with brainstorming a killer list on a napkin. "No matter, there are no bullet points for motive, means, and opportunity for anyone else on his list. Just Mom." An icy bath seemed to pour over my shoulders.

"Too bad we can't have the pleasure of kicking Alan out of Thistle Park." My sister sighed.

Olivia's family had just moved out of the B and B yesterday. The first model home had been finished, and they were using it as their temporary living space until they could rebuild the cabin in some iteration. Before my discovery today, I was sad to see them go, but it had been a bit cramped with four unexpected guests.

"Let's get the heck out of here." Rachel's eyes got wide as we heard footfalls. The whole office floor was suddenly drenched in revealing light. We dropped the offensive napkin into the trash and hightailed it down the hall.

"What're you guys doing here?" Olivia stared at us with surprise in her eyes.

*Thank goodness.*

I gestured toward Goldie's office, where we'd just been caught. "We wanted to surprise you for the bridal shower. I knew you'd been showing your mom some ideas. I thought we could take a look without either of you knowing."

I held my breath as Olivia seemed to ponder my explanation. A wide grin broke out on her delicate face. "You guys are the best!" She leaned in and pulled my sister and me in for a hug. I tried not to look too obvious as I turned around to find Justine. She was gone.

My sister, Olivia, and I chatted excitedly as we left the building. I felt my heart beat so hard in my chest I feared Olivia would see, but she seemed none the wiser. Rachel and I made a big show of climbing into the Butterscotch Monster and starting the engine. We waited a few minutes after Olivia drove off in her Acura.

"Ahh!" I screamed as Justine gently tapped on my window.

"That was too close." The woman shook her head. "I'm sorry I dragged you two into this."

I clasped her gloved hand. "No way, this was all my idea."

Justine made her way to her car and drove away. And not a moment too soon.

"Uh-oh."

My mom's rental car screeched to a halt behind us. I took in a deep breath as she slammed the door and appeared at the window. She was clad in her own all-black ninja outfit, the better to out-sleuth us.

"What in heaven's name are you two doing here? Performing some impromptu surveillance?"

*She doesn't even know the half of it.*

"I suspected something, and I was right." My mother's superpower was definitely her special ESP that was attendant to her daughters' nefarious hijinks.

"I have tried my whole life to take care of you girls." My mom was just getting started. "I built up my business after your father disappeared. It wasn't just a hobby. I want you two to respect my work. And this isn't a good way to show it."

I slid down in the worn leather of my station wagon, utterly crushed. "I'm sorry, Mom," I whispered.

But Rachel wasn't having it. "But Mom, we found—"

"I don't want to hear it, girls! You broke your mother's trust." Tears coursed down Carole's face. She turned back to her rental and drove away.

Rachel's voice grew small. "She'll be okay."

But I wasn't so sure.

"This is gonna be fun." I glanced at the cuckoo clock in the kitchen and nervously awaited Alan March's arrival.

"Yup. Not too cozy sharing a kitchen with the dude who thinks Mom is a stone-cold killer."

I sighed and took inventory of the ingredients Alan had asked me to amass. I was going to learn how to make some of his family's Czech recipes. I'd spent the morning vacillating between feeling guilty for picking through Alan's trash and feeling vindicated by discovering his accusatory thoughts about my mother.

"And Miles said he'll be late." Our sweet cook was smitten with Rachel. He'd be upset if he knew he'd missed a chance to talk to her today. He was going to taste Alan's recipes and discuss any changes or adaptations for Olivia's big day.

"Well, I'm sorry I'll miss all of the excitement. But now that Rudy's on the mend, Clementine has resumed teaching her yoga class." Rachel tucked her mat under her arm and sailed out the back door in her big silver parka.

Moments later the doorbell clanged.

"Come on in, Alan."

Olivia's dad advanced into the hall and stopped short. "Whoa. What's in the tree?" He stared mystified at the colossal evergreen.

"What do you mean?" I tried to follow his line of sight. Two glittering, ochre eyes caught the light from the chandelier just so and glowed an incandescent green.

I burst out laughing. "That's just my cat, Soda. She loves sitting in the big tree."

Alan relaxed with a chuckle and shrugged off his overcoat. To my surprise, he approached the tree and talked softly to its feline inhabitant. Soda stretched one orange paw out, then another, and calmly advanced down a thick branch. Alan finished coaxing my cat from the Christmas tree. I could hear the little orange fluff ball's purrs from three feet away.

"Aw, she likes you." Soda was actually a pretty good judge of character. I considered reassessing him. Maybe he wasn't so bad?

Alan followed me to the kitchen and gently deposited Soda in the window seat. He washed his hands, rolled up his blue shirtsleeves, and donned an apron. He certainly did appreciate the finer things. His fine suit pants and Italian leather shoes looked too nice to cook in.

"Thanks for getting all this." Alan gestured toward the ingredients amassed on the island. He got to work, nimbly adding ingredients and stirring with gusto.

"We'll have twelve dishes in keeping with the Christmas Eve tradition, albeit one day early." Alan stopped and ticked dishes off on his fingers as he named them. "First up is rybí polévka, which is fish soup. Then smažený kapr, the fried carp. And of course, potato salad, bramborový salát." Alan continued to mention various dishes. My head was spinning as I tried to observe and write down his methods and ingredients. His hands flashed as he assembled the dough he'd asked me to make ahead of time, and twisted ropes of the stuff into an elaborate braid. The gorgeous braided dough reminded me of Judge Frank's crown of hair.

I found myself warming to Alan as we chitchatted. He might like the finer things, but he wasn't afraid to get his hands dirty, either.

"I'm delighted that Olivia wanted to honor my heritage." Alan spoke while his fingers helmed a flurry of chopping knives. "I was Alan Krylenko once, before Clementine and Rudy convinced me to take their family name." He gave a bitter laugh and neatly slid some green onions into the stockpot bubbling away. "My heritage may not be Olivia's explicitly, but she has always honored it." His expression turned pensive. "I guess we'll never know exactly how Olivia came to be with our family. But it was the greatest thing to happen to us."

"Finding her in the manger," I said.

"Yes." Alan looked up from his food ministrations with a surprised look on his face. "Olivia's actually not too fond of the story of how she was found. It was in all of the papers all over Pennsylvania, but that was nearly thirty years ago. She must've told you, though. I'm not surprised because you two are so close."

I squirmed a bit, not wanting to reveal that the judge had spilled the beans to me first.

"Olivia is so stressed. I just want my daughter to have a lovely wedding, and even better, a wonderful life with Toby. He's a great guy. I wouldn't have

picked anyone else for Olivia." He stopped bread-
ing a piece of carp and frowned. "Now if they
could just sort out the mess about where they're
going to settle down."

I decided to wade into it. "Then why don't you
help her make her decision and let her take on the
legal matters for March Homes?" My heart sped
up in anticipation of his reply. I didn't want to
seem impertinent, but he'd opened the door.

Alan wiped his hands on his apron, but not before giving me a shrewd glance. "Our business is
aboveboard, make no mistake about that."

*I almost believe him.*

"But we can be aggressive," he continued. "We
drive hard deals, and we can be very . . . persuasive. Olivia doesn't need to see that."

I tried hard to suppress my eye roll. I wanted to
say Olivia was a big girl but settled on highlighting
her professional experience. "I'm sure your
daughter could handle seeing how your business is
run and not think less of you for it. Have you forgotten how much she's recognized as a litigator?"

Alan began to blush. "That's true. I just want to
protect my baby. When you have your own kids,
you'll understand."

We stood in pensive silence finishing off the
dishes. A thought floated through my brain. I wondered if he was aware of the three thousand dollar
deposit his wife had been making all these years.

"Sorry I'm late." Our shaggy-haired cook, Miles,
closed the back door against the cold December
air. "Good to see you again, Mr. March."

"Please, call me Alan."

The pair had met when Alan was staying at the B and B. Alan quickly caught Miles up on the dishes he'd made and the bread and cookies he was making. Miles didn't seem to make notes as he nodded and asked questions validating his culinary expertise. The clock struck three and Miles glanced up.

"Is Rachel around?" He seemed so hopeful I wanted to give him a hug.

"Nope, she's at her yoga class. But she should be back soon."

Miles glanced at the door in anticipation. I wish my sister would give the sweet cook a chance, but the heart wanted what the heart wanted, and Rachel's scheme du jour was to be with a doctor.

"Hi, guys." Rachel sailed in and shucked off her giant, puffy silver coat. Her curvy and toned frame was on full display in her skintight yoga gear, leggings and a tank top with a snowflake pattern. "Evan has invited me to be his plus one at the surgeon's Christmas party!" Rachel waved her phone under my nose so I could read the text.

"Asking you out over text, how romantic," Miles said drily.

Rachel narrowed her eyes. "Evan happens to be hopelessly romantic, I'll have you know."

"I do know. We were roommates at Quincy College. We were both chemistry majors."

Rachel did a double take. "You were a chemistry major?"

Miles nodded. "I was premed and finished with a grade point average of 4.0. But I realized after I'd gotten into med school that my real passion was cooking. So I started culinary school the day I was due to start med school, and the rest is history." Miles raised his brows at my sister and took his leave.

Rachel seemed lost in thought, her hand resting on her chin. It took a lot to render my sister speechless.

Alan caught my eye, and the two of us giggled as we finished up his recipes.

*Maybe I was wrong about him.*


Later that evening I caught up with my sister. We had an hour until the March family would descend upon Thistle Park to sample the meal Alan had made for an impromptu tasting. I found Rachel poring over her laptop with a dreamy expression in her green eyes.

"Whatcha looking at?" I caught a flash of diamonds and metal.

"Nothing!" Rachel clapped the lid of the laptop down with startling force and cringed. "None of your beeswax, that is."

"Come on. You've been hankering for me to get married for ages. And I even told you about Truman and Summer's ridiculous plan for me to propose to Garrett."

Rachel rolled her eyes and flipped open her laptop. "Fine. I'm perusing my options." She turned the laptop toward me, and I took in Tiffany's iconic robin's egg blue background.

"Your options?" Confusion clanged in my head.

"I need to see what kind of ring I want, so I can give Evan some hints."

"Um, *what?*" I stared at my sister with alarm. "Is there something you're not telling me?!"

Rachel relaxed into a fit of giggles. "Don't be such a stick in the mud. I can just tell that Evan is the one. So I'm getting a head start on our happily ever after."

"So where will you wed, Rachel?" Our mother appeared at the top of the stairs to our apartment. She seemed weary from her day at work.

"Don't encourage her, Mom," I said.

Our mother offered a warm smile. "Rachel can be very persuasive, Mallory. If she sets her sights on this fellow, there's a good chance anything could happen."

Rachel beamed, and the two of them began to chat about the merits of Rachel and Evan tying the knot at Thistle Park or elsewhere. Their frenzied matchmaking attempts were amazing, like some kind of crazy modern-day Jane Austen novel.

"They're ridiculous!" I roped my stepdad into the fray. "Aren't they?"

"I think they're just fatigued from fixating on your relationship," Doug said evenly. "But you take things at your own pace, Mallory."

I felt like tossing my hands in the air in frustration. "I'd love to make a decision about what to do, if Garrett and I were on the same page."

My sister and mother stopped their excited planning and turned to me expectantly. It was a trap. Now they were all ears, waiting to put my relationship under the microscope. And I wasn't sure I was even ready to see that.

"I guess I want more." My voice was small and timid. "I was okay with things the way they were before. But now I want a bigger commitment. But why do I need that? Our relationship should be able to thrive on the weekends, even if Garrett moves to Pittsburgh."

I gulped, not even believing myself.

"Sweetie, have you told him this?" My mother moved to sit next to me on the poofy striped couch.

"No," I said softly. "I'm just figuring it out as I go along. And in keeping with the way it's been the last year, we're both too busy to have a serious talk."

"These modern relationships." My mother made a tsk sound. "You and Olivia both. One thing I've learned is you can't have it all." Her face grew soft, and she reached across the coffee table to give Doug's hand a squeeze. "You really do need to prioritize love and people first."

"Then it was all a lie," Rachel said glumly. "You even taught us, Mom, to go for the careers we wanted, to dream big, and try to cram in as much life as possible. Are you saying we can't manage careers and family life, too?" Rachel's speech was accusatory.

"Well, it would help if you young people decided to live in the same town, for starters." My mother made her pronouncement in a dry voice. I motioned for my family to follow me down the back stairs to the kitchen. It was time to warm the dishes Alan had showed me how to make.

"Yup. No offense, Mallory, since I know Olivia is your friend." Rachel seemed to tread carefully, both in her conversational accusations and as she made her way down the creaky stairs. "But come on! How can they have a real relationship when they both seem to work a bajillion hours, and they don't even live within an hour of each other? Why even bother being together if you never spend any time together?" She made her last breezy pronouncement with an air of dismissiveness.

"It's different working at the firm." I tried to stand up for my friend, or at least explain where she was coming from. I slid the carp into the oven to warm and heated the fish soup on the stove. "I'd worked for some partners who bragged they hadn't seen their kids in a few weeks because they left before they woke up and got home after they went to bed. And women who spent most of labor on their phones in the hospital answering email." I shrugged. "It wasn't the life for me. So when I inherited this place and had a chance to trade it in, I did. Olivia might not be so lucky."

*And it would all come down to Garrett.*

I took a deep breath. "And I can't cast any stones at Olivia and Toby when I've been living in my own house of glass."

I'd been unwittingly careerist, choosing to grow my business over spending time with Garrett. I'd replicated my life at the law firm, just with wedding planning as the substitute. "How can I scrutinize Olivia and Toby, when Garrett and I are doing the same thing?"

We were all silent for a moment. My mother began to say something, no doubt considerate and consoling, when the doorbell clanged.

"Saved by the bell." My mother shrugged as we all went to let the Marches in. Olivia, her parents, and grandparents shrugged off their heavy coats and followed us to the kitchen. I normally would have a tasting in my office or the formal dining room, but since they'd spent a few days at the B and B, I kept it more casual. They tasted each dish in the kitchen. Half an hour later, every last morsel of Alan's meal had been devoured.

"This will make a fine wedding meal," Clementine grudgingly said.

"It'll be super." Rudy clapped his son-in-law on the back. "Olivia, you made a fine choice."

Olivia beamed at her grandfather, who now seemed no worse for wear from his near perishing in the cabin inferno.

"And now we can all enjoy a little surprise." I ushered the family into the parlor and revealed a tray of Czech wines, some red, some white. I pulled Olivia aside as her family oohed and aahed.

"And some champagne for the bride." I beamed as I handed Olivia a flute of sparkling, pale gold liquid. I leaned in close to her ear. "It's grape juice."

"Thank you." Olivia smiled with relief and paused before she took a sip.

"Na zdraví," Alan said a toast in Czech, and the Marches each took a sip. We all drifted toward the elaborately tiled fireplace, fashioned in a mosaic peacock pattern. The warm flames danced off the iridescent tiles in shades of teal, lavender, and gray. Two Christmas trees flanked the fireplace, and electric candles danced on the mantelpiece. I'd also hung a jaunty row of stockings, one for each of my family from the mantel.

I noticed Rudy kept a healthier distance from the fire than the rest of his family.

*I don't blame him.*

Clementine noticed too and went to twine her arms through her husband's.

"What the . . ." Goldie let out a sharp slip of her tongue and softly cursed. She recoiled from the set of stockings. I never thought I'd hear her swear.

"Mom?" Olivia made a motion to join her mother, when Goldie held her back.

"It's nothing."

"Wait a minute." I made a beeline to the stockings.

"Who put up this extra one?" Rachel reached the fireplace just as I did. There was a knit snowflake stocking for Doug, and a magenta, pineapple-embossed stocking for Mom. Rachel had a glittery, sequin confection of a stocking in blue and purple. And I had a tartan plaid one. There were even stockings for Whiskey, Soda, and Ramona.

And a new, eighth stocking had made an appearance. I picked up a green satin stocking with script embroidery done in contrasting red thread.

"Who is Joy Christine?"

Goldie dropped her drink, the pretty cut glass goblet shattering into several long shards. "I'm sorry." Her voice came out barely above a whisper.

"Your original name." Alan turned to Olivia with sorrow in the depths of his eyes. Goldie seemed to recover and shot her husband a murderous glare.

But not as angry as Olivia's expression. Her initial shock had transformed to fury. "My original name? What are you talking about?" She stared from Alan to Goldie like an accusatory tennis judge. "You told me you knew *nothing* about my whereabouts, just that I showed up in the manger,

and you were the first ones to leave the church."
Her chest rose and fell with each intake of breath.
"What else do you know?"

She had morphed from a blushing bride, happy
to spend the evening with her family, into an eagle-
eyed and sharp-tongued litigator. I wouldn't have
wanted to be on the receiving end of her courtroom questioning and neither did her parents.

Alan looked downright miserable while Goldie
seemed defiant.

Clementine decided to wade into the fray. "Your
parents changed your name to match the March
family botanical theme," Clementine explained.

Goldie nodded. "There was a note hidden
among the folds of your blanket," Olivia's mother
admitted. "It said just those words, Joy Christine."
She winced. "Obviously your name. But nothing
more."

Alan cleared his throat and gave his wife a
barely perceptible nod.

"Fine." Goldie huffed. "That ridiculous glass
angel. That was in the manger, too."

"Mallory, I'd like to see the angel." Olivia ignored her family and pivoted on her heel. I
gulped and went to get my purse in the front hall.

*It's not there.*

A sickening wave of dread coursed through me
as I pawed through my big purse. The glass angel
was gone.

"Never mind. We'll just have to get a ladder. But
why did you put it there?" I returned to follow
Olivia's pointing index finger. There atop the
highest tree resided the angel, staring down at all
of us.

"I didn't put it there," I whispered. "And I obviously didn't hang up the stocking, either."

Which meant someone had been in Thistle Park uninvited. I glanced at Rachel, who seemed to realize, too. She made for the security system.

"It was off," she whispered to me.

"Did the police thirty years ago check the note and the tree topper for fingerprints?" Olivia was pacing now, her sparkling grape juice long forgotten.

"Of course!" Rudy nearly roared.

"And none of this matters, sweetie." Goldie tried to sidle up to her agitated daughter. "If there's one thing I know, you're one hundred percent March." She'd spoken the phrase before, back when we'd had the initial tasting for what was to be a spring wedding. It seemed a hundred years ago, not a mere week and a half.

"No one could fathom who would leave behind a baby as lovely as you." Rudy's eyes shone with genuine love for his granddaughter.

"I can't either," Olivia said flatly. She cradled her still nearly flat stomach and raised her eyes defiantly to her family. "Especially now, since Toby and I are going to have a baby of our own."

Her big news created a splash of silence, followed by a whoop of joy, and a flurry of congratulations. But the bride was having none of it. She tore from Thistle Park, down the front stairs, and into her car—leaving her family in her wake.

# CHAPTER ELEVEN

"It's a beautiful snowy day." I peered out the window in the library and observed the scene before me. Four inches had fallen overnight. The branches of the trees glittered in the weak sunlight, each crystal sparkling. The Christmas lights popped against the white background, and cardinals fought over their place at the bird feeder, a pleasing red blur against the dazzling winter canvas. You never knew what kind of weather would show up in Western Pennsylvania for the holiday season. It could be as classic and snowy as a Christmas card, or, more likely, just cold and gray and dreary. But the mercury was firmly below freezing, so this snow would probably grace us with its presence for a while.

"Too bad those crazies probably ruined Olivia's shower today by holding back details about finding her in the manger." Rachel joined me at the window and handed me a steaming mug of peppermint coffee. I had to silently agree. As of the last text message I'd received, Olivia's small bridal shower would still go on today. But the bride wasn't feeling merry and bright after the revelations her parents had kept from her for three decades had come to light yesterday.

"I still haven't figured out who got in here to put that angel on top of the tree and slip in that stocking." I shivered despite the roaring fire and the heat coursing through Thistle Park. Someone had come into the B and B uninvited, unnoticed, and unwanted.

"I didn't turn the security system off." Rachel gave me a look and raised one perfectly plucked brow. "And Faith didn't find anything, either."

Truman's partner Faith had stopped by to walk the perimeter of our property and house. Nothing seemed tampered with or out of place.

"Then it had to be one of them." The March family flummoxed me. "Who would want to spill the beans to Olivia? Definitely not Goldie. She was so ticked."

Devastated was more like it.

"Well, no one looked happy yesterday."

While we pondered the possibilities, Olivia arrived.

"Sorry I'm early."

I beamed at my friend. It was customary for the person being feted at a shower to be the last to arrive. "Nothing we're doing is traditional. Come on in."

Olivia beamed at the setup in the library. Rachel and I had tied simple arrangements of evergreen and silver Mylar balloons around the already decorated holiday space. I'd opened the door of the wooden unit concealing the large flat screen. A whimsical slideshow featuring pictures of Toby and Olivia together ran in a loop.

"I wanted to get here a little before my mom and grandmother to discuss some things." Olivia sank into an armchair and happily accepted the steaming cup of cocoa Rachel brought her.

She rubbed her belly in an absentminded way. "We actually made up last night. My whole family." Her eyes grew misty. "My mom explained to me her reasoning in keeping some details from me all these years." She sighed. "I can't blame her. And everyone is ecstatic about the baby." A look of relief flooded her delicate features.

"How did your parents justify keeping those details a secret?" Rachel plopped down on a loveseat, her jaunty ponytail bouncing in time.

"Rachel!" I was outwardly once again astounded by my sister's lack of tact. And inwardly happy she'd busted out a question I wished I had the nerve to ask.

Olivia chuckled. "It's a fair question. Alan and Goldie couldn't have children of their own. They'd given up and were in the process of looking into adoption. They were told it would take years. Then they got to church late Christmas Eve. They had to take the last seats in the last pew. My mom told me she prayed for a miracle. They were the closest to the back door and the first to leave. And the first to hear me crying in the manger."

"It was meant to be." I brushed a tear from my eye and caught Rachel doing the same.

"It was, in a way," Olivia carefully agreed. "But even though we've all made up, I sense there's more to the story." She gently turned the emerald ring

Toby had given her around on her finger. "My mom made me promise to accept the information she was forced to reveal last night. But I'm not ready to stop there." She set down her cup of cocoa. "Mallory, can you investigate my adoption? All I have to go on is my original name and this." She pressed the angel tree topper into my hands. It had been void of any prints, according to Faith, wiped clean no doubt by the person who had found it in my purse and placed it atop the tree.

Olivia continued, a frisson of nerves laced through her words. "I'm afraid it'll get back to my parents if I'm the one doing it. They have a lot of connections and friends in high places through their business dealings over the years. You still have those research skills from your years at the firm. I know you can do it."

*But do I want to wade into this?*

Lacey Adams was dead. The stager had perished at a party thrown by none other than yours truly. And someone had seemed to set my mother up to appear to be the perfect perpetrator. Rudy March had almost died in the inferno at the March family cabin. And someone had snuck into this very house to send Olivia and her family a message. Not to mention, it all started with the spray-painting of Olivia's car.

But Olivia was nearly family. She'd held my hand through my breakup with my fiancé and helped me get back on my feet after I left my first career. I couldn't let her fend for herself now.

"I guess I could look into it."

*Truman's gonna love this.*

But he would never know. He couldn't know.

"Thank you!" Olivia leapt to her feet and gave me a quick embrace. "I bet when you agreed to plan my wedding you never imagined it would come to this."

"You'd be surprised," Rachel grumbled. Olivia and I laughed and headed to the kitchen to set up for the shower.

An hour later, a small gaggle of ten women close to Olivia and her family noshed on petit fours, savory sandwiches, and piping hot dips meant to be spread on little triangles of bread. Word had spread fast that Olivia and Toby were going to have a baby in the summer. Her gifts were a silly blend of lingerie and baby gear.

"For he's a jolly good fellow!" Clementine raised her glass of pink champagne as Toby sheepishly made an appearance. He was followed by Rudy and Alan. The surgeon groom had a rare day off, and the two March men had taken Toby out for midday drinks in lieu of a formal bachelor party.

"Here's to a wonderful marriage and family for two amazing people." Alan looked for a drink to punctuate his toast and selected a pretty electric blue martini from the tray at the bar we'd created atop a waist-high bookshelf.

"Um, Rachel, did you make that?" I nudged my sister as Alan's speech grew longer and longer, waxing and waning about the qualities that made his daughter and Toby a good match.

"Heck no. That looks like—"

But I was off before my sister could confirm my suspicion.

"So here's to two people I love. To Olivia and Toby." Alan raised the martini to his lips.

"Argh! Have you gone mad?" I made it across the room in a flash, skidded on the rug, and crashed into Olivia's father. The drink sloshed all over the floor, but I managed to wrestle the martini glass out of his hand for safekeeping.

"We didn't make this drink." I was nearly panting.

"What?" Alan recoiled from the blue puddle marring the herringbone-patterned hardwood. "Is this the same kind of drink that Lacey . . ." He trailed off. The small party of merry-makers had gone silent.

"Yup." I held the martini glass away from my body as if it were a liquid cup of kryptonite. "Let's call the police."

The next day I worked out the stress kinks in my neck with a fun morning in the snow with Summer. The back of my property connected with the Davieses' backyard, and Summer made the trek through the woods pulling a sled behind her. We made a wonky snowman, created snow angels, and whooshed down the tall hill on the west end of my property until we could no longer feel our fingers.

I whooped and hollered and let out steam I hadn't known was gathering. But at the back of my mind, I kept picturing Alan March about to take a swig of a mystery drink that may or may not have been poisoned. Truman hoped he could rush results on the drink but didn't make any promises. Something was rotten in Port Quincy, and he didn't seem any closer to finding out. And neither did I.

"See you later, Mallory." Summer beamed as she

retrieved her sled from the trunk of my station wagon. I turned back to Thistle Park, took a long, hot, restorative shower, and headed out to the Candy Cane Lane Christmas store to get the final items I'd need for the Marches' toy drive and Olivia's wedding.

"Hello, Nina. I didn't expect to see you here."

The once-jolly proprietress was standing behind the glass counter with red-rimmed eyes. The Christmas music was no longer jaunty but set to more solemn tunes. I heard the lament of Frank Sinatra croon "I Wonder As I Wander," the notes pensive and serious. Lacey had been buried mere days before. The store had lost its sparkle with the loss of Nina's remaining daughter.

"Lacey would have wanted me to get back in the swing of things." The shop owner wiped her eyes with a tissue.

"I genuinely enjoyed working with your daughter on Paws and Poinsettias. She was a lovely woman." And her drunken performance the night of the gala had seemed completely out of character, according to those who knew her.

"I don't know if I'll ever find out what happened. First Andrea was taken from me, then Lacey." She gave a weary sigh. "My daughter didn't drink. She was on a waitlist for a new kidney. Someone spiked her punch and poisoned her at the same time."

I nodded, not wanting to reveal that Truman had already told me as much.

"She was hiding her issues from her employer." Nina grew thoughtful. "The March family didn't know she was having dire kidney complications;

they just realized that she'd used up almost all of her leave for medical appointments."

I cocked my head. That was an interesting tidbit of information.

"She told me she'd planned on drinking Hawaiian blue punch all evening." Nina gave a mirthless chuckle. "She said it looked festive and was a dead ringer for an ice blue martini. No one would suspect anything. Well, now there are no suspects."

*Save for my own dear mom.*

I swallowed and let her go on in her grief.

"It's funny. Lacey's sister Andrea was the one who decided to give the girls' cousin her kidney. My niece was in dire need, and Andrea rushed out to get typed. She was a giver, that girl. But it turns out she wasn't a match. My niece luckily found another donor, and she lives today. As for my poor Andrea . . ." Nina trailed off. I followed her gaze to a small, holly-bordered photograph of the woman in happier days with her two girls. There was the once-jolly purveyor in this very shop, behind this very glass case. To her left was a young Lacey, grinning behind an elaborate gingerbread house. And to her right was a pretty young woman I guessed was her missing daughter, Andrea.

"I can't begin to imagine your pain."

"It's the not knowing that gets to me. Everyone wants me to accept that Andrea must be dead. But I still hold out hope. I suppose that's one thing to be grateful for, that I know that Lacey is truly gone. Now that she isn't here, my mind can't stop replaying the last few days I saw Andrea."

"What happened when Andrea disappeared?" I spoke the question in a near-whisper.

Nina squinted and sighed. "Andrea was a perfectionist. Lacey was always in her shadow. Sometimes it just happens that way with children, no matter what you do to try to make things even and fair. Lacey really came into her own after her sister disappeared. The girls had an epic fight the day Andrea went missing. I love Lacey, but I always wondered."

I shivered at the near accusation hanging in the air by a slender silver thread. Did Nina Adams really think her younger daughter had a hand in the disappearance of her older daughter? A mini film of all of the scuffles Rachel and I had been in over the years played through my mind. Some of our sisterly fights had been real doozies. If Rachel had vanished after a few in particular, I never would have forgiven myself. No matter what had happened between Lacey and her sister, it would have been a grave weight for the stager to carry around for the last decade.

"The police latched onto the theory, too." Nina shook her head. "It was a theory of convenience, according to me. Lacey always had a temper. It was the perfect foil. Blame the one sister for the other's disappearance. But Lacey was only fifteen."

"What were the other leads? A lot of time has passed, but maybe Andrea's disappearance has something to do with Lacey."

It was a stretch. But stranger things had happened.

Nina made a face. "This shop originally belonged to Andrea. She had a particular customer who stopped by a little too much. Over the course of a few months, it morphed into full-blown stalking and harassment. She had a restraining order and everything. It was Greg Gibson."

"The same guy suing his parents for selling their land to the March family?" The name had rung a bell.

"Yes. He's always been a hothead. I was happy the March family seemed to like my daughter, well, except for Clementine. I really thought they'd give her the boot after what happened with Toby, but I guess her relationship with Goldie was strong enough to withstand it." Her mouth twisted down in a frown as she mentioned Olivia's fiancé.

*Say what?!*

"You mean Toby Frank?" She had to have been mistaken.

Nina looked at me as if I had four heads. "Yes, Toby Frank!" She was nearly hysterical. "That man strung my daughter along for over a year. He claimed he couldn't take their relationship to the next level and give her a ring because her main tasks staging were in Pittsburgh. He dumped her a fortnight before the Marches announced they'd carved out enough of Allegheny County like the locusts they are and were setting their sights south. Lacey begged Toby to take her back once she knew she'd be relocating to Port Quincy for the foreseeable future. But it was too late," she spat. "He'd already taken up with Olivia."

"This was back in June." I heard the miserable tone in my voice.

"How did you know?" A sharp tone pierced Nina's grief as she gave me a cool once-over.

"Um, no reason."

Yeah, right. I'd just gotten the gig planning Toby's

surgery department's holiday party. I'd thought he'd be a good match for my friend and introduced the two just six months ago. And the rest was history.

"I told Lacey to drop it and that Toby had moved on." Nina sighed. "But she kept trying to make Toby see reason."

A realization spilled over my shoulders in an icy bath. Unless Toby had shielded Olivia from the knowledge of his previous relationship, she had to have known her mother's favorite employee had once seriously dated her fiancé. Then why hadn't she told me?

It was really none of my business. Unless, that is, this was an important clue to the puzzle of Lacey's murder and maybe even the fire at the cabin.

*A great clue for Truman to have.*

My subconscious gently reminded me that sleuthing was not technically my purview. I should leave the real investigating to the experts and stick to planning weddings.

"So," I started, my voice falsely bright. "Do you have any more artificial garlands?"

Nina seemed to stare through me. I was done trying to see how the pieces all fit together, but it would seem she was not finished yet. "Lacey was a smidge stalkerish, if I'm being honest with myself." She seemed to deflate. "She couldn't handle that Toby had broken up with her a week before she learned she needed a new kidney. Not only was she sure he wouldn't have ended the relationship if he'd known she was moving back home, but she was also certain he definitely wouldn't have cast her aside when she was so sick."

My heart went out to the departed stager. She'd borne the double whammy of getting dumped and learning she'd need a transplant all within a fortnight.

"The last straw for Toby was when Lacey pressured him for a ring. She wouldn't have done it if she'd known." Nina gave a shrug. "But after she found out about her kidney, and had started calling Toby morning, noon, and night, he did help her." A wistful look crossed her face. "He used his medical knowledge to research options for her health care while she waited for a donor match. My daughter accepted his help, and even more importantly, accepted that he'd moved on."

"That's wonderful," I breathed, desperately searching behind her for the garlands in question.

"But then Lacey found out." Nina's eyes grew flinty, her anger more arresting than the redness from crying.

"Found out what?" I stopped trying to surreptitiously scope out decorations and turned my full attention to the woman.

"About Olivia's pregnancy."

*Okay, now you have my full attention.*

"Lacey was at her doctor's in Pittsburgh for her annual exam. As it so happens, Olivia used the same physician's office. Olivia was checking out. A nurse took her copay and said congratulations to her. It didn't take much for my daughter to put two and two together."

I gulped in response, as much as a comment as I could give.

"It was the biggest slap in the face of all. Here Toby claimed he couldn't continue to see my

daughter because she wasn't committed enough
to him. She wouldn't take on a two-hour commute
and move back to Port Quincy. And two weeks
later, Toby had started a new relationship with another woman who worked two hours away. One
busier than my Lacey. And six months later, this
woman had a ring, and a baby, and her whole life
ahead of her. While Lacey had nothing, living on
borrowed time."

"It would be a pickle." I croaked out my lame response and abandoned my quest for ornaments.
"May I use your restroom?"

I took the slender key Nina proffered and disappeared into the back of the store. My head was
spinning. I splashed cold water on my face and
gazed at my reflection.

I now had a hunch who had spray-painted "gold
digger" on Olivia's car and placed the manger
there. Maybe it had nothing to do with the incredible story of how Olivia was found in the nativity
scene and everything to do with a woman scorned.

A glimmer of red caught my eye in the last
vestibule in the back. I glanced toward the front of
the store. I heard Nina talking with another customer and took a deep breath.

*Holy tamale.*

There lay all the purloined toy drive presents.
There were bikes and scooters and dollhouses and
baseball bats. If I hadn't inventoried the stolen
and replacement gifts, I may have mistaken the
cache of toys for something else. I decided to wait
for Nina to come to me. And five minutes later she
did.

"I can explain…" she began.

"I can't wait to hear it." My voice was cool and even. I couldn't decide what emotions were appropriate. Empathy and understanding for a woman who had just lost her second daughter, fear for a woman who had every reason to hurt Olivia, or anger at someone desperate enough to steal from a youth toy drive.

"I did steal the toys. But I did it early enough for them to be replaced." Nina held up her hand as I began to speak. "I took the toys to get the police to look into March Homes." She took a series of deep breaths when she knew she had my attention. "Lacey was poking her nose into things there that weren't her business." Nina's voice was nearly a whisper. "I have every reason to think they poisoned my daughter."

"What was Lacey looking for?"

Nina twisted the red-and-green striped apron she wore with her left fist. "She didn't say," she moaned. "She said she wanted to protect me. Too bad she couldn't protect herself."

"We'll have to tell the police about the toys." I whipped out my cell phone, my finger hovering over the programmed number for Truman. The poor man had to hear from me nearly once a week.

"No!" Nina made a swipe for my phone, but I nimbly spun away from her and clutched the device to my chest. "Just give me twenty-four hours to make it right. I promise I will."

I blinked and took in her desperation.

"I just buried my daughter."

"Okay. But I'm going to take a picture." The camera on my phone flashed and it photographed the toys in bright relief in the dark back room.

"Mallory."

"Yes?" I'd sidestepped the woman and started to make what I'd thought was a fast getaway.

"I'd be careful, if I were you. If I weren't suspicious already about the Marches, I'd have a perfect suspect for who killed my Lacey. None other than your mother."

I left without another word and threw myself behind the wheel of my station wagon. My hands were shaking and not from the cold.

"You what?" Rachel shook her head in disbelief. "The old Mallory I know would have had Truman on the horn in two seconds flat about those toys."

"But she made good on her word." I squirmed under the censure of my sister's glare and held up my cell phone. The front page of the *Port Quincy Eagle Herald* had been updated with a quickly written account of how the March Homes toy drive proceeds had been miraculously found. There was a quote from Faith about the anonymous tip that there were toys inside one of the homes that had just been built out by the highway.

"All's well that ends well," I nervously said.

But Rachel just gave me a smirk. "If you were me, you'd tell yourself to just spill to Truman."

I wanted to. But the anguished look on Nina's face kept coming back to haunt me.

"Let's just enjoy the toy drive."

It would be a truly bountiful Christmas for those in need. After the *Eagle Herald* got some shots of Rudy and Clementine counting gifts in their Santa and Mrs. Claus garb, Rachel and I would hand over the updated spreadsheet of recipient children and families. With twice the toys, those Nina had stolen and returned, and their replacements, we were able to include each family on the waiting list that had not made the initial list. The Marches would begin personally delivering the goods after the photographs.

"Clementine and Rudy have eclipsed your and Garrett's status as Port Quincy's 'it couple.'" Rachel motioned to the grandparents decked out as Mr. and Mrs. Claus. Rudy went ultra-traditional, in a red velvet coat and pants, shiny black boots topped with fur, and a jaunty red hat. He already had the beard, twinkling eyes, and a belly that looked like he enjoyed a cookie or two. Clementine's take on Mrs. Claus was predictably more daring. She wore a green velvet dress to accentuate her hair, a faux fur stole, and a retro pair of reading spectacles. Clementine and Rudy made a big show of stacking toys in a large brown cloth sack and transporting some of the goodies to a sleigh that had appeared in the lobby of March Homes's headquarters. The newspaper photographer was eating it up.

"Mallory and Rachel, please join us." Rudy stopped yukking it up to motion my sister and me over. We dutifully joined in the photo shoot as the hosts for the toy drive. I couldn't help but imagine Lacey in her rightful place.

"You done good, kids." Rudy sent us a wink and a smile. He transcended simple American mall Santa and exemplified the real deal, as imagined in my youth before I'd found out on the playground the big guy wasn't real.

"Thank you for hosting the toy drive. I hope this is the first of many to come." I couldn't help but beam at the older man.

"As long as we're not run out of here first." Clementine's megawatt beam that had appeared for the photographer slid from her barely lined face. "I'm just going to shimmy out of this." She unzipped her green dress right then and there and slid it off, revealing a tight black yoga cat suit.

*Phew.*

Clementine caught my eye and erupted in laughter. "Didn't know what was under there, did you?"

Rachel and Clementine chatted amiably about their shared gym while Rudy slung his giant arm around my shoulder. "You've really taken care of my Olivia." His eyes twinkled merrily beneath the faux white fur trim of his hat. "She's so special to us."

I flashed a smile. "She's special to me, too. She deserves every happiness."

"And I want her to be happy, too." Rudy took a deep breath. "I understand your beau is weighing his options." He quickly amended his phrasing when he took in what must have been my alarmed expression. "Career-wise, that is. If he doesn't end up inviting Olivia into his practice or handing it over to her, I think we can find a place for her at March Homes." Rudy studied my reaction to his news.

"That's fantastic!" I tried to keep my voice buoyant and enthusiastic. As I would have been before I heard the rumors that the real estate developers might not be on the straight and narrow.

"Alan doesn't want her to join the family company, but if it'll make my granddaughter happy and give her a way to move here to start her new family with Toby and continue practicing law, I'll find a way."

The jolly old fellow gave me a clap on the back and ambled over to see his wife.

"Mallory and Rachel, I'd like a word." I jumped as Truman appeared at my elbow. He seemed immune to this staged version of a holiday tableau.

"Yes?" My sister and I leaned in.

"Alan's blue martini?" Truman raised a single, bushy gray brow. "Chock full of antifreeze."

I felt a cold chill steal over me. The blood in my veins may as well have been made of the stuff.

# CHAPTER TWELVE

"Okay, this is getting downright creepy." I bit into a crispy brown figure.

"I couldn't agree more." Truman reached across the table to grab his own cookie.

He had followed us back to Thistle Park in his police cruiser. Rachel, the chief, and I noshed on cardamom men and sipped peppermint tea. I felt like the trappings of Christmas this year were being tainted with murder and mayhem and wondered if it would ever be the same. I absentmindedly picked up Whiskey, who had been twining around my legs, begging for a morsel. She'd survived as a stray for I'm not sure how long before Summer found her under the porch at Thistle Park. She'd developed a fine repertoire of batting her big kitty eyes and purring to ensure you shared your food with her.

"Cats don't eat cookies." Truman gave me a disapproving look as I broke off the tiny hand of the cardamom man.

"This one does."

Sure enough, Whiskey pranced over to the morsel and gobbled it up. She rewarded me with a rumbly, outsized purr and settled onto my lap. I was happy to have the cuddly little calico fluff ball to pet and hopefully calm me down.

"Focus, people." Rachel rolled her pretty green eyes and took a swig of peppermint tea. "We're talking about antifreeze."

Truman's rush request on the contents of Alan's drink had been approved.

"It was the very same antifreeze used to poison Lacey," he said. "Well, at least the same brand and composition."

"So we can assume we have the same perpetrator." I petted the calico and reached for the legal pad I liked to use to plot out my thoughts. I enjoyed using my tablet and phone to manage some aspects of my wedding planning business, but there was nothing like the tactile experience of musing over something with paper and pen.

"No, you can't make that assumption. Every big box store, hardware store, and some grocery stores in town carry several brands of antifreeze this time of year." Truman glared at my notation on the legal pad until I crossed it out.

"Well, that's why you're chief of police," I replied testily.

"And I'm just here to interview you two in my official capacity since the drink was served by you, technically. Don't get any ideas about deputizing yourself in my investigations."

I squirmed in my chair, causing Whiskey to jump down in a kitty cat harrumph. I avoided the sly glance from my sister. She no doubt wanted me to spill the beans on Nina Adams stealing and then returning the toys.

Truman cleared his throat. "But while I'm here, I may as well run some theories by you."

Rachel and I exchanged triumphant glances.

"So we need to think about who would want to do this to Alan." I glanced at Truman. "And how they got in here. And why."

"Maybe someone who is mad about their big real estate plans did it," Rachel put in her theory.

"Yes, and I've questioned several people who fit the bill." Truman nodded.

"Including Greg Gibson." I brought up the name that had kept coming up in my own informal conversations. "He's mad his family sold their farm to March Homes."

*And he used to stalk Andrea Adams.*

I felt a blush creep up my neck. Truman definitely wouldn't approve of me trying to tie in the current nefarious goings-on in Port Quincy with a ten-year-old crime. Or possible crime, that is. I'd typed Andrea Adams into a search engine and read the stories in the newspaper that cropped up each year near her disappearance. It was never definitively proven she'd been a victim of foul play.

"Greg knows he's being watched and is behaving like the perfect little altar boy." Truman smirked. "He hasn't engaged in his usual drunken disorderlies or other petty crimes in the last month."

"What about Toby?" Rachel's voice was small and apologetic.

I laughed out loud. "C'mon. You can't be serious."

But she was. My sister's face fell. "I'm dating his best man. And he talks." Rachel asked Truman for wordless permission to go on. He gave her a barely perceptible nod. "Toby is pretty ticked off at Alan. With Garrett's decision up in the air, he's not sure how Olivia can keep up her career, relocate to Port Quincy, and take care of their baby." Rachel seemed to give me an apologetic look. "Toby doesn't like how Alan's been bullying his daughter into accepting the partnership at her firm in Pittsburgh."

"So, you think he tried to poison his soon-to-be father-in-law? That's so silly." I stood from my chair with a loud scrape on the black-and-white tiles. "You can do better, Rach."

"You just don't want to see it, Mallory," my sister countered me with no satisfaction. "I'm just not sure what Toby poisoning Alan would have to do with someone else poisoning Lacey, unless he meant it to be a copycat killing."

A trill of panic made my heart beat faster.

*It kind of fits.*

I glanced at Truman. He remained wordless, taking in our theories. I was sure he knew what I was about to say, if not Rachel.

"I don't want it to be true. But you may be right. Because there is a connection." I detailed Nina's account of Toby and Lacey's breakup. I felt Truman's eyes bore into me as I vaguely credited the story to town gossip. Which could have been true. After all, Toby and Lacey had dated for nearly a year. Lots of people had known.

"So Toby may have poisoned Lacey because she still wouldn't take no for an answer. Especially after he may have suspected her of threatening

Olivia by spray-painting her car. Then he turned to Alan when he thought he could get away with it." I hugged my middle and stared out at the now frozen expanse that was the backyard. The snow had developed a top crunchy crust, reminiscent of sugar icing. The soon-to-be setting sun turned the western sky into a pleasing palette of pastels. But the pretty view was wasted.

*Did I set my best friend up with a stone-cold killer?*

And she was carrying his baby, to boot.

I wasn't sure how to broach the topic with my bestie that her fiancé may have killed his former girlfriend and attempted the same with her father. Truman had agreed it was the leading theory. I'd tossed and turned that night, the cats not enjoying the seismic quakes my legs created under the comforter.

But the next day dawned cold and clear, and I had more fun things to attend to.

"What're you up to, dear?" My mom gave me a hug in the kitchen as she fired up the waffle maker. Doug held up the front page of the *Eagle Herald*, featuring a beaming snap of Rudy, Clementine, Rachel, and yours truly.

"You girls are famous." He went back to his bowl of oat bran, making sure he downed something healthy before he ate a decadent waffle.

"I'm dropping off a cookbook at the Davices' house. Summer wants our cardamom men recipe." I beamed at the thought. "And later today I'm meeting Olivia to make the centerpieces at her wedding. But between then, I'm free."

"You'll make a wonderful stepmom, Mallory." My mother bestowed me with her special smile.

My face must have dimmed. "I'm not so sure I'll have the opportunity, Mom."

"Well, it's time for your fellow to make a decision." My mom's face changed from mellow and calm to annoyed in startlingly quick fashion. She angrily beat the waffle batter with a spin of her whisk. "Or I'll give him a piece of my mind!"

"Don't meddle, Mom." Rachel leaned over to bestow our mother with a quick hug as she entered the kitchen. "Mallory can handle her own love life."

I sent my sister a grateful glance. Meddling may as well have been Carole's middle name.

"Just trying to move things along, dear." My mother wasn't affronted. If anything, she seemed to enjoy the rapid-fire banter between my sister and me. She, Doug, and Ramona were slipping so nicely into our lives in Port Quincy.

"And when will you guys be moving out?" My sister took a hearty bite of a banana.

"Rachel!" I glowered at my sister for destroying the warm fuzzies with her characteristic bluntness.

My mother let out a laugh like silver bells. "I know you want your third floor back. As it happens, Doug and I are going to check out some open houses today. You're welcome to come along."

I made plans to join my parents while Rachel prepped for another epic date with her surgeon Evan. After handing off the cookbook and giving Summer a quick hug, we were on our way.

"It's this way, Dougie." My mom used her pet name for my stepdad as she squinted at the rental car's built-in GPS. The two chatted in their rapid-fire manner and I smiled from the backseat. I could barely remember my birth father and mother's relationship since he'd walked out on us so young. But within moments of meeting Doug, I'd known he was the one for my mom. They had their occasional differences, but they truly were best friends. They still held hands, and did so today, advancing up the path to the first house on their list. A generous smattering of rock salt had eaten away the ice on the stairs of the pretty Craftsman style we were checking out.

"Welcome." The realtor invited us to check out the house after we'd dragged our feet over the plush rug just inside the door.

"It's so pretty," my mom mused. "But a bit boring to be honest." The rooms were all made over in builder's beige, the better to appeal to the widest market of buyers.

"You could gussy up this place in no time flat," Doug assured her as he trailed after my mother. I could picture her at home here, selecting a palette of the muted but still vibrant tropical colors she favored, like the ones she'd decorated my third-floor apartment in.

I reflected on what it would be like to have my mom and Doug so close. There seemed to be no turning back now. And there would be no stopping the force of nature my mom could become when she set her sights on something. If some mothers were tiger moms, Carole was a sabertooth.

My mind wandered to all of the mother-daughter relationships in my midst. There were Clementine and Goldie, with their subdued and ever-simmering differences, if not dashed with a healthy helping of real affection; and Goldie's wishes for Olivia, complicated by the unusual manner in which my friend had joined the March family; and then there was poor Nina Adams, with her two girls now gone.

"You could use this time to start looking for yourself, Garrett, and Summer, you know." My mother turned around with a twinkle in her green eyes.

"What do you mean?" I tried to tread cautiously but suspected a trap. Carole just had to live up to my expectations of her as a meddlesome but well-meaning mom.

"I imagine after you two wed, he'll want to move out of Truman and Lorraine's house, and you'll cede the third floor of the B and B to Rachel."

I was stunned to realize I hadn't yet thought of what kind of arrangement would work best if Garrett and I took our relationship to a new level. I felt my mother's eyes searching my face. I felt bamboozled.

"Just give her some space," Doug gently chided my mother. So she switched gears and dropped the subject. I felt a swift blush stain my face.

"I do love the style of the new March Homes models," my mother admitted as we made our way down from the finished attic. "But nothing beats the charm of an old house."

"A drafty old house," Doug muttered. He tugged his Mr. Rogers-esque blue cardigan a bit closer. Today my mom had dressed herself and Doug in a fresh periwinkle blue. My mom's pinstriped gray pants bore threads of the blue woven through, and her cardigan nearly matched Doug's.

"It is a bit chilly." I hugged my own sweatered arms around myself.

"You could blow some insulation into the walls," the realtor offered cheerily. She'd overheard Doug's complaint. "I think the last thing you need to see is the basement." The woman flicked on a light switch atop a steep set of stone stairs and motioned us downward.

"This is where they keep the bodies," my stepdad joked.

*Um, not funny, Doug. Haven't you been paying attention to what's going on this December?*

But he was right. The rest of the house had received a slick, modern update, but the basement revealed the house's true age.

"Lots of storage." My mom tried to make some lemonade out of the situation. There were rows of neat steel shelving erected in front of the peeling paint walls and dirty, concrete floor.

And on the shelf nearest the stairs resided a single can of paint.

*Gold spray paint.*

"Do you see what I see?" I nodded my head toward the can. Maybe I'd been wrong in my hunches. Lacey may not have vandalized Olivia's car; the owner of this house could have.

"But lots of people have metallic spray paint." My mother frowned. "I always have a few cans."

"You're a stager and decorator," I said with exasperation. "This is a total scarlet letter can of paint!"

"Excuse me, is there a problem?" A beefy figure took up the frame of the top of the stairs.

"Um, no. Excuse us." I alighted up the steep steps and brushed past the man.

"Oh dear, we've run over time for the open

house." The realtor glanced at her large rose gold watch. "The owner has come back."

"Well, what'd you think of the place?" The man seemed to search my mother and Doug's faces as they gushed over the house. I wondered how much he'd heard about the paint.

"I'm sorry, I didn't catch your name?" My mother smiled indulgently at the man.

"Greg Gibson."

I froze, then recovered. Here was the man who had stalked Andrea Adams before her disappearance. The man who was suing his parents in court for selling their land to the Marches. The man who had threatened Judge Frank in her very own courtroom.

"Um, we'd better go." I placed my hand on my mother's elbow where she swatted it off as if I were a pesky fly.

"And you are . . ." Greg waited expectantly for us to cough up our names.

"I'm Carole Shepard, and this is my husband, Doug. We just moved back from Florida. I'm the head stager for March Homes."

*No, no, no!*

I tried to send my mom a telepathic message to stop her prattling. If I'd had time, I would have stepped on her blue moccasin clad foot.

"Those disgusting locusts?" Greg seemed to morph into a version of the Hulk, his chest puffed out and his eyes nearly bulging. "The people who tricked my parents out of their prime farmland, what was to be my inheritance? No way would I consider selling my house to the likes of you!"

The realtor mumbled something in the corner

of the kitchen. She looked as if she wanted to sink straight into the kitchen tile. And I wanted to join her.

"Get out of here." Greg Gibson pointed a quivering finger toward the back door.

"But—" my mother opened her mouth, no doubt to extol the virtues of her new employer.

"You heard the man." Doug linked arms with my mother and swept us from the house.

And not a moment too soon.

Greg slammed the door in our wake, making the bank of back windows shake.


I texted Truman about the gold spray paint we'd seen in Greg Gibson's basement. I figured that in the karmic scheme of things, withholding some info from the chief, like Nina's pilfering of the toys, could be balanced out by offering up other evidence.

I tried to put the scary man out of my mind as I met Olivia to craft the centerpieces. The RSVP list of confirmed guests was predictably small, since the big day would be a mere two days before Christmas. We wouldn't have too many centerpieces to make, but the work still had to be done.

"Sorry I'm late." Olivia breezed through the back door of the B and B as if floating on a cloud. "But look!" She held up a miniature Santa suit, complete with teeny, tiny black velvet booties and a white-trimmed hat. "Grandpa Rudy is already campaigning for the baby to be named after him."

I gushed over the little outfit and beamed at my friend. "But what if it's a girl?"

Olivia laughed. "He thinks Rudy would work for a girl, too."

I ushered Olivia into the dining room where I'd set up a representative centerpiece. I'd procured glass angel candelabras to sit in the middle of each table. We'd ring wreaths around each angel and place the whole shebang atop a large star mirror. The centerpieces would reflect the dancing candlelight, bring in some fresh greenery with its lovely scent, tie in the color scheme of evergreen and silver, and honor Olivia's request to include angels.

"It's lovely," Olivia breathed, reaching out to touch the wreath. "And it won't be hard to pull off this late in the game."

The nursery on the north side of town had agreed to reserve six fresh wreaths for the centerpieces as well as a healthy passel of poinsettias. The mansion was already decorated for Christmas, and we wouldn't be overhauling much for Olivia's wedding.

"Are you okay with these plans?" I bit my lip. Some brides wouldn't think there had been enough effort put into this super-sped-up affair.

"It's just perfect." Olivia gave me an impetuous hug. "Now let's make these favors."

She settled down in front of the centerpiece, and I brought in a box of favor-making bits and bobs. We'd be giving guests the same cardamom soldier cookies Rachel and I had been baking and nibbling since Thanksgiving. Each little iridescent bag of cookies would also feature a cookie cutter tied with silver ribbon.

"We'll bake the cookies the day before your wedding, so they'll be fresh. But we still need to tie a fair number of cookie cutters to each bag, make the table number signs, and design your program."

Olivia's eyes grew wide as saucers at the mini to-do list. We tucked into our work. We chatted about the rest of the plans for her wedding and then fell into companionable silence.

I decided to let her in on some perhaps good news. "While my parents and I were looking at houses today, we found a bottle of gold spray paint."

Olivia's nimble fingers froze above her cookie cutter, the metal fashioned into the shape of a holly leaf. "Oh?" She set the bag and baking implement down. "Was this Lacey's old house, by any chance?"

*Interesting.*

So Olivia assumed Lacey had vandalized her car as well.

"No. It was Greg Gibson's house."

I let the statement hang in the air. Olivia set her face in an impassive cast and picked up the cookie cutter. Her cool demeanor was belied by the almost imperceptible shake of her hand.

"So this is in retaliation for my parents' real estate development." She cocked her head in thought.

"Why did you think it was Lacey?" I had to admit I was a bit hurt. It wasn't my business that my best friend's fiancé had a stalker ex or that he'd broken up with Lacey a mere two weeks before he got together with Olivia. But once upon a time, we'd shared everything.

"If you must know, Toby and Lacey were once

an item." Olivia stared darkly into the flickering flames of the centerpiece, then observed my reaction. "But then you already knew, didn't you?"

I squirmed in my wingback chair. "Yup." I figured the truth was good enough. "But not before I set you two up. Not that it would have made a difference," I hastily added. "But I had no idea Toby and Lacey dated until a few days ago."

"Gossip is spreading now that the town knows I'm pregnant, we're getting married two days before Christmas, and my whole family is considered to be one big gang of suspects." Olivia sighed and rubbed her eyes wearily.

*Phew.*

I was glad I didn't have to spill the beans about who had told me about Toby and Lacey.

"Everyone thought Lacey was this great girl," Olivia mused. "Even my own mom. *Especially* my mom." Olivia shook her head ruefully, her glossy dark hair swinging from her shoulders. "I did Lacey a big favor by not telling my mom the half of it."

I nodded, giving my friend encouragement to go on.

"Lacey was pretty chill when I started dating Toby. I think she figured we were just a fling or that we wouldn't last because I live two hours away." Olivia cringed. "But then she realized I was here to stay, and she started contacting Toby again. It seemed friendly and innocent enough, but my radar told me it wasn't with good intentions."

"And then it escalated."

"She started calling morning, noon, and night.

I'd almost convinced Toby at one point to take out a restraining order against her. I wish I had." Olivia shivered at the memory. "But then she succeeded in getting through to him. She claimed," her voice hitched, "that she was dying of kidney failure." Olivia's delicate features turned down. "I'm not proud of what I did. I told Toby she'd just concocted it all in an effort to gain his pity and win him back. But then it turned out Lacey was telling the truth."

"It's okay, Liv." I reached out and squeezed my friend's hand.

"So Toby started talking to her, trying to calm her down and explain her options from a medical standpoint. I'll admit I got scared. I could tell he still had feelings for her, although they did seem strictly platonic. But they did date for a year. Feelings do run deep." She stared at her ring and gave a sigh. "In fact, I found out he had started contacting her about her health the day I realized I was pregnant. I considered breaking up with him right then and there." A rueful smile ticked up the corners of her cupid's bow mouth. "I'm glad I didn't."

"And I'm glad, too." We resumed our crafting in pensive silence.

"One thing I never did figure out. I was so certain Lacey had vandalized my car because she once approached me." Olivia broke the silence and seemed to consider a memory. "She cornered me in the produce section in Giant Eagle. She accused me of getting pregnant to entrap Toby." She shook her head, as if responding to Lacey in person. "But that wasn't true. I'd been taking antibiotics for a sinus infection, and they messed with my birth control. I wasn't trying to get pregnant at all. But how did Lacey know? I accused Toby of telling her, but he denied it, and I believe him."

I kept my face impassive as I stared at my favor with calm concentration. No way was I going to tell my friend I'd been discussing this very issue with Lacey's grieving mother.

"I guess the lure of gossip was just too strong for someone at my OB's office," Olivia mused. "HIPAA law be damned."

"I wonder." I stopped to try to tread extra carefully. "Does Lacey's death have anything to do with her actions?"

"What do you mean?" Olivia placed her favor atop the star mirror and gave me her full attention. "Mallory?"

My friend would have a conniption if she knew Rachel and Truman had laid out a neat theory connecting the dots of Lacey's murder straight back to Toby.

"Um, well, if Lacey was unhinged enough to go a little fatal attraction, what else did she do in her other relationships?"

Olivia relaxed at my explanation, and I let out a sigh of relief.

"I was wondering where you were going with that, Mallory." Olivia carefully assessed me. "If I weren't certain, I'd wonder if you were hinting that Toby is involved with Lacey's accident."

I gulped. Categorizing the stager's murder as an accident was an interesting choice of words.

"Maybe you were too quick to give up your practice, Mallory." Olivia's eyes narrowed. My poker face had slipped, and my anguished face had confirmed her suspicions. "You're treating me like a hostile witness."

"Hardly!" My voice came out louder than I intended. "I just don't want you to get hurt."

A delicate stream of tears began to course down Olivia's cheeks. "I'd hoped to make new traditions this year. Everyone thinks it's so neat I was found in a manger on Christmas Eve. But I've always wondered who would've abandoned me, and why?" She cradled her nearly flat stomach. "Especially now that I'm going to have a family of my own. I couldn't fathom giving up this little one." Her eyes grew flinty. "I don't want to get hurt again either, Mallory, but someone out there seems hell-bent on causing trouble for me and my family. And I'm going to give it my all to protect us and make some new Christmas memories to boot."

"I'm so sorry," I whispered to my friend.

"It's okay." Olivia wiped the tears away and gave a little laugh. "Have you found out anything about my adoption?" She'd abruptly changed the subject, a slick diversion tactic she'd no doubt used in her practice.

I shook my head and gave my own laugh. "There are only so many hours in the day, Liv. You'll have to decide what's more important to you. Finding out your history or pulling off this wedding."

We fell into a rhythm of work, the atmosphere still strange, like the air after lightning had struck nearby. It was companionable enough, but I couldn't help but think some things in our friendship had just irrevocably changed. I retreated to my own thoughts and Olivia to hers. The oppressive silence reigned, save for the gentle click of our nails on the cookie-cutter favors.

Olivia left half an hour later, and I breathed a sigh of relief. I felt I'd bungled our meeting.

"What do you expect when you basically accuse your best friend's fiancé of murder?" I muttered some self-censure under my breath before I blew out the candles in the sample angel centerpiece.

"What was that, dear?"

I jumped about a mile as my mother came up behind me. "You really need to get some different footwear, Mom. Those moccasins turn you into a stealth ninja."

My mother smiled. "There's a method to my madness." She linked arms with me and we headed for the kitchen. "You're working too hard, my dear. This was supposed to be a well-deserved several weeks off for you."

Doug snorted from his spot at the kitchen table. "Like you can talk, Carole. You're supposed to be retired!" I knew my stepdad. He was ninety-nine percent joking, but that outlier one percent showed he was genuinely upset. My mom dropped a kiss on her husband's head and pretended not to notice. He'd read three historical biographies since moving back. He took little Ramona on enough walks to tire out the pup and increase her already ample nap schedule. I wondered if my parents had discussed my mom's new career and its demanding hours.

A sharp rat-a-tat-tat at the back door broke through our cozy atmosphere.

"It's just Truman." We all relaxed as I let the chief in. My mom was at ease, although she did seem annoyed at having to entertain the man who'd questioned her so extensively. Her hello was cool.

"I'm happy to see you." I found myself trying to make up for my mother's hostility. "Can I get you something?"

"This isn't a social visit, unfortunately." Truman, with something akin to regret, handed me a sheaf of papers. My mother had already fled the kitchen to show Doug the angel centerpiece in the dining room.

"A warrant." I glanced at the contents and shook my head. "No, no, no."

"Yes, I'm afraid."

My mom and Doug watched me follow Truman straight upstairs and to their room. He neatly searched every nook and cranny of the space, his right now that a judge had signed the warrant.

"Judge Ursula Frank," I muttered to myself. Toby's mother had personally given her John Hancock allowing Truman to carefully toss my parents' room.

"What in the devil are you doing?" Doug appeared at my shoulder and made a move to enter his room.

"He has a warrant," I said miserably. "Oh, my God."

*He has the goods.*

Truman's face flashed a brief look of pain before carefully concealing it behind his professional poker face. Deep in the recesses of the closet was the same half-empty jug of antifreeze my mother had carried into the B and B the first minute she'd arrived.

"Carole?" Doug turned behind him to take in my mother.

"I did not put that stuff in there! I've been framed." My mother followed Truman down the stairs, dogging his every step. "That *is* my bottle of antifreeze—"

*Ouch.*

"And I did use most of it, but I didn't put it in my closet, for Pete's sake!"

*Stop talking!*

"Mom, as an attorney, I must say, you've got to be quiet right now."

We followed Truman like a gaggle of baby geese waddling after its mama. Truman entered the kitchen, stopped before my mom's purse, and unzipped the main compartment.

"Oh, no way! You do not go through a lady's purse!" My mom seemed more indignant that Truman wanted to take a peek than the fact he'd just found the poison used to kill one person and attempt the death of another in her wardrobe.

"It's in the warrant." Truman nodded at the paper in my hands.

"He's right." I handed the document to my mother, whose eyes went wide reading about the probable cause Truman had amassed against her.

"Anonymous tip? That's where you got this info? You've got to be joking." She slammed the warrant down on the kitchen table. And went silent.

We all held our collective breath as Truman retracted a pretty bottle of perfume from Carole's bag. She stared in horror as if the jaunty Vera Bradley holly berry print bag would regurgitate any number of unknown vessels that would implicate her.

"This yours?" Truman barked out his question. He held the pretty bottle of Ralph Lauren Blue to the light, the liquid inside a lovely shade of the titular color.

"Yes," my mom whispered. It had been a present from Rachel, and my mom thought the scent a bit young for her, but I knew she dutifully wore it each day.

Truman sprayed a measure of the perfume onto a napkin and took a whiff.

"Carole Shepard, you have the right to remain silent."

Out came the Miranda warning, and there went my Christmas.

# CHAPTER THIRTEEN

The next morning Rachel and I glumly ate our morning treat from the advent calendar. The luxe Swiss chocolate tasted like sawdust and ash in my mouth. It was December 19, Christmas a mere six days away. Our mother was firmly ensconced in the Port Quincy jail.

"I'm sorry, pup." I picked up Ramona. The poor girl hadn't understood as Truman led his person-mama away. She'd spent the evening looking hopefully out the window, her tiny curled tail quivering in anticipation of my mother's return.

Doug was in worse shape than the pug, since he knew the gravity of the accusations and the evidence found.

"I swear I put that antifreeze in the shed myself." He banged his hand on the kitchen table and made his untouched coffee jump. Except for his Revolutionary War reenactments, the man was a pacifist to a T. It upset me to see him so angry.

"I was there when Mom spritzed herself yesterday," Rachel marveled after she spit out her chocolate. "She smelled like the perfume I gave her, not antifreeze."

"Well, if it's obvious to us someone planted that stuff, it'll be obvious to Truman, too."

At least I hoped. And in the meantime, Carole was going to be calling the Port Quincy jail "home."

I decided to pull out the big guns. It was time to pay a visit to the Davies residence. I'd kept my distance, trying to give Garrett space to decide what to do with his career. But desperate times called for intervention. I decided to walk through the woods to clear my head and formulate my plan. I pulled on some plaid wellies, donned my parka, and began the trek through the woods connecting my property to the Davieses' backyard.

"I'm so sorry, love." Garrett embraced me as soon as he opened the door and ushered me in from the cold. "I know Dad didn't want to do it."

I nodded against his chest.

"He has to appear impartial, you know? And if someone thinks he'll find something, he has to investigate." Garrett looked down and winced. "And if he does end up with the goods, he has to arrest, or it'll look like your mom's getting special treatment because we're dating."

"I understand," I mumbled. "On paper, at least. But this is real. You know my mom didn't murder Lacey. Or try to poison Alan."

"And I'm sure Dad does, too." Garrett tipped my chin up and gave me a tender glance. "He's just doing his job. It stinks that this is all going down near the holiday. But with any luck, it'll be sorted out."

"I guess I just never believed he'd arrest someone close to him," I grumbled.

"That didn't stop him from arresting my mom!"
We jumped and parted as Summer appeared behind Garrett. "I'm sorry, Mallory."

It was true. Just ten months ago, Truman had
loaded Summer's mother into the back of his squad
car for her own stint in jail. "Right, Grandpa?"

I jumped again when I realized Truman was
present. "You're here? Why aren't you downtown,
questioning my mother or something?" I blanched
at the harsh tones I used unbidden.

Truman winced. "I questioned her nearly till
dawn, Mallory. She's resting now, or as much as
she can in that place, and I'm trying to as well." He
was clad in his time-off clothes, his West Virginia
University sweat suit. He wearily unwrapped a
candy cane, cursing when the cellophane stuck to
the candy. He took a loud bite, breaking off half of
the stick, and crunched it loudly between his
teeth.

"I can't think straight from this lack of sleep,
not to mention I haven't had my first cup of coffee." Truman beckoned me to follow him, and I
sat opposite him in a matching recliner.

"That's better." He smiled as Garrett wordlessly
handed us steaming mugs of what smelled like
strong coffee. Summer peeked her head into the
room before Garrett shooed her away.

"The case against your mother is pretty convincing," Truman began.

"Which you know is total garbage!"

That earned me a glare. I decided to mentally
zip my lips closed and let him state his piece.

"As I was saying, the case itself is convincing."
Truman set his coffee on a crochet coaster and
began enumerating the points against my mother.
"She desperately wanted the stager job. And because she's Carole, she was a flibbertigibbet about
it. She let every man, woman, and child in town
know she was going to get that job."

Yup. My mom's over-the-top enthusiasm had led
to a formidable forty-eight hour campaign to un-
knowingly unseat Lacey from her job.

"Next, she undid all of Lacey's work, and yours,
I might add, decorating for Paws and Poinsettias.
If that doesn't make it seem like your mom had it
in for Lacey, I don't know what does." He took a
restorative sip of coffee. "It was all too easy making
the case in the warrant. Ursula happily signed it.
Well, that is, after extracting a promise that I start
to seriously consider Hemingway's disappearance
as a 'catnapping' if he's not found by Christmas."

The judge had taken to putting up a new round
of fliers downtown featuring her pretty Persian
cat. The first round of neon fliers had been deci-
mated in the snowy weather. These plastic coated
ones greeted passersby at nearly every pillar, street-
light, and telephone pole downtown.

"And there's the matter of the antifreeze. Several people at a tasting saw your mom come in,
nattering about her rental having run out, with a
big bottle of the stuff in her possession."

So the March family had ratted out my mom.
Or, they'd just politely answered Truman's queries.
Either way, my mom's Christmas goose was cooked.

"And, I'm betting the stuff that suspiciously smells

like antifreeze in that perfume bottle will be a perfect match, as well."

"But she was obviously framed!" The springs of my recliner whined as I jumped to my feet. I retrieved my mug of coffee and began to pace the Davieses' living room. "I know it, you know it. We just need to figure out who would want you to think it's my mom, and why."

Truman saved me the trouble of throwing my dear friend under the bus by bringing up the matter of Olivia himself.

"You're not going to like this. But Olivia has just as much of a motive as anyone."

I enjoyed being mock-stunned. "First my mom, now Olivia. Who's next, me or Rachel?"

Truman ignored my comment and enumerated everything I'd quietly sleuthed out myself: Lacey's stalking of Toby, her harassment of Olivia, and Toby's ministrations once Lacey found out she was sick.

"You don't seem surprised by any of this." Truman carefully regarded my face. "You haven't been deputizing yourself again, have you, Mallory?" His tone was even, but I saw his eyebrow twitch. In anger or amusement, I wasn't sure. A small smile cracked despite himself, and I relaxed as much as possible in the situation.

"People just happened to tell me about Toby and Lacey. That's not a crime."

"Yes, the town of Port Quincy does excel at gossip." Truman's smile dimmed. "But if I'm honest, Olivia seems like a more likely candidate to murder Lacey and to try to kill Alan than your mother."

I was stunned. I knew, and Truman seemed to

know that my mother didn't murder Lacey. The chief had to follow through and honor the evidence some anonymous meddler had led him to. But I believed my mom would be exonerated. I wanted to think the same for Olivia since my bride was an unofficial suspect.

"What are you thinking about, Mallory?"

I'd stopped to peer at the bank of photographs on a credenza. There was Truman and Lorraine taking an infant Garrett home from the hospital. The faded eighties photo couldn't suppress the joy and excitement on the new parents' faces. Next were a series of photos of Summer, and it was fun to trace how she'd grown over the years. Olivia was supposed to be embarking on a similar journey, welcoming her baby with Toby this summer. It was a life worthy of protecting. And maybe she would do anything to protect it.

I shivered and wheeled around. It was time to come clean.

"Olivia poured her drink out at Paws and Poinsettias. It didn't seem like a big deal at the time."

Truman's eyes flashed with something akin to annoyance. "You're mistaken. It's a very big deal."

"Couldn't she have done it just because she's pregnant?" I grabbed any straw within my reach.

Truman considered my volley. "Sure, but it could be a thousand other things. One of which could be that it held the poison she used to kill her fiancé's ex."

"I think you're getting ahead of yourself." I returned to my chair. "There were plenty of people upset with Lacey. Clementine, for starters. She was unhappy with Lacey's work, but Goldie wouldn't let her fire Lacey. Clementine wanted a stager who's more avant-garde, like my mom, but Goldie was in Lacey's corner."

Truman nodded. "I thought as much, and it's nice to hear you confirm it. The March family gave me some hooey about them all being a happy, working family. I'll admit, it doesn't make Clementine look good to try to conceal that she was trying to fire Lacey."

"Okay, great!" The morning was looking considerably brighter. "Now just go chase down that lead, and you can formally drop the charges against my mom and leave Olivia out of it."

Truman just shook his head. "Come on, I'll drive you home. I'm not really on the clock today, but I'm glad we talked. I'll head into headquarters. I'd like to look into some other things." He excused himself to get dressed in his work garb.

I felt cheered. Maybe Truman would right the ship and head for a different course, one that didn't involve accusing my loved ones.

Five minutes later Truman reappeared in his uniform.

"Let's go."

I sat in the police cruiser with a heavy heart. My mom hadn't ridden in the passenger seat yesterday when Truman had driven her downtown. She'd been placed in the back, the metal grille separating her from Truman. Her innocence was no longer presumed.

A cell phone trilled out a tone from Truman's front pocket.

"Truman." The chief frowned as he listened. "Be right there." He jabbed the phone off with a poke of his finger. "I should have known what kind of day it would be when you showed up on my stoop. That was the dispatcher. They've found a body on the March property."

I held my breath as Truman turned on the sirens and lights. We breezed through several stoplights that were notoriously slow and buzzed our way out to the large parcel of land March Homes had begun carving up. A fancy script sign at the entrance of the rudimentary road announced this was Phase II of the March Homes developments in Port Quincy, to be christened Rushing Creek. Homes were going to be a mix of predesigned and build to suit.

"They throw these homes up fast." Lot after lot had been carved up in precise rectangles, set off with fluorescent stakes and surveyor's string. Backhoes had carved out basements on some lots, while others had poured concrete slabs and skeletal wooden frames rising up from the snow and mud.

"Unbelievable," Truman muttered under his breath as we pulled up to a lot, neatly parceled off just like the others with surveyors' string. A small crowd had already amassed, trampling on the boundary in their quest to get a glimpse of the back. "People like to listen to the police dispatches."

This plot was still largely barren, located at the back of a cul-de-sac. Houses in various states of build hulked around it. I stood back as Truman left the car and brusquely made his way through the small throng of people. The nosy nellies parted like the red sea when they recognized the chief. I realized how it looked driving to the scene with

Truman. I kept a respectful distance, though I longed to follow Truman to the back of the property.

No matter, it was easy to surmise what had happened. A backhoe stood poised and ready to resume digging. A worker in a hard hat excitedly gesticulated to Truman, pointing to the ground and a trash bag and then a tarp where a single long bone lay in repose. It looked large, possibly a femur. I felt a wave of nausea overtake me.

"Maybe it's a cow or something," a bystander hopefully put in.

"Nah. That's a human bone. I'm taking an anatomy class this semester. I'd know that anywhere." A college-aged girl next to me squinted at the bone and explained her reasoning in excruciating clinical and macabre detail.

The cul-de-sac was nearly filled with parked cars. I recognized a reporter and photographer duo from the *Eagle Herald* advance on the scene. Goldie and Alan Marches' Lexus came screeching to a halt in front of the piece of land, barely missing the ever-growing crowd. Clementine and Rudy's Land Rover was not far behind. Justine, my mother's assistant stager, sat in their backseat.

"I told you not to dig there!" Clementine was apoplectic. She blanched as all assembled swiveled their heads to hear her proclamation that seemed tantamount to a confession of murder. She thrust her bag through the open car window at Justine to hold while she waved her hands around as she shouted. "Not because I thought there'd be a body! That's ridiculous." She shook her head, sending the green tips of her hair waving and her green bead earrings swiveling like mad. "This is where I have my wildflower and butterfly garden!"

*Interesting.*

The patch of land used to build a house had actually been used by somebody in the March family. It hadn't just been fallow land.

"Now, now, it's okay, dear. We'll get this all sorted out." Rudy was still in friendly Santa Claus mode. He rubbed his wife's back through her thin yoga hoodie and waved away the remains of the corpse, as if a flick of his fat fingers could make it all go away. "That probably isn't even human. Lots of people sneak on our land to hunt. I bet it's the remains of a recently fallen deer. A big buck, probably." It was good Rudy was keeping his calm demeanor in this situation. But I assumed he would soon be proven wrong about the origin of the remains.

Clementine allowed herself to be partially soothed. "Yes, yes, the matter of the body." She screwed up her forehead in thought. "Who would dump that in my butterfly sanctuary? And who authorized phase two to leak onto this part of our property? Where will the monarchs stop on their way from Canada to Mexico?"

The group of bystanders was now staring at Clementine as if she'd gone off the deep end. Perhaps fixating on her lost butterfly garden was her way of coping with the inexplicable appearance of a body on the family land.

Clementine clarified. "What's really eating me, Rudy, is that this isn't where phase two is supposed to start. See that little creek?" Clementine pointed to a gully to the right, about five hundred feet to the east of our present location. "I personally approved the zoning and mapping plans for Rushing Creek. And I wanted to leave this little corner for my garden. The last cul-de-sac was to end on the other side of the creek, and not edge into the plot where we are now. Who changed the plans?"

This got through to her husband.

"Who authorized this?" Rudy had morphed from kind, gentle Santa Claus to something out of a Christmas horror film. The six-foot-four bear-of-a man could look pretty menacing when he wanted to. "My wife says this development was to start five hundred feet to the east. Where's the contractor?"

I noticed Alan become inordinately interested in his shoes. He edged closer to his Lexus as Goldie gave him a sour look.

A sheepish man, the same one who'd led Truman to the bones, ambled over to Rudy. "Alan changed the plan. I thought he was in charge of this particular development. At least, that's what he told me."

Rudy's face grew red enough to match his suspenders. He huffed and puffed around the grounds, seeming more akin to the big bad wolf than Santa. "Nice job, Alan." He dressed his son-in-law down as if he were a recalcitrant teen. "I don't mind you taking the initiative sometimes, but you need to run things by me and Clementine. This is supposed to be a family business."

The power struggles within the March family continued.

Rudy walked over to the bones and appeared

deflated. "God rest his or her soul, whoever this poor person is."

"You have no idea how these bones got here?" Truman's eyes swept over Clementine and Rudy, Goldie and Alan. "They definitely appear human."

Justine had remained stone silent as her employers raged around her. She had left the car and now leaned against a tree, her skin pale and translucent in contrast to her dark hair.

"She's going to faint." I made my way over and put my arm around her shoulder.

"It's intentional." Goldie's voice was clear and calm, with a thread of anger laced through. "Someone moved these bones here to frame us, just like they poisoned Lacey. No one wants us here in Port Quincy. Developing here has been a huge mistake. We should've just left our own land here alone." She burst into a flurry of tears to match the flurry of snowflakes that had just begun. Alan soothed his wife, seeming happy to fuss over her rather than be on the receiving end of Rudy's outburst.

A green Malibu came screeching to a halt in front of the crowd. A figure tore from behind the wheel and around the crowd. The woman moved with alarming speed.

"What the—"

"Ma'am, you can't go any further. You need to stand back." Faith had arrived on the scene, but her instructions and hand held up like a stop sign were no use. Nina Adams ducked and weaved around the officer like a skilled running back and finally reached the bones. She gave out a wild keening roar of infinite sadness.

"You finally found her. You found my daughter Andrea!"

When I'd left the scene of the housing development, Officer Faith Hendricks had physically restrained Nina Adams from throwing herself on the exposed bones. At first she just wanted to see the remains she was certain were her daughter's. Then the accusations had begun to fly.

"You killed my daughter! Now I'm certain of it. In fact, you probably murdered both of them!" Nina raged as her index finger of censure quivered in the air and pointed to the four March family members.

The growing crowd of gawkers winced as Truman and Faith led a weeping Nina back to her car. Her accusations swirled around in my mind as I headed home.

I tended to the mundane matters of my business that I couldn't ignore. I paid some utility bills for my hulking mansion, looked over food orders for upcoming weddings in January, and checked with vendors on open bids. But my heart wasn't in my work. I was able to do my tasks on autopilot when my real attention was focused on getting my mom out of jail and digesting the new information about the body.

It would all come down to the body's identity. Things wouldn't look good for the March family, concerning Lacey, if the body was truly her sister, Andrea. Maybe Lacey had uncovered the truth—

as sure as the surprised backhoe operator had today. And the Marches had silenced her for it.

I chased away the chill of a draft with a heavy crochet shawl. I kept my cell phone nearby as I worked. I'd double-checked the security system before I'd settled in to work in my office and texted Rachel to let her know I was here. I was taking no chances this sinister December.

The view outside my office window should have cheered me. Delicate flakes twisted down from the sky against an ever-darkening backdrop. The new snow filled in the divots and footprints of the deer, raccoons, and rabbits who had frolicked across the yard after the most recent snowfall. When the clock struck four, I gathered my things to meet with the minister who would marry Olivia and Toby. I wondered if my friend had learned about this newest disaster to befall her parents. And I couldn't help but agree with Goldie. Maybe the Marches never should have left Pittsburgh. Their splashy entry into Port Quincy as businesspeople, not mere landowners with a hunting retreat, had gone disastrously.


"Thank you for meeting me here." Pastor George Millen extended his hand. "Especially with this nasty weather." The older man was clad in a simple rust-colored sweater and jeans, the effect relaxed and welcoming.

I sank gratefully into the chair before him. I was pretty sure I'd be safe within the confines of his office. "And thank you for agreeing to marry my friend and her fiancé at such short notice. Olivia and Toby are going to write some of their vows but want to keep the main components of a Lutheran ceremony."

The pastor and I got to work crafting and nailing down the elements of the ceremony.

"And Olivia wanted me to apologize for not meeting with you personally." I bit my lip. "She's in a bit of a pickle trying to wrap up some career issues all while commuting down here to plan her wedding."

The pastor nodded. "We're all so proud of Olivia. She has turned into an exemplary woman. I hope she finds peace and the life she wants."

I hoped so, too. "Were you here when she was found in the manger?" I blurted out my query before I thought better of it.

Pastor George nodded, a small, sad smile gracing his lined face. "Thirty years ago, this Christmas season. I thank my lucky stars the Marches were the ones to find her. I think about it each season when we put out our crèche. It's the same set where Olivia was found. Our board has debated updating the nativity each year, but we just can't seem to part with it."

I blinked and considered Olivia's plea to look into her adoption. "The police never figured out who left Olivia behind." I let the statement hang in the air.

George tented his papery hands before him and rested his elbows on his desk. "It's a matter I've reflected on for thirty years. Even so far as to consider who may have been hiding a pregnancy in my congregation." He held up his hands in defeat. "But to this day I have no idea." A look of concern flashed behind his round spectacles. "There is one thing that always got me. It was extremely cold that evening. More like a January or February evening. The temperatures were hovering in the single digits. The blanket Olivia was wrapped in was warm, but no real guarantee against that kind of cold. We didn't have security cameras on our property then, and indeed, we don't have them today. But I wonder who was so certain that Olivia would be found. If she hadn't cried out, she could have just slept on, growing colder and colder." He shuddered at the thought. "It's like someone knew she would be found. Like it was guaranteed."

We wrapped up our meeting with some amiable chitchat, and I turned up the collar of my pea coat against the now whipping wind. It wasn't as cold as the evening the pastor had described, but it was close enough. The pretty flurries that had graced the ground at the start of our meeting had dissipated.

I needed to see Garrett. I needed to work out my feelings. The ephemeral nature of our relationship was no longer enough. I'd taken him for granted, and now I wanted permanence. Life was too short.

*Maybe marriage is for me.*

I didn't just want the pageantry of a wedding. I wanted a gathering to make a formal declaration and shore up a promise between two people, and with Summer, three. I was able to reflect on it all under a cold, clear black sky. There was an icy breeze, yet I was filled with warmth. It was still the December season. A time of family and love. A time for bringing together old friends and new.

Everything would be alright. I paused at my station wagon, perched in front of the church at the street corner.

*Not a creature is stirring.*

Except there *was* a creature stirring. The tiny baby Jesus crafted in wood lay in repose in the snow next to the three wise men. Then what was in the manger?

My heart beat as I caught a real, fuzzy blue blanket peeking out from the tiny cradle. The kind you would wrap around a real, human baby. I was out of the car in a flash. My footfalls startled whoever was in the blanket. A feeble cry emanated from the little manger.

*It's happening again.*

My heart sped up as I reached the wooden cradle. I gently lifted back the blanket, eager to get the baby out of the cold and into my arms.

# CHAPTER FOURTEEN

"Meow."

Hemingway's doleful amber eyes stared up at me.

"Oh, thank goodness!"

The Persian cat was scrunched in a too-small carrier. The blanket wrapped around the mesh pet carrier must have helped a bit to keep the cat warm now that the sun had dipped below the horizon, but I hustled to get him out.

"The judge sure will be happy to have you back, buddy." I unzipped the door to the carrier and the cat nimbly stepped out on his snow-white paws. His purr erupted as he rubbed his snub-nosed face against mine. He appeared to be in good health.

Except for his ear. The little furry scrap of skin was wrapped in a tiny bandage.

"Who hurt your ear, little fella?" I carefully pet his head without brushing against the white bandage, with its small amount of blood seeping through. I debated whether to call Truman. A found cat

was not an emergency. Judge Frank might think
so, but I didn't. Then again, someone had con-
sciously mimicked the circumstances in which
Olivia had been found thirty years ago. The situation did not trump finding a skeleton, but Truman
had to know.

I took the purring Persian to the Butterscotch
Monster and cranked the heat. Hemingway pranced
around on the bench leather seats, giving practice
scratches with the polydactyl paws that had inspired his name.

"You're lucky this upholstery is already shot," I
murmured to the big cat as he dug his nails in. He
answered me with a soft meow.

"This had better be good." I could hear Truman's near growl even through the rolled-up window.

"I found Hemingway."

If Truman rolled his eyes any harder, they'd
jounce from their sockets. "Mallory, I have more
important things to do than fetch the judge's lost
cat back to her. I thought you had some sense, but
now I'm not so sure."

I patiently let him go on and pointed to the soft
fleece blue blanket still in the manger. "Hemingway was in that carrier, in that blanket, wrapped
just so in the manger. So that when you heard him
meow, you'd think he was a baby."

"Oh. Well, that's a horse of a different color."
Truman set off to examine what was now to be
considered evidence.

Half an hour later, I had been officially deputized to take care of Hemingway. Truman had to

get back to the station to pull some overtime associated with the found remains. I headed north of Port Quincy to the fancy animal hospital located a stone's throw from the highway. They had an emergency department that consented to examine Hemingway under the unusual circumstances.

"Let's take a look at him." The veterinarian gave me a reassuring smile as he gently palpated the white cat. Hemingway was a pretty chill guy and consented to the examination with nary a hiss or meow.

"And you didn't put this bandage here?" The vet bent in to examine the gauze before he gently removed the tape.

"Nope. That's why I'm here. To find out if Hemingway is okay before I bring him back to Judge Ursula Frank."

"Ah, yes." The vet smiled and gestured to the corkboard within the examination room. "She begged us to put those up."

I stared at Hemingway's visage in black ink on fluorescent green card stock. I vaguely wondered if the judge would take down all her fliers now that Hemingway was back.

"Well, Mr. Cat, you seem to be in fine health. I'd bet you've been inside and cared for these whole two weeks. You're fat and happy and seem none the worse for wear."

I had to agree, as Hemingway was purring again.

"Now let's just see what's under here." The vet pulled the gauze with infinite patience as it slowly unrolled from the cat's ear.

"Hm. It appears his microchip was removed."

"Microchip?" I stared at the small nick on Hemingway's now naked ear.

"This little guy had a microchip implanted in his ear. The judge did mention it. If someone had found him and not recognized him, a shelter or veterinarian could scan his ear, learn his identity, and reunite him with his owner."

It was a clever system. So long as no one absconded with your cat and removed the microchip.

"Do you have pets? You should consider getting them microchipped."

We discussed the procedure, and I left the animal hospital but not before I'd made appointments to have Whiskey and Soda microchipped. There were two openings on Christmas Eve, and I thought, why not get it over with? By then the hullabaloo from Olivia's family, a situation I'd begun to categorize as March Madness, would be done.

I made my way to one of the grand Victorians not far from my own home. I'd decided not to put Hemingway back in the cramped carrier, and besides, Truman wanted it for evidence. I advanced up the path to Judge Frank's porch with the big fellow resting placidly in my arms, his six-toed little paws happily kneading them.

"Mallory. What brings you here?" The judge fumbled with her lock and chain. She hadn't yet seen Hemingway.

I wordlessly handed her her cat as she flicked on her porch light.

"Oh! My sweet baby boy." The judge dropped the needlepoint hoop she'd been carrying and it rolled around her hallway floor. "Come in, Mallory, and tell me how you found him!"

I offered her a kind smile and demurred. Truman had tasked me with getting Hemingway checked out, but he hadn't gone so far as to allow me to interview the judge. He'd asked me to withhold the information about how Hemingway had been found until he'd be able to formally question her. I let her know he'd be contacting her soon.

"Mallory." Garrett appeared behind the judge. *What is he doing here?*

"You don't have a minute to come in?" Garrett offered me a warm smile and held the door open further. "The judge and I were just chatting."

"Yes, I'm trying to convince Garrett to take that job offer. The deadline to decide is in, what, a week?"

Garrett had the good sense to blush a bit under the collar.

I found my blood coursing in my ears. I was growing impatient with his weighing of his options, without weighing our collective feelings and relationship.

"I've got to go, Garrett. Let me know when you've made your decision." And with that I trotted down the steps, leaving my confused boyfriend in my wake.

"I think I messed up."

"It'll be okay, sweetie pie. And it is time for that man to make a decision, whether he includes you in the process or not."

I found myself engaging in girl talk with my

mom. It was just like old times. Except for the fact that our fireside chat was taking place in her cozy little jail cell.

Rachel, Doug, and I were no closer to bringing Carole home for the holidays. Christmas was in less than a week. We were facing the very real reality of spending the day with Mom in jail.

"I have my own regrets." My mom took a sip of the horrid coffee Truman had let me bring in from the vending machine in the headquarters lobby. "I regret moving to Port Quincy. I was too eager to jump in and get both feet wet. I landed in an icy puddle."

"The pickle you're in is much bigger than a puddle," I said with a laugh. One that soon died out. The guilt and pathos and despair I felt welled up and spilled over into tears. I recalled the bright and cheery decorations at Thistle Park, inspired by my mom's love of Christmas. She should be there, enjoying the season with her family, not detained in a drafty concrete cell.

"Let's just have another cookie." My mom wiped away her own set of tears and reached for another cardamom man. Her preoccupation with my waistline was gone, as she had bigger issues to attend to. It was literally the only perk of her being incarcerated. She choked down the little figure with the help of a swig of the wretched coffee.

"You were a Christmas Wonder Woman growing up, Mom. If we can't have you home for Christmas, we'll bring Christmas in to you."

I'd already called in my chips with Truman. He'd grudgingly agreed to let me smuggle in a small ham and other dishes on the holiday, provided I only used plastic cutlery and ran the whole feast through the metal detector. I'd rolled my eyes and consented. But I hoped it didn't come to that. Especially since the chief himself seemed to be working hard to spring my mom.

"Believe it or not, Truman is trying to find out who planted the antifreeze in your purse."

My mom gave a harrumph. "I'll believe it when I'm home with you girls, Doug by my side, and Ramona in my lap."

The one thing Truman hadn't approved was bringing in the sweet little pug to see her mistress. Ramona had settled into a motherless existence, her little curly tail a bit less sprightly, her big pug eyes more doleful.

Doug had rallied in Mom's absence, reminding Rachel and me to eat our square of advent chocolate each day, to bake Mom's special snowflake lace cookies, and keep up some semblance of normalcy. I was forever grateful he was my stepfather. This month had made me reflect on what it meant to be a family. And I loved mine.

But Garrett, Summer, Lorraine, and Truman were also my family. And I might lose them. I'd had it all, and felt it slipping away.

"Hello." The soft voice of Justine Bowman made me jump. "I thought I'd fill you in on what's going on at work." She nodded her thanks to Faith as the officer opened Mom's cell and allowed Justine to slip inside.

My mom shook her head. "I don't want to know, Justine." She set her jaw and looked hopeful. "When I finally break out of here, I think I'll resign." Her resolve dissolved into hysterical laughter. "That is, if the Marches haven't already fired me. I wouldn't even know."

"Oh no, they're eager for your return." Justine made a face. "Clementine only has eyes for your designs. It's tough deciding whose orders to follow, hers or Goldie's. I have to admit, I've enjoyed working as a stager there with you as the buffer. But with you gone, it's hard to live up to their expectations."

"Clementine's a lot of hot air," my mom offered. "In truth, if I really did follow all of her suggestions, the model homes would look too over the top. Her design choices really do need Goldie's more prosaic choices." She offered Justine a smile. "I let Clementine dictate the initial design. Then I work with Goldie a day or two later to smooth it out and ground it in reality."

Justine gave a grateful laugh. "That system works. I'll have to put it into play. That is, until you get back."

My mom's face fell, and she glanced at the utilitarian clock nailed high on the wall. "I think this visit will be coming to a close soon."

Just as she'd predicted, Truman's heavy footfalls slapped on the linoleum in the hall outside the cell. His eyes were rheumy and red from lack of sleep. "Time to go, ladies."

"Any news on my case?" My mom's eyes grew heartbreakingly hopeful. I didn't want to see the bubble of anticipation popped and deflated.

"I'm sorry, no." Truman gave my mom a look of genuine good will. "And the news for Nina Adams isn't great, either."

"So the body is her daughter." My heart fell.

"No." Truman shook his head. "That would have been some final closure for the poor woman. This skeleton is definitely male."

I turned to leave with Justine, but the woman was already gone.


I swung by Thistle Park to pick up my sister. She'd visited my mom the day before. We'd decided to take turns visiting her in jail, not knowing how long her stay would be. Rachel and I buckled our seatbelts and headed north to Pittsburgh. We had a wedding planning errand to attend to with Olivia's parents.

"If the body on the property isn't Andrea Adams, who in the heck is it?" Rachel bit a shiny gold acrylic.

"It could be anyone. And despite the fact that Clementine used that section of the property as a garden, it would be the perfect place to dump a body. Up until now, they only used the cabin at Christmas and for weekends in the summer. People in Port Quincy had to know when they came and went."

Nina Adams would be left in the dark once again when it came to the demise of her daughters. It was a dark and muddled drive as my sister and I considered how it all fit in with the impossible events this month. We were no closer to an answer as we concluded the nearly two-hour drive north. I didn't envy Truman the task before him to unravel this complicated knot.

I pulled to a stop in front of the large house in Sewickley, a suburb of Pittsburgh where Olivia had grown up. The tasteful and rambling home was made of aged, gray stone, complete with a turret and a little moat out front. I could see echoes of this house in the cabin that had gone up in flames.

"This place has Goldie written all over it." Rachel wrinkled her nose as we advanced up the wide slate steps. I made a motion to zip it, and we rang the bell.

"Come in, come in." Goldie opened the wide front door. Her mind seemed to be elsewhere, as evidenced by the spacey look in her eyes. "I'm sorry, I'm trying to process what's happened down in Port Quincy."

Alan appeared at her side and offered her a heavy tumbler of cut glass. It was filled nearly to the brim with a smooth, amber liquid. "Here, honey. Drink this." The nutty fragrance of cream sherry emanated from the drink. Goldie raised it to her lips and downed the drink in one fell swoop. Rachel and I exchanged glances.

*Whoa, slow down.*

"I know she's having a horrible December, but this isn't a kegger." Rachel arched one brow as we allowed Alan and Goldie to lead us down a long hallway at a safe distance out of earshot.

Alan watched with concern as his wife shoved the goblet back to his chest.

"Let's get this over with." Goldie's usual politeness and propriety were all gone, apparently. I gulped and followed Goldie into a sunken living room. A full grand piano stood before a bank of glass windows overlooking a wide yard. An eclectic mix of modern and antique bird feeders provided shelter and food for a menagerie of cardinals, blue jays, and fat squirrels. March Homes was in the business of building domiciles celebrating new money. These included the big split-levels they'd constructed in the late seventies, to the colonials they'd erected in the eighties, and the McMansions they'd made in the nineties and aughts. But for their own home, they celebrated their old money.

Alan offered us drinks, and Rachel and I requested simple glasses of water.

"This December just keeps getting worse and worse." Goldie sank into a plum-colored couch in front of a book of old Polaroid pictures. "And I think I know why."

I was all ears. I'm sure Truman would want to be, too.

"I enjoyed working with Lacey. She was like a second daughter to me. I'll admit, I would get testy that Olivia seemed to spend so much time at the firm. But I ended up monopolizing Lacey's hours in a similar fashion. I enjoyed being her mentor and spending the day with her bouncing ideas around. But I should have fired her as soon as I found out she was harassing Toby."

I wondered if this was an opening to weigh in. "It must have been a tough decision."

"I knew how sick Lacey was." Goldie took in my surprised face. "I was the only one she'd told at the company. I think other than me and her medical team, only her mother knew. Then she eventually told Toby. She needed a kidney, and she needed it fast." Olivia's mother appeared to have aged ten years in the last week. "I felt bad for Lacey, what with her sister having disappeared all those years ago, and then her health problems. I know it's a hard surgery, too."

Rachel blinked. "You *know?*"

"I had my own kidney replaced."

"Excuse me?" I thought I'd misheard her.

"Ten years ago my kidneys finally gave out. I've had renal issues my whole life." Her face grew wistful. "It prevented me from having a biological child, as a matter of fact. My doctors said a pregnancy would kill me."

"I'm so sorry." I felt for the woman who had had to make an odd choice of allegiance between her own daughter and the woman who was as close to her as her own daughter.

Goldie's eyes grew thoughtful. "Christmas time usually brings blessings to my family. We've had two downright miracles occur. First we found Olivia outside the church. Then a kidney became available years later on Christmas Day, just when I didn't think I'd be able to see my little girl graduate. I had the transplant the day after Christmas. It was a new lease on life."

"And now Olivia and Toby will have their own new start in life." I gazed at the large framed picture of Olivia and her fiancé that took up a large part of the stone mantel.

"Yes. I'm sorry I'm mired in all that's going on this month. Let's get to it."

Goldie, Rachel, and I poured over pictures of Olivia as a baby. The photographs gave way to her as a chubby toddler and finally a lovely, young woman. We selected twenty photos to make a slide-show to play in the great hall at Thistle Park after the wedding. I dimly wondered if the busy judge would follow through with my request to produce similar pictures of Toby growing up. I thought I'd have a fighting chance of receiving the photographs now that I'd reunited her with Hemingway.

"Don't forget these." Alan entered the room with one final album. "There are some real keepers in here." He gave his wife's shoulder a warm squeeze, and she sent him a grateful look.

We flipped through the book in record time, selecting two more adorable photos of a young Olivia. Goldie shut the album with a satisfied smile. My eyes trailed a photograph that fluttered out from between the last page and the binder, fluttering to the floor.

I picked it up and glanced at the composition before I handed it over.

*Justine.*

The picture had definitely been taken decades ago. The five people in the photograph wore eighties outfits—the women with big bows on their blouses under their chins, shoulder pads, and hair teased to dizzying heights. I pushed aside the quick thought that my naturally curly, sandy hair would have been more at home back then when women paid to transform their straight hair into kinks and corkscrews. The photograph appeared to be in an office setting. And in the back stood a young Alan March, laughing and conversing with a gorgeous, incandescent Justine Bowman.

They could have been coworkers sharing a joke. But the look of love or lust that transpired between the two was evident to see. Rachel was tired of waiting to see what was taking me so long, and bounced up to my side to take a look.

"Jeez Louise." Rachel clapped a hand to her mouth, a second too late.

"Mallory, hand me the picture." Alan appeared by my side, a true look of alarm on his slender face.

"What's going on? Mallory, give that to me." Goldie appeared on my other side, leaning over my arm to take a peek.

I gulped, frozen, and held the picture flat against my front.

My sister had about nine inches on me, and plucked the photo from me. "Um, I'm not sure either of you need to see this."

It was an awkward and farcical standoff. Goldie finally ended things. "Give me that photograph, Rachel Shepard, or the wedding is off."

*Gulp.*

Rachel laid the dog-eared picture in Goldie's outstretched palm. I felt Alan take in a pendant breath beside me.

Goldie studied the picture with intent eyes. She flicked them up after a moment, the depths of her gaze laced with sadness, disgust, and knowledge.

"I thought there was something odd about Justine Bowman. A certain familiarity or some kind of hidden agenda."

Alan squirmed like a pinned bug. Then he decided to try a different tactic. "Yes, I knew Justine once. She worked in your parents' South Hills office, the one in Mt. Lebanon. She was one of the decorators your parents used on a contract basis."

He decided to toss his wife a haughty look. "And what of it?"

"I'm exhausted. I think I'm going to take a nap." Goldie's hard voice could cut glass. All at once her hardened face softened a mere degree. "Thank you, Mallory and Rachel. The slideshow will be lovely." And with that she left the room. An awkward silence reigned.

Rachel and I mumbled our goodbyes to Alan and got the heck out of there.

# CHAPTER FIFTEEN

"They were totally an item." I wrinkled my nose as we left the North Shore and crossed to downtown Pittsburgh on the Fort Duquesne Bridge. The electricity between Alan and Justine in the old photograph had been almost palpable, transcending time and space.

"I'd be ticked, too, if I was Goldie. If Alan really had nothing to hide, he would have mentioned to his wife that he'd worked with Justine before. Even if it was dozens of years ago." Rachel shook her head in disgust.

"This changes things. Goldie seemed to have just realized Alan had a prior relationship with Justine. But maybe she found out earlier—"

"—And gave him that antifreeze-spiked martini," Rachel finished.

"Or," I wondered, "maybe Justine wanted to start things back up with Alan and he refused. So *she* tried to poison him."

We tossed our various theories around as I

wended my way down below the earth in a subterranean parking garage. We were headed to the Clark Building to pick up Toby and Olivia's rings. The edifice contained some of the nicest jewelry stores in town, all located in an informal kind of jewelry district housed under one roof.

"I miss it here, but I love Port Quincy, too." Rachel gazed at the skyscrapers as we emerged from the garage. I took in the hustle and bustle of people crowding the sidewalk at lunchtime. And lasered in on one couple in particular.

"Uh oh."

Rachel followed my gaze and made a face. "Ugh, fancy running into Keith and Becca here."

My ex-fiancé and his new bride spotted us as well. Becca sauntered over with a smile, her arm possessively twined through Keith's.

"What brings you two here?" Becca swung a bag over her wrist from the priciest jewelry store in the Clark Building; owning a bauble from this store almost rendered the bag a piece of jewelry in and of itself.

"We're here to pick up rings for a client," I stated, offering nothing more.

"Olivia March." Keith smirked and gave me a quick once-over. "How are things with Garrett?"

I felt my eyes narrow. What was Keith getting at?

"Just fine, thank you."

"I hear he may be leaving Port Quincy," Becca offered. "Good news travels fast, doesn't it?"

I didn't bother to conceal my disgust this time. "He's considering a wonderful offer to direct a law clinic at Pitt, so yes, he might be relocating." I heard the acid in my voice.

"The judge always finds a way to funnel all the best outcomes to Garrett," Keith mused with a sinister smile. "Just look at each and every case he's had before her. It's not even worth putting in an appearance in court if the judge is Judge Ursula Frank, and Garrett is the opposition." He saw my shocked expression and went in for the kill. "Everyone knows that. Everyone but you, apparently."

I stood speechless on the sidewalk. Keith had basically just accused my boyfriend and his mentor of an improper bias, at best, and fixing cases, at worst.

"No way." I felt my chest rise and fall. "That is a very serious allegation, Keith. Are you sure you want to get behind it?"

I felt Rachel's glower descend upon my ex-fiancé.

Keith dropped his voice. "I'll stand behind what I said one hundred percent."

And with that the couple did an about-face, wheeling around on the sidewalk to leave me sputtering in front of the Clark Building.

"The nerve of those jerk faces!" Rachel's exclamation drew the curious stare of several passersby. "Keith is full of it, Mallory. You know it, and I know it. You'd think he and Becca would be more gracious after we worked so hard on their various wedding plans."

I gulped and tried to gather my composure, which was laying on the sidewalk, dashed to smithereens.

*What if Keith is right?*

I shook my head, scolding myself for taking the

bait. I had once been engaged to the odious little man, and he knew how to get my goat. There was nothing more to it.

"Let's get this taken care of."

Rachel and I entered the building and took a brass medallion elevator to the third floor, where we picked up the rings Olivia and Toby had selected and had sized.

"And anything for yourselves, ladies?" The pretty clerk patted the gleaming glass cases.

"Ooh, I think I will." Rachel accepted the invitation with a bounce on the balls of her feet. She rubbed her hands together in anticipation and asked to see the engagement rings.

"Do you know something I don't?" I raised my eyebrow at my sister's unbridled enthusiasm.

"Evan is the kind of man who will pop the question within a year."

"Okay, maybe that's true." I tried to suppress a laugh. "But that's in about 365 days, Rach."

"It doesn't hurt to figure out what I want early," she hissed in return. "Not everyone drags their feet in the relationship department like you have. Then you don't have to worry later if it's all going to fizzle out."

I felt my face fall and the sharp pain of tears starting to form when you try to reign them in.

"I'm so sorry, Mallory. I didn't mean to upset you." Rachel slung an arm around my shoulders, suffocating me with the treacly scent of her cupcake and jasmine perfume. "I'm sure you and Garrett will work things out."

*Yeah, if it turns out he's not fixing cases with Judge Frank.*

I shook my head, feeling dizzy. I'd let Keith get to me, and Rachel knew it, too.

"I think I need some air." I pushed through the glass doors of the jewelry store and leaned against the wall, taking deep, restorative breaths. A minute later Rachel joined me, and the two of us spilled out onto the sidewalk.

My cell phone vibrated in my purse, and I plumbed its depths to extract it. "Doug told me you were in Pittsburgh today. As it happens, I'm here with Summer, too. Do you have time to meet?" My heart accelerated at the text from Garrett. I'd stormed off from Judge Frank's front porch last night in a snit, and here was a chance to make things up. I texted that we should meet soon, and we arranged to go ice-skating.

In half an hour's time, Garrett, Summer, Rachel, and I whipped around the great big tree at the center of the small rink at PPG Place. It was too small to rival Rockefeller Center, but what it lacked in size was made up for by its location within a black glass castle. It was intimate and ethereal in the waning light, surrounding the skaters with acres of obsidian glass. It was truly a glittering, shimmering space. As the sun set and night encroached, I felt as if we were one with the great, big, black bowl of a night winter sky.

Summer laughed as her father attempted to catch up with her blinding fast skating speed. Rachel made figure eights in the ice, and I watched the ones I loved. My heart ached. I couldn't lose Garrett, or Summer.

"What brought you to Pittsburgh today?" I caught up with a panting Garrett, the wind in his dark hair, and an exuberant smile on his face. I tried to keep the accusatory tone from my voice as I skated with Garrett. It had been a while since I'd laced on a pair of skates, and we kept bumping into each other as we attempted to skate holding hands. I'd forgotten my mittens and was grateful to enclose my small hand in his.

"Summer and I were picking out some Christmas gifts," he said evenly. "And Doug told me you were getting Olivia and Toby's rings."

I nodded my assent, willing the creeping doubt Keith had planted in my head to fly far, far away. I didn't want to press things further, and it appeared Garrett didn't, either. We skated until we were all hungry and tired, trying to prolong the magic of the early evening. The four of us grabbed sandwiches and made our way to our separate cars. It had been a perfect afternoon, unplanned, with no pressure or ultimatums.

"You have nothing to worry about." Rachel leaned over and patted my knee as we left the parking garage and headed back on the long drive to Port Quincy.

"I hope so." I flashed my sister a smile. But I wasn't quite so sure.

The next day was blessedly quiet, with nary a dead body discovered or family member accused. Rachel and I got to work finalizing the small details for Olivia's big day, which was a mere two days away. But before we could wrap up our obligations to the March family, we had one more event to put on.

"It's weird throwing a party I'm also invited to," Rachel said as she tore through her closet.

I sent my sister a smirk. "So long as you don't use it as an excuse to wiggle out of your duties."

"Like I'd ever do that." Rachel stuck out her tongue and made me laugh.

We'd taken on the gig for the surgery department holiday party way back in July. The day after Toby stopped by my office to go over the details and drop off a check, I'd set him up with Olivia. July seemed ages ago, not a mere six months ago. So much had happened for my family, for Olivia and Toby, and the little family they'd created. I felt a wave of emotion surge through me. I was a bundle of nostalgic nerves lately, but that was to be expected around the holidays.

"Look at this." Rachel made a face and thrust her phone under my nose. "The Marches are advertising for a new assistant stager, but not a head stager."

"So they're still keeping Mom's job open for her, even though she's in jail. But they've fired Justine." I knew the bad news would outweigh the good when we talked to my mom later on for her one allowed call.

"Wouldn't you, too, if you'd discovered Alan's old affair?" Rachel dug through the pile of party dresses on her bed, flinging frocks hither and yon.

"I guess. Another stager bites the dust." I shivered. "I guess it's better that they fired Justine than the alternative."

"I need to look perfect tonight." Rachel bit her lip and continued digging.

"Just pick a dress." I was growing impatient. "We need to set up in time. You look fabulous in everything, and you know it, too." It was true.

"But none of this is right." Rachel held up one dress in her right hand, a spangly metallic number with spaghetti straps in a daring purple sequin. In her left was a green chiffon confection featuring a daringly high slit. The dresses were perfectly Rachel. Which wasn't who she wanted to be when she was with Evan.

"Can I . . . ?"

*I know where this is going.*

"Yeah, yeah, yeah. Borrow whatever you want. Just make sure to return it this time." I rolled my eyes and led my sister to my room. She renewed her digging, this time taking marginally better care of my clothes.

"Okay. I've found it. Let me get dressed, and I'll show you the full effect."

I left my sister in my room and paced in the hallway outside. Ramona joined me, thinking walking in endless circles was quite fun. "She's gone mad, old girl." I picked up the pug and gave her a snuggle. "And she's going to make us late to boot, if she doesn't hurry."

Rachel flung open the door. My towering sister was channeling the elegance and demure poise of a petite Audrey Hepburn. She was wearing a dress I hadn't donned in years, a stretchy midnight blue sheath with a pretty yet modest v-neckline. The dress was solidly tea length on my frame and hit Rachel at the knees. The effect was tasteful and flirty. She'd paired the dress with a pair of simple black velvet heels, a few inches lower than she usually dared. Her honey waves were carefully pulled back from her face, trapped in a smooth chignon. She'd abandoned her usual daring makeup palette for a simple look. She wore muted sable and cocoa eye shadow and simple pink gloss. Her dress was less va-va-voom as it was understated elegance. I noticed she'd helped herself to my string of blush pearls and a few sprays of Chanel Number 19. The woodsy fragrance was the antithesis to the sweet scents she usually favored. My sister didn't even *smell* like herself.

It was a gorgeous look, just not one my sister would have ever picked out for herself unless she was trying to snare her surgeon.

"You look lovely." My voice was small. "Like . . ." I searched for words that would be complimentary of her look, yet not critical of the reasons behind it.

"Like I could be Evan's fiancée!" Rachel spun around in a circle like a teen in a sixties movie and fell back on my bed.

"Fair enough. Now let's just set up for the party."

Forty-five minutes later, our work was complete. We'd ferried food out to the carriage house for the party, clad in our snow boots rather than heels. We lit hundreds of candles and placed them on two sideboards, away from areas where passersby could jostle them. The long tables in the back of the room held big bowls of Christmas ornaments in shades of lavender, green, and blue. We'd left the two massive trees in the room simply decorated, the boughs wound with small white twinkle lights. The murals of old-time cars and carriages marching around the room seemed to move in the dancing glow of the flames.

"This is perfect, Mallory and Rachel. I can't wait to see what you've come up with for our wedding." Toby appeared with Olivia by his side. My friend was flushed with excitement, but exhausted, too.

"I quit the firm!" She nearly bounced in her low kitten heels.

"You what?" I was sure I'd misheard.

"The managing partner stopped by. It's official. I earned my partnership." Her face turned bitter-sweet. "But no matter what happens with Garrett's decision, whether I practice here with him or take up Rudy's offer to work for March Homes, I want to be here. I love you, Toby. I choose Port Quincy. I choose us." My friend turned to her fiancé and he swept her up in a scorcher of a kiss. Several of his colleagues whistled, and the couple broke apart with sheepish grins.

"Now that's the kind of speech I hope to hear someday." Rachel made a beeline for Evan, who took in her new look with appreciative but some-what cool eyes.

*Uh-oh.*

I wondered if my sister had misjudged. But I barely had time to give it a second thought.

"I'm sorry, Rachel, but you seem to have gotten the wrong idea. It won't matter how long we date. You are super fun and drop-dead gorgeous, but I'd never marry you." Evan gave a callous little shrug that seemed to wound Rachel to her core. "I need a helpmate, a life partner." His eyes raked over my sister, taking in her transformation. "I appreciate what you're trying to do. But I need a different kind of woman."

I opened my mouth to give him a piece of my mind, when Miles emerged from behind the buffet.

"You'd be the luckiest man on this planet if Rachel Shepard deigned to give you even a minute of her time." His white-hot glare melted as he turned to look at my sister. "She's the smartest woman I've ever met. She's beautiful, creative, and an amazing businesswoman. She has the biggest heart you'll ever come across. I'm sorry you can't see that." A small smile ticked up the corner of Miles's mouth. "Never mind. I'm *thrilled* you can't see that."

Rachel's quivering lips slowly turned up in a beatific smile. "Miles. That was lovely."

The cook traced a thumb across Rachel's cheekbone, drying a rivulet of tears. "It's true."

My sister linked arms with Miles and abandoned her duties for the rest of the evening. Evan pouted in the corner, and Rachel and her new beau cut a rug. I grinned as I watched.

# CHAPTER SIXTEEN

"I've been so blind." Rachel nearly danced out of the carriage house in her heels, forgetting to switch to her boots.

We broke down the holiday party together. I said nary a word, letting Rachel expound on how she was lucky to have found her real true love match with our redheaded cook.

"Miles has been chasing you for over a year, Rach." I couldn't help but point out the obvious.

"And I've been a fool." The stars in my sister's eyes mirrored those above in the impossibly clear black sky. "A darn fool."

I bade my sister goodnight. She glided into her room on a gust of puppy love, and I booted up my laptop with a smile. It was just before midnight. Tomorrow would be December 22. And my mother was still not home.

"Come here, girl." I scooped up my calico cat Whiskey to keep me company as I delved into some newspaper research in the *Eagle Herald*'s on-line archives. I opened up several browser tabs, one for each subject. First up was Andrea Adams's disappearance. It took reading a few old articles to pinpoint the exact date. It can take a while for a missing person to truly be considered missing. The first article pondering her whereabouts appeared two weeks after Nina Adams had told the police her daughter never came home.

My second tab sought stories regarding Judge Frank. Keith's heinous accusations about Garrett and the judge were still bothering me. I'd taken my boyfriend's word that the woman was above reproach. But I realized I didn't know much about her. I'd seen her in court, her approach and demeanor formidable. But she didn't have time to attend a single planning meeting for her son's rapidly impending nuptials.

"Oh my." A hit from a now defunct Pittsburgh Paper, the *Pittsburgh Press*, appeared in my search. There in a grainy photo were the judge and Goldie March, arm in arm at a gala in Pittsburgh. I had no idea the two women had known each other before their children became engaged.

Then again, it was no smoking gun. The March family did own property in Port Quincy. It was possible Ursula Frank and Goldie March ran in the same social circles in the 1980s and had grown apart.

My final tab searched for news about Olivia. She wasn't called Olivia then, just the baby found in the manger. Goldie and Alan had stumbled upon the softly crying infant outside the Port Quincy Lutheran Church on Christmas Eve thirty years ago.

The missing link I'd hoped to find wasn't there. I nearly clapped my laptop closed in frustration, but my purring cat stopped me. A tiny, itchy detail asserted itself in the back of my head.

Toby had once mentioned following in his father's footsteps. My fingers flew across the keyboard.

*Pay dirt.*

Another society page took up my screen. The scene was similar to the one tonight, the resplendent holiday party for the McGavitt-Pierce Memorial Hospital's surgery department. Front and center were the hosts for the evening. The chief of surgery, Dr. Tobias Frank, and his wife, a newly appointed judge, Ursula.

My mind swirled with possible theories and ideas. I felt like I was getting tantalizingly close, but to what, I couldn't tell.

Soda pawed open my door, her little orange creamsicle face peaceful and sleepy. I prepared for bed and nestled up to my cats, the wind roaring all around me in my aerie nest of an apartment. I felt as if the eventful last few days were akin to being in the eye of the storm. I closed my eyes and willed myself to sleep, trying not to anticipate what the rest of December would bring.

"I thought she'd be free by now." The cold reality of a new day came in on the coattails of the arctic front hovering over Port Quincy. My sister buttered a cranberry muffin and took a resigned bite.

"I thought so, too, Rach." Our mother was steeling herself to spend Christmas, her favorite day of the year, in jail. I'd been certain some miracle would appear to prove my mom's innocence. She was stuck in some weird limbo with evidence that showed her to be Lacey's poisoner, yet no one really believed it.

Doug was beside himself. He paced the halls of Thistle Park muttering about antifreeze and plotting to raise my mom's spirits despite her incarceration. Ramona was resigned, perhaps believing my mom would never return. Yet each night, according to Doug, the little pug curled up in what was my mom's side of the bed.

I heard my stepfather conversing with someone as he made his way down the back stairs.

"It's not as good as springing her out. But it'll do." Doug touched the screen of his cell phone and met our eyes in turn.

"It looks like Carole is really going to spend Christmas in jail." His eyes were dejected. "But I did convince Truman to allow us to bring some more of the holiday to her."

He detailed that Truman was waiving his moratorium on decorations, food, and music for my mother. We could even bring Ramona in for short visits. The denizens of Port Quincy were largely behaving this year, and my mother was the only person left in the facility's temporary wing.

My sister and I got to work prepping food and gathering decorations. We would spend the next few days bringing as much Christmas cheer to my mother as possible. It was an imperfect solution, but it would have to do. Half an hour later, we strung blinking lights around the metal bed frame in my mom's cell. Doug pulled out a tiny MP3 player and a set of tinny speakers. Soon the make-shift sound system blasted out Bing Crosby's "I'm Dreaming of a White Christmas."

"This will help me get in the spirit," our mom quavered. "Thank you, girls." She pulled us in for a hug. "And thank you, my love." She saved her biggest embrace for my stepdad.

I opened the picnic basket I'd lined with fabric patterned with snowflakes. "And we saved the best for last."

Ramona had remained still as we set up the dec-orations. Now that the picnic basket lid was opened, she bounded out.

"My sweet baby!" Mom held the pug to her, Ra-mona yipping and trying to lick her face. We'd dressed the pup in one of the holiday sweaters my mom favored. This was a new one, a blue number with a wooly abominable snowman embroidered on the back.

I laughed and brought out the cooler that con-tained the food we'd brought. "Truman also al-lowed us to bring you some holiday goodies."

"We can bring them every day until . . ." Rachel began, trailing off when my mom's face fell.

"It's wonderful. I just really thought I'd be home for Christmas."

Truman's footfalls resounded in the hallway. "Mallory, a word please."

"I'll be right back." I followed Truman to his of-fice. It was pretty spare, with pictures of his family along his desk, but no nods to the holiday.

"I wanted to apologize in person. This is an

abomination, but as it stands, Carole did use the antifreeze, and her prints are all over the bottle, the perfume, and even Alan's glass."

I groaned at the last tidbit of information. "And they would be. She helped us get glasses ready for Olivia's shower before she left for work. This just keeps getting better and better. When you and I both know she didn't poison Lacey." I frowned in thought. "Did you ever trace the call that made the tip about finding the antifreeze in Mom's purse?"

"Of course!" Truman nearly boomed. "It was a disposable cell phone. It had been used to make just the one call. Probably abandoned by now."

We sat in weighty silence. I broke it with my theories.

"I can think of a million people who had the motive, means, and opportunity to kill Lacey. And none of them are Mom."

Truman nodded. "And if I could make an airtight case against any of them, we could release your mother."

"There's Clementine March. She butted heads with Lacey. But Goldie wouldn't let her mom fire the stager. Maybe she took matters into her own hands." It was weak theory and I knew it.

"Goldie herself is a better candidate. She has said herself she felt bad she kept Lacey on the payroll even after she had evidence that the woman was harassing Olivia's boyfriend. Maybe the guilt ate away at her." Truman folded his hands in front of him.

"Especially after someone vandalized Olivia's car. Goldie probably thought it was Lacey."

"But if Goldie March killed Lacey, she did a bang-up job framing your mother for it instead." Truman took a sip of coffee and seemed to weigh his next words carefully. "The only other person I can think of who has motive to kill Lacey is your bride."

"I know." I had to agree. "But just because she had a reason didn't mean she did it."

"She must have been crushed to have found out Toby was still in contact with the woman who was stalking him. And right after she found out she was carrying his child. It could be enough."

"But Olivia must've found out she was pregnant back in September or so," I mused, doing the math in my head. "Why wait all that time to kill Lacey?"

Truman frowned. "I admit the theory is imperfect. But I don't like the detail you told me, that she poured out a drink at Paws and Poinsettias. I don't know if you noticed, but each potted plant in a large tub in the lobby of March Homes is now gone. Your mother told me Clementine changed her mind and ordered them to be removed the day after Paws and Poinsettias."

*Interesting.*

But it was no matter. None of these theories truly exonerated my mother. Whoever had wanted her out of the way, bearing the torch of suspect numero uno, had done a good job.

The landline on Truman's desk rang impossibly loudly. I jumped and stared wordlessly at the chief. He nodded, giving me permission to stay.

"Mm-hmm. Okay. I wasn't aware you could do it

with such granularity. Perfect. Well, this is the first good news all December."

He hung up, including me in his grin. I couldn't imagine what would make me as elated as him.

"That was the crime lab. First, I apologize this took so long. But I have good news. The antifreeze in the rental car had silicates and phosphates as part of its chemical composition. It's more of a traditional blend. It matches the liquid in the big jug your mother and Doug brought to Thistle Park, precisely, just as you would expect. It also matches the antifreeze in her perfume." He couldn't tamp down his excitement and stood from his swivel chair. "But the antifreeze that killed Lacey and the antifreeze found in Alan's drink doesn't contain any silicates. It's the kind of stuff European cars use."

"In plain English?" I was excited with where this was going.

"The antifreeze used explicitly as poison does *not* match the original antifreeze that was in your mother's possession."

"So this proves she didn't do it."

"This proves she didn't do it!"

Truman and I practically raced down the hall. Rachel, Doug, and my mom were engaged in the saddest Christmas carol sing-along I'd ever heard. My mom barely lifted her head when we appeared at her door.

"Carole, you're free to go."

"Pardon?" My mother looked up from petting Ramona with a confused look on her face.

"This had better not be a joke, sir." Doug rose to his feet.

"This is for real. What are you waiting for?" I flung open the door while my family cheered. Ramona barked and turned around in a circle on her hind legs. The little pup led the way, her head held high, and my mom triumphantly followed as we all trooped out of the jail and into the sunlight.

# CHAPTER SEVENTEEN

Olivia and Toby were going to have a magnificent day. The layer of snow from the earlier storm remained on the ground, providing a quintessential white backdrop. Yet the sun bathed the mansion in pretty, clear light. All was calm, all was bright. It was two days before Christmas. My mother was home, and I was about to facilitate a ceremony and party for one of my dearest friends. I was surrounded by the ones I loved.

*Except Garrett.*

We'd made plans at least to see each other on Christmas Day. Springing my mom from the clink had filled me with courage and cheer. I'd called Garrett as soon as my mom was settled back in and invited his whole family over for a Christmas Day visit, after the Davieses had their own delicious meal, of course. Garrett had run the idea by Lorraine and accepted. It would be our first official Christmas together as a couple, with his family and mine assembled. I felt better. No matter what was going to happen with his possible relocation, I was making my intentions known. I wanted to spend more days, and especially the important ones, with Garrett and Summer and his family.

I smiled at the thought as I lit the last candle in the final angel candelabra in the carriage house. After the surgery department's party, Olivia and Toby had requested that we move their ceremony and reception to the same space. It was no trouble to set up the six tables for the small number of expected guests with the star mirrors, wreaths, and angel candelabras. Rachel and I transported hundreds of poinsettias into the space, and it looked just as festive as it had for the work party, but decidedly different.

Guests began to filter in, exclaiming over the magnificent space. Pastor Millen arrived and shook my hand, awaiting the couple under a trellis we'd brought in and stationed at the front of the carriage house. The white wood was adorned with holly and boughs of fresh evergreens. I'd affixed the very angel ornament that had accompanied Olivia in the manger to the top of the trellis, in keeping with her theme.

"It's almost go time." Rachel cast a nervous glance at her watch. No matter how many weddings we had under our belt, I still experienced a welcome frisson of excitement at the start of each event.

Miles sent my sister a wink from the back of the carriage house, and she sent him one in return. He'd recreated all twelve of Alan's Czech dishes for guests to dine on after the ceremony. Toby walked his mother to her seat and took his place under the trellis to await his bride.

"Are you ready?" I opened the door to the Marches' Land Rover. Olivia hovered inside the warm vehicle, awaiting her turn to go in.

"More than ever, thank you Mallory, for making this day possible." She wiped a set of tears from her eyes, her makeup flawless despite the tears, thanks to Rachel's expertise.

Alan offered Olivia his arm, and the bride swept from the car, resplendent and ethereal. She walked into the carriage house and beamed when Toby caught her eye.

The ceremony itself was spare and heartfelt. The pastor blended elements from a traditional sermon while Toby and Olivia made their own declarations to each other before all assembled. And when Toby leaned in to kiss his bride, the room erupted in cheers.

"We should throw smaller weddings more often." I leaned in to share my opinion with my sister. The party was in full swing, all fifty guests chatting, dancing, and merrymaking. It was intimate and festive, low-key and wonderful. Alan's twelve dishes-inspired dinner was a hit, as was the cookie table groaning with confections.

"Mm-hmm." My sister sent Miles a dreamy look and then left me to join him without another word. I usually cautioned my sister to put on the brakes, but in this case, I just laughed.

"Nice work, Mallory." A woman who looked familiar shook my hand. "I'm the organ transplant coordinator for the hospital."

"Oh! And your daughter is getting married here next June. Clarissa Fields, right?"

The pretty, plump woman beamed. "Yes. We're going to have an outside ceremony near the gazebo. But," she turned in a slow circle, "after seeing this space, I'm going to ask my daughter to reassess. This wedding planning is more complicated than I thought." She gave a chuckle. "The medical industrial complex has nothing on the wedding industrial complex."

We chatted amiably for a few minutes, turning to what made us love our jobs most.

"I get to make brides and grooms' dreams come true for their big day, but you get to literally save lives." I gushed to Clarissa after she explained the procedures of matching up organs, facilitating their transfer on ice, and arranging for the long operations to follow.

"It's a unique position, for sure." The woman nodded. "But the doctors are the real miracle workers. I do admit it gives me a thrill each and every time I contact a family with news that there's a match. Especially around this time of year."

"I'd imagine that would be extra special. I've just heard of a woman who got the news on Christmas and had her transplant on the following day. But I'm sure she had it done up in Pittsburgh."

Clarissa's bright visage dimmed as if a cloud had passed overhead. "I've had one of those, too. A long time ago."

I couldn't resist. "It wasn't Goldie March, by any chance?"

"Oh! Excuse me." We leapt back as Clarissa dropped her drink. The pretty cut glass goblet miraculously held and rolled toward the corner. She made a move to chase after it, when I placed my hand on her arm. "Don't worry about that. I'll get you a new one."

Clarissa looked around as if she were afraid someone would hear her. "In fact, it was. I don't like to talk about that one." She gave a little hiccup, and I realized she was a bit tipsy. "That one was . . . not per protocol."

I raised one brow, hoping she'd fill the silence. "She was desperate. We typed her and waited for a match. Just like everyone else. And one day, Christmas Day, a kidney magically showed up. It was a perfect match for Marigold March. This kidney had no provenance. It was from nowhere. But I pushed it through."

"So Goldie got her kidney, and there were no more questions to ask."

Clarissa nodded miserably. "But a year later I was reading the *Eagle Herald*. There was a piece about a woman who'd gone missing the year before. I must not have seen it the first time around." Her voice quavered. "I recognized the woman. She'd been typed in a bid to help her cousin. She wasn't a match." She hungrily grabbed at a new goblet of holiday punch as a server went by with tray held aloft. She took a fortifying swig and went on. "She disappeared a few months after she was typed. Just before Christmas a year prior."

"Andrea Adams." I made a statement, not a question.

Clarissa nearly dropped her second drink. "Yes! How on earth did you know?"

"Lucky guess."

Clarissa looked ill. "I thought about going to the police but a year had passed since that girl disappeared. I convinced myself it was just a strange coincidence and put it out of my mind. Excuse me, I think I'm going to be sick." She left to find her husband, who thankfully seemed to have just been imbibing water as their designated driver.

I felt a prickle of dread trill down my spine. Goldie March stared at me from across the room, gripping her drink, her face a mask of stone.

I tried to run my revelations by Rachel as we broke down Olivia's wedding. The happy couple had ridden off in a carriage bedecked in holiday greenery, to the whoop and hollers of the guests. I'd put away the delicate angel tree topper first, for safekeeping until the bride and groom returned from their honeymoon. Then I commenced with the rest of the decorations.

It was early Christmas Eve before we were done. Rachel yawned when we got back to the main house and held up her hand for me to stop. "You'll have to let Truman know. But maybe give it a rest for one day, y'know? It's Christmas Eve, for goodness' sake."

"You're right. We can just take the cats to the veterinarian later today when we wake up and relax the rest of the time." We went to bed soon afterward.

I awoke several hours later with the sun now above the horizon. It had been a whirlwind two weeks. I loved Olivia like my own sister, but I was relieved to have her wedding in the rearview mirror. I felt safer with the March family and all their shenanigans out of my hair. Our mother was weighing whether to return as their stager in light of Justine's firing. Nevertheless, Rachel was finally with a gem of a guy, and I'd decided to lay it all bare with Garrett. I'd tell him tomorrow, on Christmas, that I wanted to take our relationship to the next level. I was nervous, but relieved as well. I hoped it would be a very merry Christmas.

But first I needed to take the kitties to the animal hospital. I apologized to Whiskey and Soda as they meowed in their carriers.

"I know this isn't the nicest way for you to spend Christmas Eve."

"Don't worry." The veterinarian opened the door to the waiting room and beckoned me back. "It'll only take a minute. We use a tiny needle to insert each chip, and that's it."

He was as good as his word. The kitties sent me mutinous glares as their chips were slipped into their ears subcutaneously, but within minutes they were no worse for wear. They spent a few happy minutes sniffing all of the surfaces in the room, no doubt catching whiffs of other kitties and doggies.

"You're the second customer of the day, actually." The veterinarian smiled. "Judge Frank brought in Hemingway to get him re-microchipped. She gushed about how you found him."

I smiled in response. "All's well that ends well."

"It's funny, he really could be a Hemingway cat." The vet gave a chuckle.

"I beg your pardon?"

"I pulled his original microchip records before placing the new one. You can still access the information in the database, even when the chip itself is missing. Anyway, that kitty originally came from a shelter in Key West."

I blinked my confusion. The vet must have noticed.

"I asked the judge if she'd lived in Florida. She said the cat had been a gift from some dear friends, ten years ago this Christmas."

I only knew of one couple who vacationed regularly in Key West. My mind cycled back to my mother's initial conversation with Clementine when the spirited yoga instructor had regaled her with tales of the Florida community.

"Thank you so much for helping me take care of these two." I loaded my curious cats into their carriers and wished the vet a merry Christmas. Then I hightailed it out of there, itching to investigate.

# CHAPTER EIGHTEEN

I settled my cats in with treats and conciliatory catnip. Mom, Rachel, and Doug were chatting in front of the fire in the parlor.

"Come join us, sweetie." My mom held her mug of eggnog aloft.

"I will in a bit. I just need to check on something."

I closed the door to my shared office and flipped my laptop open.

"Okay, what are you sleuthing now?" Rachel appeared in the doorway. She carried two glass mugs of eggnog and pressed one into my hands. "You need to put that thing away, cuddle our cats, and join us."

"I think Goldie March bought a black-market kidney, and somehow Judge Frank is involved."

*Now I've got her attention.*

"Okay, spill it." Rachel sat down for the juicy details.

"I heard last night from the organ donation facilitator at the hospital where Andrea Adams was typed to give her cousin her kidney. But she wasn't a match. She disappeared a few days before Christmas. Then bam, a kidney showed up for Goldie. One without a provenance. Goldie lived, Andrea never came home. It fits."

"Whoa, whoa, whoa." Rachel held up her hand. "It does fit, but it doesn't have to. It could all just be a coincidence."

"True." I chewed my lower lip. "But I just found out that Judge Frank was gifted Hemingway on Christmas ten years ago. This would have been when Goldie had her transplant. Hemingway came from a shelter in Key West, where Clementine and Rudy vacation."

"This is getting murky." Rachel took a swig of eggnog and sat down in front of my desk.

"I just want to see if there are any connections before I bring this all to Truman. And—" I held up my hand before my sister could protest, "I definitely won't bother him with this now. Not even tomorrow when the Davieses come over after Christmas dinner."

My sister was pacified. My fingers flew over the keyboard. I called up the tabs I'd closed the other day and brought out a yellow legal pad to mark my notes.

"Fact. Ursula Frank's husband was a surgeon. He passed away eight years ago. So he was still around when Goldie had her transplant." I reran the search for the judge. An article on the third page, a link to an archived newspaper story, caught my eye.

"Holy tamale. Judge Frank presided over Olivia's

adoption." The story was a little blurb, a feel-good fluff piece that celebrated the adoption of the baby found in the manger. The writer did not mention the new name chosen by the adopting parents nor their names for that matter. But the small article did feature some quotes from the judge who handled the adoption, one Ursula Frank.

"But Judge Frank doesn't usually handle family court matters," I mused. "Her docket is always criminal."

Rachel gave me a shrug. We were no closer to what had happened.

"There's one other thing that's bothering me." My voice sounded so small.

"You're thinking about what that toad Keith said." My sister knew me well. "Don't even give it a thought. You'd believe some stupid bee Keith tried to put in your bonnet over your trust in Garrett?"

I squirmed as my sister put it that way. But I needed to put the accusation Keith had made to rest. I pulled up the Westlaw legal database and put in my old credentials. The search I was about to do would cost a small fortune. I put Garrett's name in as the attorney in the search field and Ursula as the judge. Garrett had appeared in her court for over sixty matters. And each and every one had been decided in his favor. My heart rate accelerated.

"It could be a coincidence," Rachel muttered.

"I don't think so. Garrett is a phenomenal attorney, but this percentage is too high. At best, she's deciding in his favor because she's his mentor and she feels some kind of loyalty. At worst, they have some kind of formal arrangement going on."

"Well, you can't just accuse Garrett," Rachel warned. "I know your relationship is at some kind of a turning point. But this would turn it for the worse; you have to know that."

"I know. That's why I'm not going to ask him. Yet."

I nosed around in Westlaw for a few minutes more, searching for all of Judge Frank's cases. A troubling pattern began to emerge.

"I don't like this. There are some cases where the judge accepted a plea bargain grossly off from the initial charges. I have to wonder if she's receiving payoffs." A thought clicked into place. "Oh my goodness. The payments made by Goldie started thirty years ago. Maybe she's been paying the judge for facilitating the discovery and adoption of Olivia." My voice got faster and faster. "All that in addition to getting Goldie a kidney."

Rachel shook her head. "I wouldn't want to cross that lady, Mallory, even on a good day. You'd better watch your step."

I ignored my sister's advice and texted Garrett. My beau appeared, rosy and handsome, a mere ten minutes later. He leaned in for a delicious kiss on the front porch. I paused before bringing him inside.

"What's wrong, Mallory?" Garrett tipped my chin up and peered into my eyes. I longed to turn back the clock. Before I'd taken on any events for the

March family. Before the judge had brokered Garrett's job offer at the clinic. Before all of the death and mayhem had rained down this December like a sinister snowfall.

But it was too late. So I waded into the fray.

"I'm a little worried about some things I've uncovered." I paced the front porch and noted Garrett sitting down on the wide swing.

"You've been sleuthing again." An amused smile lit up Garrett's face. "My dad won't be happy, but I think it's fun." His face dimmed a degree. "As long as you're staying safe, Mallory. I don't know what I'd do if something happened to you."

My heart melted. Then I steeled myself to have the hard conversation I didn't want to have.

"Judge Frank presided over Olivia's adoption."

Garrett frowned and stood, the chains from the porch swing clanking in the cold air.

"Did she? What does that have to do with anything? Other than being a fun coincidence that her son ended up marrying Olivia."

"It's just odd. I looked up each and every one of her cases. She has presided over criminal matters exclusively, not adoptions. All except for Olivia." Garrett raised his eyebrows. "Goldie March has made a sizable cash payment mailed to a post office box in Port Quincy for precisely thirty years. They began soon after the Marches found Olivia."

Garrett shook his head. "I don't like where this is going, Mallory. This sounds like a lot of loose coincidences."

I sent him a pleading look. "Judge Frank's husband was the head of surgery at the hospital. Do you know what kinds of surgeries he usually performed?"

Garrett seemed to consider my question. "I think he had a gift with transplants, actually. But Tobias Frank has been dead for eight years or so."

I nodded, a chill running down my back. "Andrea Adams disappeared the day before Christmas ten years ago. And a day later, Goldie March had a kidney transplant. You'd think she'd have had her operation in Pittsburgh, where she lives. But she had it here."

"These are very serious accusations, Mallory, and quite frankly, I don't really see how they're tied to Judge Frank."

I'd anticipated Garrett's fierce allegiance to his mentor.

"Why does the judge seem so keen for you to leave Port Quincy? Do you think she thinks things are coming to a head?"

Anger flashed in Garrett's lovely hazel eyes. "I think she offered me her class at Pitt because she knew I once had aspirations to teach law. Nothing more. If the school wants to offer me a job directing a clinic, that's their business."

I took a deep breath and hoped my relationship could withstand my next observation.

"The judge's record is there for all to see. Including some plea bargains that are a bit outside the range of normal. I have to wonder if she's accepting favors or payments to reduce sentences."

Garrett had had enough. He opened his mouth to speak. But I wasn't finished.

"There are rumors about your practice, as well.

All of the issues and matters you've presented before her have been adjudicated in your favor."

Garrett's anger melted into something akin to sadness. "I've heard those rumors, Mallory. And while I do have many cases in front of Judge Frank, I can assure you we have no deal or arrangement. I just practice to the best of my ability. Faithfully and with integrity. And I thought you knew that, too."

He brushed his thumb against my cheek. "I had made my decision. I should have involved you more in the process, and for that I apologize. I was going to reject the clinic offer and stay here in Port Quincy. But now I'm not so sure."

"I'm sorry." My heart sank into my feet. I felt a rivulet of tears course down my face, but Garrett didn't wipe them away.

"I need your trust. And I don't have it. I love you. I do. But I think we need to stop seeing each other."

I nodded my reply. I had no words to offer. I watched his figure advance down the front stairs, into his car, and out of my life.

# CHAPTER NINETEEN

I slipped back inside and grabbed my pea coat. I couldn't bear to join my jolly family before the fire. I had ruined the relationship with the man I loved, all over some suspicions that may or may not even be true. My sister had been right. I should've just calmed down, enjoyed the holiday, and run my theories by Truman the day after Christmas.

I left Thistle Park, walking in a blind stupor toward downtown. I passed the pretty rows of Victorians in my neighborhood, each one bedecked in holiday finery. I realized with a start I was near Judge Frank's own house. I definitely thought there was something hinky going on with her cases. But maybe it wasn't my place to wonder.

"Mallory, do you need a ride? It's far too cold to walk."

*Speak of the devil.*

A Tahoe pulled over and Ursula Frank beckoned me inside.

"I'm fine, thank you." I blinked up at the judge. "Merry Christmas."

"Don't be ridiculous," she snapped. She could be as commanding outside the courtroom as within. "I haven't thanked you properly for the wonderful wedding you put on for my son and Olivia."

I stood on the sidewalk at an odd kind of standoff. Finally I pulled open the passenger door and climbed into the SUV. I'd ruined my relationship with Garrett over accusations with the judge. I may as well seek some clarity.

"Where are you headed?" I frowned as we headed away from downtown and out to the western side of Port Quincy.

"I wanted to check out my new home. My retirement is going to be all about new beginnings. I bought the Victorian with my husband ages ago, and we raised Toby there. But it's time to get some new digs. I'm going to be moving into one of the first March Homes. The house is nearly finished."

Alarm bells rang in the back of my head as we traveled further from the city. True to her word, the judge pulled into a housing development, this one marked at the entrance as Phase I, Juniper Ridge.

"And here we are." The judge had selected a pretty rambling ranch of a home. Smooth salmon brick rose in a pleasing composition of triangular roof peaks. It was a modern structure, very different from her current abode. Ursula gave me a mini tour, her excitement palpable.

"Hemingway will like looking at all the nature," I began carefully. The judge ushered me into the kitchen. The room was almost finished, but there were some missing elements. The kitchen cabinets still bore tape holding their doors closed, and there was no refrigerator. I could see the big back-yard through a set of French doors.

"Tell me, how did you come to adopt Heming-way?" I'd slipped my cell phone from my pocket. I hoped to be able to dial my sister if I needed to.

The judge surprised me. She folded her hands neatly in front of her and raised her eyebrows in invitation. "I think you already figured it out, Mal-lory. Why don't you tell me?"

So I gave her the same spiel as I had done with Garrett, this audience very different.

"I think you and your husband facilitated Goldie's kidney transplant. Andrea Adams had been typed to explore giving her organ to her cousin. She wasn't a match, but Goldie was. So you killed Andrea, Goldie got her kidney, and you got Hemingway as a token of thanks from the March family. Did I miss anything?"

The judge laughed, her smile suddenly disin-genuous and cunning. "Well done, Mallory. But some of your details are off. I didn't kill Andrea Adams. In fact, I have no idea where that kidney came from."

She made note of my guffaw. "Oh, fine. If I'm honest, I'd guess that's where they got it. But I didn't ask and neither did Tobias. He just performed the operation."

I almost believed her. "What about Olivia's adoption? You stepped out of your purview of criminal cases to handle that. Why?"

The judge sighed. "Before I became a judge, I had a thriving practice. I handled a few cases for the March family. I knew Goldie couldn't have her own children. Her kidneys were always a problem."

Her story so far echoed Goldie's.

"I knew of a woman in a troubled marriage who was having a baby of her own. I got her in contact with the March family."

"You tried to broker the sale of her baby?"

The judge recoiled. "No! The adoption of her baby. What kind of a person do you think I am?"

*A person who obviously skirts the fine line of ethics and legality.*

I rolled my eyes at the judge.

She sneered and continued her tale. "As it turns out, she wasn't interested in giving up her baby. But she did eventually need my help. Her husband attacked her, and she murdered him in self-defense. I arranged not to charge her, or even report the crime, if she gave up her baby."

A sickening wave of dread washed over me.

"Olivia."

"Yes." The judge gave a callous laugh. "The funny thing is, I didn't even need to broker that deal. It's truly ironic. The killing of her husband clearly was in self-defense—a pregnant woman trying to save herself and her baby. But the poor woman didn't realize. So, the Marches got their daughter, and I got a nice, fat check each month."

"I'm sure this is illegal." I slipped my phone from my pocket, not sure how rational the judge would be. "You can't get away with all of this."

Ursula smiled. "I get away with it all, Mallory. Although your snooping was a bit much. I tried to get you off my trail at lunch that day. And I'd almost succeeded in convincing Garrett to take the position in Pittsburgh. He really is an exemplary attorney. I hear the rumors about deciding too much in his favor. But that's because of his skill, not some arrangement. At least you should know that."

It was a small good thing in a sea of odious and unethical actions. If I managed to get out of here, the judge would surely pay.

She pulled open a drawer in her new cabinet and extracted a pistol.

"The one thing I can't figure out is who took my Hemingway. I did assume it was someone who didn't like one of my rulings. But removing his microchip? That muddies the waters."

I heard my breath as it accelerated. The judge was yammering on, waving the gun this way and that. If I approached it just right, I bet I could kick it out of her hands. In the meantime, I swiped my fingers across the smooth glass case of my phone. I didn't dare remove the device from my pocket, but hoped the screen was still up and ready to dial my sister.

"Ursula, what in the heck are you doing?"

We both wheeled around, coming face to face with Santa himself.

# CHAPTER TWENTY

"Rudy, thank goodness." I sidled up to the man in red and willed my heart to stop racing. Olivia's grandfather wore a red Arkansas Razorbacks sweat suit. With his bald pate, big belly, and prodigious white beard, he looked like Santa taking a day off.

"Mallory, you sure have waded into a mess here." Rudy shook his head, his eyes no longer twinkling. "And Ursula, you've said too much."

I grimaced as the judge raised her pistol and pointed it at Rudy.

"Don't play your little Kris Kringle gambit with me, Rudolph March. You're in this up to your eyeballs."

*Uh-oh.*

I'd unwittingly chosen to jump straight from Judge Frank's frying pan into an even more dire fire. I attempted to put some physical distance between Rudy and me, but it was too late.

"I'm sorry, Ursula. But I should have done this a long time ago." Rudy pulled a revolver from the back of his waistband and shot the judge. She crumpled to the floor with a moan, her blood staining the pretty subway tile.

"Oh no, oh no, oh no," I chanted.

"Chill out, Mallory." Rudy's voice was weary. "When it's your turn, I'll make it quick. Now, let's just have a little chat about how you figured this out."

I closed my eyes against the wave of nausea cresting in my throat. "If Judge Frank didn't kill Andrea to get a kidney for Goldie, then you must have."

Rudy nodded sagely. "If you have children some day, you'll see. You'd do anything for them. And I was tired of watching my baby Goldie get so sick. All the money in the world wasn't healing her; she just needed that kidney."

"So why didn't you offer Andrea payment for her kidney? I don't think that's allowed, but it would be better than killing her."

Rudy shook his head in a mournful manner. "I tried, believe me. But she didn't want to sell. So she had to go. I told Lacey the same thing the evening of Paws and Poinsettias."

"She was snooping around and figured it out."

Rudy shook his head. "Not quite. It was ridiculously ironic. Lacey never figured out I'd murdered her sister. What she'd uncovered concerned Goldie's transplant. Lacey needed her own kidney. She tried to blackmail me into procuring one just as I had for my daughter. I had to burn down that cabin to hide any traces of records." The man laughed. "Like I'd go out of my way for someone who isn't family, blackmail or no! So for Lacey, I used the antifreeze I had in the trunk of my Land Rover. It wasn't until later that evening I realized your mother had brought in a jug of the stuff that first day I met her. It was too good of a coincidence to pass up."

His smile was still kindly, his manner still avuncular. But as I heard Ursula moaning on the floor behind me, I knew this was the sickest incarnation of Father Christmas I could ever imagine.

"And what about Olivia?"

"That was more complicated but worth it just the same." Rudy smiled. "I love Olivia. And she was meant to be a March." A dark cloud crossed over his jolly visage. "Or at least a Krylenko."

The name rang a distant bell in the back of my brain.

"Alan's original surname before he changed it to March. Oh my God, Alan is Olivia's biological father. Does he even know?"

It fit. Olivia resembled both of her parents, despite being adopted. Now I knew in the case of her father, it especially made sense.

"He was starting to poke around that actuality. He asked me if I knew anything else about Olivia's whereabouts before he and Goldie found her." He sighed. "So I let myself into your house and made Alan a special drink. He likes blue drinks, so I hoped he'd drink it. And I wasn't wrong."

"But you could have poisoned anyone at Olivia's shower with that antifreeze!"

Rudy shrugged. "That was an acceptable risk. I admit I bungled that one, though." He ran a hand over his balding scalp. "Turns out I bungled burying that body, too."

"The man found on your property."

Rudy nodded. "Patrick Bowman was an abusive jerk. I would have killed him myself, but it turns out, I didn't have to. But I did tip him off about his wife's affair with my son-in-law."

"Justine," I whispered. It fit.

"Yes, Justine. I nearly had a heart attack when she waltzed into March Homes as your mother's new hire. And I think she suspected Olivia may have been her daughter, but I don't think she was sure."

If he had thought she was, he may have already taken care of her, I thought with a shiver. I realized my teeth had been chattering since Rudy shot the judge. I wondered if I'd have any enamel left on my teeth if I made it out of here unscathed.

"I told Patrick his wife was carrying my son-in-law's baby. That psychopath tried to kill Justine that very evening. Turns out she's a fair mark and got to him first. Ursula approached her and agreed to keep things quiet if Justine handed over her baby. And the rest is history."

"No, you're history. Put your hands up, fat man. I've got a gun."

It was my mother's finest moment. I nearly fainted from relief as Carole pressed an icicle into Rudy's back. He was so shocked he dropped his revolver.

Rachel whipped around the corner and trained the weapon on Rudy. Doug hogtied the old man with his own suspenders. It was an uneasy few minutes until the sirens wailed into the housing development, and Truman and Faith stormed the house.

# EPILOGUE

New Year's Eve was the coldest night of the year so far. But Thistle Park was cozy and warm by day. I wish I could say the same for each night. I'd tried to put the events of a week ago behind me, but my dreams were still riddled with mayhem and murder. I pet my cats each time I retired for bed and prayed for easy sleep, but it hadn't yet come.

Before he was formally charged, Rudy led Truman to the plot of land where he'd buried Andrea Adams. Nina finally had some closure about the death of her first daughter. But it was something of a cold comfort when she learned both of her daughters had been murdered to fulfill the machinations of Rudy March. She'd buried Andrea next to her sister Lacey, two daughters lost a decade apart.

Olivia and Toby had returned from their honeymoon in Iceland to find her grandfather locked up in my mother's old cell, with enough counts and accusations to keep him firmly behind bars until the end of his days. The one bright spot, in addition to Olivia's baby, was Olivia's opportunity to get to know Justine better. She forgave her for placing her in the manger all those decades ago and was grateful to finally know her history. It turns out Justine had figured out that Olivia was her daughter, and had placed the angel atop the tree at Thistle Park, as well as the stocking with Olivia's original name.

Judge Frank was no longer on the bench to accept a greased plea in exchange for a reduction in Rudy's jail time. She was still on this side of the earth, though. She'd pulled through nicely from her abdominal surgery and awaited her own trial for her years of fixing cases. Thankfully the ethics committee that had pored over her cases had affirmed that there was nothing untoward going on with the matters Garrett had presented before her.

My mother no longer worked for March Homes. She'd soured on working for the March family and was going to strike out with a new partnership. She and Justine excitedly made plans for launching their new decorating and staging business.

"Happy New Year, sis." Rachel left her perch next to Miles and crossed the room to give me a hug.

"And a happy New Year to you, too." I tried to sound cheery. I was anything but. I hadn't spoken with Garrett since that fateful conversation on Christmas Eve. I gave my sister a weak smile and escaped the merrymaking. It was too much watching my mother cuddle with Doug and Rachel canoodle with Miles.

The cold air outside was a welcome shock. Each breath I exhaled brought a stream of steam, and I focused on it for a while, willing my heart to slow down. I gazed upon the twinkling stars high above. It was a gorgeous night, cold and clear and calm. I closed my eyes against the night sky splendor.

"Penny for your thoughts."

I didn't dare to open my eyes. I was surely imagining Garrett's presence. But there were his arms, warm and strong and true, wrapped around mine. And his familiar scent of citrus and spearmint.

"I was thinking of you, of course. And of us. And how I messed it up."

I turned around to gaze into his hazel eyes.

"You did nothing of the sort." Garrett bestowed me with a tender, if nervous, smile. "I'm sorry I left the other day. I don't ever want to leave your side again."

I pressed my cheek against his chest, and we were still for a few minutes.

"I'm staying here in Port Quincy. Tomorrow I'll make a formal offer to Olivia to join my practice."

I pulled back and searched his face, trying to determine if that's what he really wanted.

"I almost lost you, Mallory. And I don't want it to happen again."

"And I realized what's important. It's you, and Summer and my family. I don't ever want to lose you, Garrett."

A wave of relief crashed over him. He bent down for a tender kiss. Then he was on his knee, a tiny box in his hand.

"Mallory, will you marry me?"

A pretty diamond ring nestled within. I smiled at my beau, my heart nearly bursting.

"Yes, yes, yes!"

Garrett slipped the cool metal over my finger, then picked me up and kissed me again.

We stayed on the porch for a few minutes more, savoring the calm night sky. Then we returned to the fire inside to share the good news.

Later that night I chatted excitedly with Summer, Truman, and Lorraine about the formal melding of our families.

"I bet you can't wait to plan your own wedding," Lorraine beamed.

But I wasn't focused on that at all. I was just reveling in my new commitment with Garrett: an assurance and a promise to live, learn, and love each other.

The ball dropped at midnight, and we all trooped up to the widow's walk to watch the fireworks go off over the Monongahela under the glittering stars.

"This year was something else," Garrett laughed, leaning in for another kiss.

I heartily agreed. "And I can't wait to see what's next."

# Recipes

## Cardamom Men Cookies

1½ cups flour
1 teaspoon cardamom
1 teaspoon cinnamon
¼ teaspoon nutmeg
½ teaspoon baking powder
¼ teaspoon salt
¼ cup coconut oil
½ cup brown sugar
¼ cup molasses

Preheat oven to 350 degrees. Line a cookie sheet with parchment paper. Sift together flour, cardamom, cinnamon, nutmeg, baking powder, and salt. Mix coconut oil, brown sugar, and molasses in a separate bowl. Combine with flour mixture. Chill cookie dough for one hour. Roll dough flat on a floured surface between two sheets of plastic wrap or parchment paper. Use cookie cutters to cut out shapes, including gingerbread men. Bake for approximately ten minutes, or until cookies are brown and crispy.

*Icing*

⅔ cup shortening
1 teaspoon vanilla
3 cups powdered sugar

Beat shortening and vanilla until fluffy. Mix in powdered sugar until blended well. Place icing in piping cone and use to decorate the cardamom men.


## Blue Ice Martini

3 ounces blueberry vodka
3 ounces blue Hawaiian Punch
Sea salt for martini glass

Dip martini glass rim in water. Next dip the rim of the glass in a plate of sea salt to salt the rim. Combine vodka and blue Hawaiian punch. Shake. Pour into a martini glass over ice.